Shieldmaiden's Quest

The Fae, book two

Alex McGilvery

Shieldmaiden's Quest
Alex McGilvery
Copyright 2022
ISBN: 978-1-989092-74-3

Celticfrog Publishing

Chapter 1

Robin rubbed her eyes and stifled a cough. The large tent filled with her thirteen commanders swirled with smoke from the braziers. The nights had chilled the past week, but she preferred the chill to the smoke.

"We should be putting things to order." Paychen, a commander of five hundred, almost banged the table but caught himself. The fines for yelling and hammering the table made the nightly meetings quieter if no less unruly. "The Ancans need someone with a firm hand to prevent civil war."

"As soon as we fight, the doom will fall on Caldera." Revont, the other commander of five hundred had yet to pay a fine, but her voice cut through the chaos like a knife.

"Then what are we here for?" Paychen scowled and clenched and unclenched his fist.

"We are here because the King ordered us to accompany Lady Robin." Marshal Hapten scanned the room, and a brief silence fell over the tent.

"That's all very well and good," Themson, a commander of a hundred, drawled. "But the men are asking what Lady Robin is doing."

All eyes on the tent turned to her. She leaned forward to speak and coughed. Sargent Temajin handed her a water skin. She took her time drinking the water.

"I am here because the land has called me." Robin had been over this a dozen times in the week since they left Fhayde. "I've ordered the soldiers to take their time and rest after the battle, but we will be at Marques Povost's manor tomorrow. He is the first imperial nobility we have met since leaving Fhayde. The men and women of the thousand will be prepared to parade when we arrive. We must make a good impression."

"And what of us, Lady Robin?" Timost, the Ancan commander asked. "Are we to parade ourselves before this Marques as well?"

"You are our escort; I would invite you to be part of the formalities when we arrived."

"Formalities, for a Marques." Timost didn't quite sneer, but it was a close thing.

"For the father of the Voice of the Emperor." Robin's cough at the end of her words stole what little emphasis she had tried to give them. But Timost nodded reluctantly and leaned back, his arms crossed.

They'd all been around this circle before. Timost was a Baron's heir, if his father's people hadn't risen against him. They'd heard rumours of rebellion and fighting other places from the scouts Timost had sent out.

Timost's hundred men kept to themselves, though many spoke enough Calderan to make themselves understood. Most of them were scouts or sweeping for trouble. Robin struggled to learn the Imperial Ancan language.

"Once we've arrived, detail some experienced farmers to be instructors in our techniques."

"We are here as soldiers, not farmers." Marshal Hapten said.

"You are here as representatives of Fhayde." Robin spoke firmly. "There is a reason you are here. When you learn what it is, you may regret wasting the opportunity to rest." She stood up, and the rest of the men and women scrambled to their feet. "You will have your people in full dress when we arrive tomorrow, and you will have a squad prepped and ready to teach what we know about farming."

"How are we to pick out a squad from a thousand?" Revont frowned.

"If I may be so bold," Sargent Temajin stepped forward. "That is a task for your commanders of a hundred and their staff."

"Assign it to a commander," Robin nodded at Marshal Hapten. "Tomorrow, the commanders will attend a formal dinner with the Marques. Ask the cooks to make it a memorable meal."

***

The Marques Povost had his guards dressed in formal uniforms to meet them. Robin thanked the Land the commanders had taken her orders seriously. The thousand snaked back along the road with pikes held almost vertically.

"Attention." Themson fired the word like an arrow from a bow. His hundred snapped to rigid stance, feet together, shoulders back, pike held in front of them absolutely vertical.

Robin marched forward with Sargent Temajin at one side, Ham on the other. Marshall Hapten came behind with her staff, one of them holding the Legion's colours, another a white banner.

"Welcome." The Marques spoke Calderan with only a hint of an accent. He smiled, but there was tension around his eyes. "I received word you were coming. To be honest, we have food enough for our people, but little to spare for a visiting army."

"We carry our own necessities with us." Robin bowed slightly. "It would be impolite to show up expecting our hosts to feed us."

The Marques didn't relax.

"I would like to invite you, and whatever guests you wish to include, to a meal this evening." Robin smiled, trying to look less intimidating.

The Marques bowed but still didn't look happy. "I would be happy to accept."

"Marques Povost," Robin tried to project her voice like Sarge taught her. "The Voice of the Emperor has entrusted me with a letter to deliver to your hand."

Sargent Temajin handed her the folded and sealed letter. Robin held it out to the Marques. One of the men at his side stepped forward and took the letter, then handed it to Marques Povost.

"My thanks, Lady Robin." His smile looked more genuine now. "Perhaps you would honour me by joining me in my chambers, along with your guards."

"It would be my pleasure." Robin bowed slightly. "Marshal Hapten, please set the Thousand at ease."

Marshal Hapten saluted and sent a man back to the column.

"If you have an empty field where my people may make camp, we will get out of your way." Robin wanted nothing more than to relax with Sarge and the boys, but that would come later.

A man stepped forward and bowed deeply to Robin.

"If you would follow me." He spoke with a strong accent.

"Marshal, I will leave you in charge."

"Very good, Lady Robin." The marshal nodded to her staff, and they returned to the column.

"This way Lady Robin." The marques's man led her to a double door into the manor, guards standing at attention on each side. He ignored them and swept into the building and through a large foyer to a smaller room.

"Please sit." The Marques waved a hand at the waiting chairs.

Robin hid a sigh of relief that she'd listened to Sarge and not worn her full armour. She settled into a chair while Sargent Temajin and Ham stood on either side of her. The Marques sat in a more ornate chair, but well worn. He opened the letter and scanned the contents quickly.

"Jequilane speaks well of you and your King. She is still bound to search for the fae by order of the emperor."

"The fae have vanished, yet are all around her." Robin said. "We all carry the blood of the fae with us."

"Some of you more than others." He tapped the letter on his knee. "You look very like the tales the old woman tell of the fae."

"So I am told." Robin said.

"If I may be blunt," the Marques waved the letter. "Jequilane's letter and your white banner proclaim you are here peacefully, even so, you carry weapons and march in order. An embassy doesn't require a thousand guards."

"Jequilane asked for aid for the Empire, a thousand can do work a handful of soldiers cannot. We have heard of your failing crops, and if you are willing, we have people who can teach you the methods we use for farming. Methods which began with the fae and have been handed down and improved for generations."

"I would be foolish to reject such advice, whether we can convince the people working the fields is another matter."

A woman came in carrying a tray with a bottle and cups on it.

"Perhaps you would join me in a cup of wine." He opened the bottle and poured deep red wine into each cup. The woman brought the tray over for Robin to choose a cup. She picked one up and took a careful sip. Wine wasn't something she was used to drinking.

The Marques took his wine and sipped it. "You didn't come with a thousand soldiers just to teach us how to farm our own land."

"I am called north." Robin shrugged. "I do not know yet why, but the Legion has a purpose beyond being my safety."

"I see." Marques Povost leaned forward. "You have heard the capital went up in flame and the emperor is missing? I have as many people as I can afford watching the roads for trouble."

"We heard rumours to that effect."

"You wouldn't be planning to take the capital and claim the Empire for Caldera, would you?"

"That is not what the land wants." Robin swirled her cup and sipped at it. The taste was a strange mix of bitter and sweet.

"You speak to the land?" The Marques lifted an eyebrow.

"Rather say the land speaks to me and only what it wishes to. We travel under the white banner and will take no part in any fighting, other than defending ourselves if the banner is ignored. I am not here to set the empire to rights.

The empire has fallen, and it will be generations before an emperor sits on the gold throne."

"I see." The Marques slumped in his chair. "I had hoped it might be repaired. I must see to my people and keep them safe." He lifted a hand, and a guardswoman stepped forward.

"Captain, see that the borders of my land are secure and have people ready to fight at a moment's notice."

"Yes, my Lord." She saluted and walked out of the room.

"The captain saw with her own eyes Ancanopolis in flames. She has prepared for the worst but I hesitated to implement her recommendations."

A runner came in a knelt at the Marques' feet. Robin couldn't make out the rapid exchange in Ancan.

The Marques sat up straight and stared at Robin.

"It seems your people insisted on harvesting the field before they set camp and are at work on other fields."

"Most of my people are foresters and farmers before they are soldiers. I wouldn't expect them to trample unharvested grain."

"You are a strange person, Lady Robin. An army marches with you, but you don't wear plate. You come under a white banner and talk of helping us. Such things make me nervous."

"At supper tonight we can talk more of what the land is asking of us."

"Us?" His brows raised.

"You don't think you have a place serving the land?" Robin set her cup down on a table beside her. "What the land wants is peace, and a powerful ruler in this place is essential to that peace."

"And if this strong ruler doesn't believe a thousand soldiers march solely to aid their enemy?"

"Breaking the white banner will leave your land and people in worse shape than your capital, even if we didn't lift a hand in our defence." Robin held his gaze without flinching and he sighed and waved a hand.

"I am not foolish enough to bring a curse upon me by attacking a white banner held by an army of a thousand."

"I am grateful. There will be fighting enough by the end, I'm sure, but not here." Robin stood and bowed to Marques Povost. "I must see to my people and prepare for the meal we will share. Sargent Temajin will come and guide you."

***

The supper loaded the tables in the enormous tent. The scents filling the space made Robin's mouth water.

"Let the Marques' people sit wherever they like. The Marques, his Captain and one other he designates, will sit at the head table. Marshal Hapten, Paychen, and Revont, you will also sit at the there. Sargent Temajin will be standing by if we need anything. The Master-Sargent will sit at beside me. Lencely and Rud will serve. The rest will serve themselves." Robin glanced around the tent. "Am I missing anything?"

"Relax," Marshal Hapten grinned at her. "You're making me nervous. This isn't the thousand's first banquet."

Robin took a deep breath. "I've sent Sargent Temajin to the Marques to inform him the meal is ready. We'll have the formalities but keep them brief. I want the Marques relaxed enough to quiz him on the state of the empire around this area."

"Lady Robin, Commander Timost asks for a minute of your time when it is convenient."

"Very well, lead me to him."

Command Timost lounged outside the tent but straightened when Robin walked over to him.

"Commander, you have my ear."

"There is a large force, my scouts guess about six hundred, camped within a day's march of us. The scouts haven't been able to determine who they belong to. They aren't wearing any colours or flying a banner."

"I see." Robin flexed her hands. "At a day's march they aren't an immediate threat, monitor the situation and keep me posted. Try to get more information, but don't risk your men."

"I pay my men to take risks." Timost met her eyes.

"The general has ordered you and your men to escort us. You can't do that if your men are dead or captured."

"Understood."

Robin couldn't read his face. He might have been looking at her with respect or disdain. It didn't matter as long as he filled his role. "Dismissed, don't hesitate to interrupt me if you feel the situation demands it."

He bowed and walked away. Robin put her concern aside. Unlikely to be treachery on the Marques' part if they were a day away. On the other hand, if she knew they were there, most likely the commander of that force knew they were here. She walked to where a young soldier kept guard duty by the feast tent.

"Pass the word to the commanders. We go to a double guard, no idle chatter."

"Yes, my lady." He dashed off. Robin re-entered the tent.

"Revont, is the honour guard ready?"

"Of course, Lady Robin." She frowned at her. "I have done this before."

"Very good. Tell them I've put the camp on alert. There is a possibility of trouble."

"May I ask what kind of trouble?"

"The kind that comes with an army barely a day's march away."

"With respect, I would suggest you send the honour guard immediately to meet the Marques and his entourage. They are more vulnerable than we are here."

"Excellent suggestion." Robin nodded. Commander Revont bowed and stalked over to where her staff chatted in a corner. Whatever she said galvanized them into action.

Sarge walked with his cane to the head table and sat himself as Lencely and Rud made sure he was comfortable. Robin headed over to him.

"How are you doing?"

"I'm just fine so long as I move at my own pace." Sarge winked at her. Lencely still limped slightly, but all his attention was on the old man. Robin forced herself to not ask if it pained him.

The boys took their duty to Sarge seriously. They wore his drab green and gold colours on their arm.

"Pardon, my lady." A young Ancan soldier stood stiff beside her. "Your presence is requested at the front gate."

"They must have made better time than expected," Robin mused.

"Aye, my lady." The young soldier bowed stiffly and jogged away.

"Why is an Ancan carrying messages?" Sarge asked. "Commander Timost and his staff are the only Ancans I've seen in camp."

"You're right." Robin shrugged. "But it is too late to ask him. I'll check with the commander later." She strolled out of the tent and headed for the gate.

"What do you need, Lady Robin?" The senior guard looked worried.

"I was told you needed my presence at the gate."

"We're fine. The honour guard left a few minutes back, and we've doubled the watch as you asked."

Robin peered down the road, though it was too early to see anything. A searing pain in her leg caused her to stagger to the side. An arrow struck the earth behind where she'd been standing.

"Watch for arrows." Robin shouted. The ghost of the pain still ached, but at least the arrow hadn't hit her. Two guards jumped out with shields held up to cover her, but no other arrows appeared. She stayed in cover and watched for motion in the air, but all was quiet. Had the land sent the pain to save her? *Thanks.* Robin sent a thought toward the land. She didn't get a response. The Ancan land hadn't talked to her since it asked for her help.

"Lady Robin, you should retreat." The guard had sent a runner off to the next sentry station in each direction.

"Right." The guards walked her back to the tent, shields held to cover her, but nothing happened.

"Find Commander Timost and ask him to come immediately." Robin dismissed the guards. The pain in her leg was completely gone, as if she'd imagined it.

"What was that about?" Sarge asked when she returned to the table.

"Arrow out of nowhere." Robin rubbed her leg. "My leg cramped and pulled me out of the path. I hope the Marques and the others are safe. I locked the camp down, no one in or out."

"Assassination attempt?" Sarge frowned while Rud's eyes widened and Lencely's mouth dropped open. "Low risk, high reward. You wearing your armour?"

"My chain mail all the time, but I think I will add the breast and back plates to it."

"Good idea."

They didn't wait as long as Robin expected when a runner came from the gate announcing the Marques, his entourage, and the honour guard had arrived. Shortly after, the honour guard escorted the Ancans into the tent.

The Marques didn't look happy, so Robin went over to see if she could calm him.

"I didn't expect to be escorted like a prisoner." He frowned and glared at her. "I should leave right now, assuming you allow it."

"No one attacked you on the way here?"

"No, of course not, unless you count your soldiers surrounding us on all sides."

"There was an attempt on my life, Marques Povost. I was concerned for your safety. You are free to leave if you wish, but I will insist on sending an escort to keep you safe."

"And I am to believe this nonsense?"

"My lord," his captain dropped to her knee in front of him. "Someone was watching us from shortly after the Calderans arrived. It would have been a long shot from cover, but possible."

The Marques stared at her, then nodded.

"Does this have anything to do with the six hundred soldiers camped a short day's march from here?" Robin asked.

"You are aware of them?" Marques Povost shook his head. "Of course you would. They probably belong to him." He pointed at the approaching Commander Timost.

"He was the one who warned me about them." Robin said. "Commander, a young Ancan soldier told me they needed me at the gate. There someone shot an arrow at me, and by good fortune, missed."

"So I heard." Timost nodded to the Marques. "I expect the troops belong to the next lord over, who has a longstanding gripe with Marques Povost."

"Who just happens to be your father."

"I didn't have any choice in that, my lord." Timost almost snarled. "It is this kind of nonsense that made me join the army."

"Timost." Robin caught his eye and held it.

"My apologies, my lady, my lord. If you don't mind, I have work to do." He spun and stomped out of the tent.

"Their family has always been hot-tempered." Marques Povost sighed. "I feared you had made a pact with Timost's father, the Baron, but I should have known if he was one of your commanders, it was unlikely."

"We will talk further about this." Robin waved her hand at the table. "Or we can pack up and leave you two to fight it out."

"I am here. We may as well talk."

***

Robin heaved a silent sigh of relief. Once the Marques calmed and ordered his entourage to be alert, but not hostile, the banquet went well. He was fascinated by Sarge and asked countless questions.

"Now that we have eaten," Robin pushed back from the table. "It is time to talk. Tell me more about this gripe you have with Baron Timost. Since I appear to be caught in the middle of it, I would like to understand what is going on."

"It is something we inherited from our fathers, maybe our grandfathers. There is a small village with a well on the border between our lands. Baron Timost claims the village is part of his barony. It has been under Povost rule since before I was born. There is a request for the emperor to solve the problem, but the bureaucracy has been grinding through the paperwork for decades with no resolution in sight. Now with the emperor missing," Marques Povost spun his cup between his fingers, "there is little chance of anything happening, so the baron is taking matters into his own hands."

"Perhaps we should invite the Baron for a chat," Sarge suggested, "but I think we should have an object lesson. I don't like the attempt to assassinate Robin."

"What do you suggest?" The Marques frowned. "He isn't a man easily intimidated."

"Robin, if he attacks the white flag, can we defend ourselves?" Sarge leaned on the table.

Robin closed her eyes and listened.

"I'd hate to risk it. It isn't just us, but all of Caldera."

"But he doesn't know that." Sarge's eyes glinted.

"We do." Robin rubbed her temples. "What if he calls our bluff?"

"Anyone who attacks a white flag will be cursed." The Marques' frown deepened. "Even the Baron knows this, but he may not care anymore. If the empire really is collapsing, then you can't depend on anything." Marques Povost leaned back to stare up at the tent. "I will assemble my men. I only risk the emperor's anger, not a curse of destruction."

"You will want to hurry." Sarge sipped his water. "I expect he will try something tomorrow. Generals who ignore white flags aren't the most patient of creatures."

The Marques left, escorted back to his manor by an honour guard under a white flag. Marshal Hapten met with the commanders and Robin.

"I will listen, but you understand better how to set up for battle." Robin looked at the group of commanders.

"But you're our general." Marshal Hapten raised an eyebrow.

"Not exactly." Sarge stifled a yawn. "She is more an ambassador backed up by muscle. Lady Robin will decide whether you fight, but the fighting is up to you."

"Understood." Marshall Hapten looked around at the commanders. "We will form a pike line. There is a field only an hour's march from here. Commander Timost says it is the only place to set up a line between the Baron and the Marques."

"Remind us again why we're getting into this mess at all." Commander Betrice leaned back. "We could get out of the way and let them fight it out."

"We could." Robin stood up. "But we aren't going to. The king asked me to do what I could to prevent the empire collapsing into civil war. I will not back away from the first hint of trouble without at least talking to the two of them."

Chapter 2

Robin rose with the Fhayden force before dawn and marched to the chosen field of battle. Timost's scouts were watching for an attack through the forest.

"Relax for now." Marshal Hapten ordered them, "But stay where you can form up in a hurry. We don't want to get caught with our pants down. "

Fortunately, the day was cool and cloudy. The men and women wore armour but kept their helmets at their sides. Dice and card games started while others lay on their backs and rested. The sun rose and lit the field in shades of grey, then colour seeped in as the light grew.

Marques Povost and his forces arrived and arranged themselves behind the Fhayden thousand.

Just before noon, a shrill whistle came from the forest.

"Form up," the commanders shouted, and the lounging soldiers became a double line of pikes across the field, far enough back to be out of range of bows. Soon after, the sound of tramping feet grew until it echoed across the field.

The opposing army erupted into the field, setting up their own lines.

"That's more than six hundred." Robin shielded her eyes with her hand.

"Crafty old bugger," Marshal Hapten smiled tightly. She nodded and strolled out past the lines of pikes with Robin, the Marques, and a squadron of the Marques' men.

"We're here under a white flag to talk." Robin shouted through a speaking trumpet.

"Fire!" A cloud of arrows flew toward them. The Thousand's soldiers held up large shields and blocked them. One woman fell with an arrow in her knee, but the others lifted her as the shield wall backed through the pike line.

"Hold fast," commanders shouted. The front line held shields up and blocked the arrows as the enemy line marched forward, swords and shields as the ready. The arrows stopped as the lines grow closer together.

The two lines of pikes lowered to create a spiky barrier between the opposing forces. The enemy line faltered.

"Forward!" Shouts came from the enemy. "They're just sticks."

They continued their march until the points of the pikes were at their throats, then the front line of the enemy broke and tried to force their way back away from the iron tips of the long spears. Chaos destroyed any semblance of an ordered attack as the enemy fought itself to get away. The Fhayden line didn't move.

Shouts from the enemy tried to restore order, but when the soldiers couldn't get back through their lines, they fled into the forest and away.

"Alright, we'll talk. Lower your weapons." A trumpet blast stopped the forward movement of the baron's army, but didn't slow the flow of soldiers away from the battlefield. An immense man in armour, flanked by others with shields, walked forward under a white flag and a banner Robin guessed was the Timost coat of arms. They had to weave past wounded and groaning men and women, injured by their own panic.

"You always were a coward, hiding behind the emperor and now behind your mercenaries." The baron shouted. "Come out and fight me, Povost."

"A bit late for that." Commander Timost strolled out of the forest. "Attacking another noble house is treason, father. Even you know that." The baron's army split to allow him to reach the spot where the baron still pushed his way forward.

"Treason against what?" The baron pointed at his son. "The emperor is dead, or as good as dead."

"Treason against the Ancan people." Commander Timost shrugged as he stood toe to toe with his father. "Seize him and I will let you and your families live."

The baron moved to draw his sword, but his own soldiers piled on him, dragging him to the ground.

Incoherent shouting became muffled as the baron's face jammed into the ground.

"Take him and hang him." The new Baron Timost pointed at a tree standing out from the forest. The old baron fought to get loose, but even his enormous size couldn't overwhelm six men. They tied his hands behind him and dragged him to the tree to hang him. Once the rope cut off the baron's curses and pleading, the men returned to kneel in front of Timost. He looked at them like a man faced with an inevitable but troublesome task.

"Command us, Baron Timost."

"Aid the fallen, send messengers to tell the peasants they are free to return to their farms. I won't lose any more of my people to this nonsense."

"There is still the matter of the village." Marques Povost walked with Robin and Marshal Hapten out of the still motionless pike line to join the new baron in the field.

"Consider it restitution for this act of treason." Timost waved his hand. "I have too much work to do to fuss about a village, no matter what strategic importance it may have had to my father."

***

Robin kept the Fhayden forces in the Marques' field for a week while they worked with both Povost and Timost farmers on preserving the soil through techniques they'd learned from the fae.

The soldiers didn't mind the down time and many of them helped with the harvest and getting the land ready for the winter, but the commanders argued.

"If we are going to do mostly farm education, we should split up and spread out. Send small teams like scouting squads. It would be much more efficient." Commander Betrice insisted.

"Smaller groups would be more vulnerable." Revont leaned forward. "The only reason the Marques gave us the time of day was because we are a sizeable group."

"Small groups would be less threatening. We were lucky the Marques didn't run us off his land. We don't have a letter from all the noble daughters to introduce us."

"The Marques and Baron Timost have said they will write letters of introduction."

Those two were the most vocal, but all the commanders had an opinion.

After a meeting ending with a shouting match, Sarge challenged Robin. "You're going to have to decide."

"I'm not sure. There is so much truth on both sides."

"A wrong decision is better than no decision." Sarge thumped his cane on the tent floor. "It is bad for discipline and worse for morale."

"What if I keep the main force together and ask for volunteers to move out in small groups? If we send out a hundred in groups of five, we get twenty times the reach."

"Dividing the force is risky." Sarge gazed at her with unflinching eyes.

"Yes, it is, but we aren't here for a picnic." Robin retorted. "We have a job to do, even if I'm not sure what it is yet."

"Still nothing?"

"Just a growing certainty we need to move north."

"There are going to be more nobles setting out to address old grievances." Sarge shifted in his chair. "Not to mention those who will try to carve out their own territory to rule."

"We were lucky both the Marques and Commander Timost were following the law. There will be more like the old baron who decide they are free of all that." Lencely brought Sarge a cup of water, his ears red. He was much more reserved after his brush with death.

"Good point, Lencely." Robin nodded at him, then stood up. "I need to sit under a tree for a while."

"Now?" Lencely's eyes widened. "It is black, dark out."

"Now. Lencely, run and bring Ham and Sargent Temajin. I will need a guard."

"I will come too." Lencely ran out before Robin could argue with him.

"Will you be all right with just Rud?"

"It's 'bout time I hit the sack." Sarge yawned. "I will get the lads to walk me to my tent before you go sitting in the dark."

The gibbous moon hung over the camp as Robin walked to a large tree on the edge of the forest. She sat with her back to the tree facing away from camp.

Meetings with commanders and resolving minor issues in the force ate into her time. If she could grab a few minutes alone with Sarge, she counted herself lucky. Once before, being disconnected from the land had caused trouble.

The night started still, but as she sat without moving, small animals rustled in the leaves. A squeak told her an owl had caught its dinner.

The land here was less sure, more fearful. Robin crooned to the land like she would to a wounded soldier. A weight around her neck turned out to be the amulet Gris had given her. As she held it, a soft glow filled her hand.

The land was dying, fractured and sick from breaking the covenant with Fhayde. Violence dotted across it added to its pain. Robin ignored the tears on her face and listened. The emperor had abandoned the golden throne, and his absence was an open wound. Robin had been certain the empire was doomed, but she'd never imagined the connections holding the land's consciousness together were so fragile.

The moon set, and Robin still sat and listened. It reminded her of sitting with her aged grandmother toward the end. The elderly woman had rambled across time and relationships before they found her dead one morning.

They didn't have much time to do anything. The only clue was the emperor, and he'd been seen last heading north from the capital. She had to find the emperor and convince him to retake the golden throne and somehow heal Anca. Knowing where the emperor was would have helped, but she'd depend on the tug from the land to guide her.

Robin stood and dried her eyes. She had work to do.

***

"We will split our forces." Robin announced and held up a hand to still the response. "I've been reluctant to do so, but I was wrong. Our task is more urgent than I had realized. The land here is sicker than I thought. But I can't allow the whole thousand to be slowed by helping landowners with healing their soil."

"How do you see this working?" Marshal Hapten tapped her fingers on her jaw. "Command will be decentralized. If you need help, you won't be able to call for it."

"If I need help, I won't have time to call for it." Robin took a deep breath. "Betrice and Hurold's hundreds will follow the border east to the mountain and west to the ocean. Talk to the nobles, tell them you're there to help, show them the letters from the Marques and the Baron. You'll travel under the white banner and leave the pikes behind. They will slow you down."

"We can do that." Hurold nodded vigorously. "Will send a message to Fhayde telling them what we're up to. What about you? What report do you send to the Duke?"

"The rest of us are heading north to find the emperor."

"One commander of five hundred will need to stay back to take reports and keep the supply lines open." Revont stared into space. "I'll need another hundred. With your permission, I will train the locals to use the pikes."

"The pikes don't make you invulnerable." Sarge looked around at the commanders. "A disciplined infantry can get under the pikes and break the wall. It is most useful against calvary, and a smart commander will send the calvary around the flanks."

"I will keep that in mind." Revont rolled her shoulders. "Now if you don't mind, I've some organizing to get at." She stood and nodded to Betrice and Themson. The three of them left the command tent.

"The pikes slow us down and make us look more of a threat. We'll bring a wagonload of them, but no more. We don't stop to chat, other than telling the nobles they can ask for help from the hundreds stationed here."

"Very good." Marshall Hapten slapped her knees and stood up.

"One other thing." Robin held up a hand. "I've been spending too much time on things the commanders should have a handle on. If you haven't done your best to deal with something, don't come talking to me."

"What will you be doing?" Sarge asked.

"What only I can do, listen to the land. We are here for the land. It is vital for me to take time to listen to it."

"I don't understand, but that isn't my job." Paychen sighed, then caught Marshall Hapten's eye. "We can take it from here."

"We march at dawn." Robin yawned, the sleepless night catching up with her. "If you need me, I will be in my tent."

Chapter 3

Hob crawled out of his tent, his breath hanging in the air. Stirring the coals to get the flames going again, he looked around to see who else was awake.

Willow appeared from the woman's tent and shivered.

"I'll be glad when we get north, and it is warmer."

"We are high in the mountains too. It is a good thing we had Duncan to drive us over the pass." Hob put a pot on the fire to warm for tea. It didn't get properly hot up here. One of the many things he looked forward to on arriving home.

"Talking about me again?" Duncan stood up and stretched until his joints popped. "I'll admit that was scarier than I expected."

"It was better than the first crossing." Hob poked at the ice in the pot. "I thought I'd died and gone to hell."

The others woke and moved around to get warm. Tad and Gren checked on the horses and fed them a bit of the hay and oats they carried on the wagon.

"They come through the night fine." Tad reported, while Gren adjusted the blankets on the beasts.

"Good."

They drank tea accompanied by a hunk of bread before Hob kicked the fire apart and hung the pot in its place on the wagon.

"Let's go." Hob brushed the grey dust from his clothes, a new set of browns, just as the others wore. "We'll be warmer walking."

Trab and Spen hitched the horses. Trab climbed up onto the seat with Duncan. They would all learn how to drive the wagon. Duncan was comfortable if not fluent in Ancan, so talking wasn't a problem. What to talk about was a mystery Hob had yet to solve.

As they meandered down the mountain, it grew warmer. Willow heard running water and took the pot to fill it. Hob accompanied her. Duncan's suggestion was they go nowhere alone.

"What are we going to do when we get home? They won't be expecting us."

"No. We will see when we get there."

The sun was setting when they arrived at the still nameless village Lord Huddroc's son had built. An enormous building in the centre loomed over the huts made of cut and barked logs. A high-born woman came out of the building and hooted loudly. Soon a crowd surrounded Hob and the others.

"I am Maysan, second in command. Lord Vipal is hunting with some others, so I welcome you in his name. Supper is not yet ready, so there is time to refresh yourselves." Villagers chattered at the visitors as they showed them to another building.

"The water comes out of the ground hot. It will warm you up and soothe your aches." A man led them in and showed them where to put their clothes. Steam rose off the water. It had an odd smell, but none of the men in the pool paid any attention.

Hob rinsed himself off with a bucket of tepid water, then lowered himself into the pool. His muscles immediately relaxed, and he let out an 'ah.'

He could have fallen asleep, but his guide, Don, nudged him. "It's dangerous to sleep in the pool, and you'll want to be awake for supper."

The meal was almost as good as his first meal with Lord Huddroc.

"We confiscated it from the Ancans who would have just dropped it into a gorge." Don kept putting more food on Hob's plate. "No need to go hungry here."

Maysan came by and asked Hob if everything was all right. He had to stop himself from kneeling in front of her. He was one of the Free, no more kneeling to overseers and masters.

The next day, Duncan and Lord Vipal dug through the wagon, checking all the gear. Lord Vipal insisted on loading yet more supplies.

"No telling when you will next get a chance to restock. Heard things are tough down the mountain."

"It has always been hard." Hob said. "Many more of my people are peasants. A village could live for a month on what is in the wagon."

"Good, you won't starve then." Lord Vipal slapped him on the back and walked away, shouting something in Calderan Hob couldn't follow. He hadn't seemed angry, and the blow was too light to be punishment.

"He's like that with everyone." Duncan dusted his hands off. "Doesn't care if you're commoner, Free or Ancan."

"I see." Hob rolled his shoulder. He didn't know what to think of being equal to Lord Vipal.

***

They reached the flat plain where the Ancan army had gathered. Splashes of green broke up the dust. After they'd set camp, Hob wandered through the plain. An overseer's whip lay discarded. He found a knife with the tip broken off and a few other things broken and half covered with dust and sand.

"I expected to die." Willow came up beside him and put a hand on his shoulder. "I didn't know what to do, so I just obeyed orders. No one ordered anyone to pick something up." She took the knife and turned it in her hands.

"Keep it." Hob said. "It is a good enough knife, even without the tip. It didn't deserve to be left behind."

He and Willow strolled back to the camp. "Strange, not needing to run everywhere." She took his hand and squeezed it.

In the morning, a breeze came up, and they had to tie kerchiefs over their mouth and nose to avoid choking on the dust.

"There's a village about a day away." Hob pointed down the road. "Best to arrive at first light. It will keep us from needing to guard the wagon all night."

"Right then, an easy pace and we camp early." Duncan snapped the reins lightly, and they rolled down the road. The only thing they could see was the flat plain of dust. The wind died when the sun was high, and as annoying as the dust could be, it at least helped to dry the sweat.

They camped far enough away from the village it floated in the air like an illusion.

The sun rose like a huge red ball while they drove the last stretch to the village. Curious peasants came out to meet them, carefully not looking up at visitors wealthy enough to be driving a cart and horses. A fat man burst out of the one house.

"Shoo, shoo, away with you." The guards on either side of the man slapped clubs against their palms.

"What may I do for you, my Lord?" The man scowled at Hob, but said nothing to him.

"I don't speak Ancan well." Duncan stammered out. "My man will speak for me."

"We are merchants." Hob let the well-practiced lie slip off his lips. "Whatever you wish to buy, we can make a deal."

The fat man caught sight of the youngest of them, a girl named Spen. "I'll buy her."

"You misunderstand." Hob said. "We are merchants, not slavers. None of us are for sale."

The guards frowned and stepped forward, clubs raised.

"Perhaps you are interested in fresh venison, not three days old." Willow came around the wagon to stand between Spen and the guards. "We have greens as well, hardly wilted."

The fat man's attention moved from Spen to Willow, and he licked his lips. "We've had nothing but lentils and beans. Hardly better than a slave's diet." He clawed at his pouch and dug out a few coins. Hob nodded and a bag of greens and a leg of venison traded hands. The guards held them like they were gold as they scurried back to the house with their treasure.

Hob opened his hand and stated at the coins. He'd never held money before. A peasant owning coin meant death, just as anything which didn't serve the masters meant death.

Peasants appeared as the man slammed the door behind him.

"Food, we need food."

They crowded around.

"We are merchants. We have nothing to give away. Ask your master for food." The peasants growled, but when Hob didn't flinch, they slunk away. One stayed longer than the others glaring at Hob.

"You're a peasant like us. What did you do to deserve to live like lords?"

"We survived." Hob slapped the man on the back. "And claimed our freedom."

The man staggered back as if Hob had delivered a full blow with a club and stared at him wide-eyed.

Hob swung up onto the wagon and checked quickly that everyone was on board. "We will leave now."

"What do you mean, freedom?'

"No overseers, no fat man eating all the food while you starve. It doesn't come easy."

"They will kill us."

"What are they doing now?"

Duncan snapped the reins, and they rolled out of the village.

***

In the next village, there was a well and overseers guarding it while peasants filed by to scrape what meagre harvest they could get from the dusty ground. Another overseer counted every grain of food to be sure no one dared steal it.

Hob drove the wagon through the village. He didn't feel like stopping. Nightmares of his time in the canyon fighting the straw men haunted him.

"We may as well stop and get rid of the last of the venison," Duncan said. "Or we'll have to dump it."

"Yes, Duncan." Hob said like he would have said 'yes, master.' Duncan didn't notice, but something burned in Hob's stomach, like he'd swallowed a live scorpion.

The man who came out this time was thin and tall. He stared down his nose at them.

"What are you doing here?"

"We are merchants—" Hob started before the overseer beside the man whipped him across the face.

He turned back to the thin man. "We are merch—" Hob caught the whip and wrenched it out of the overseer's hand. "—ants, we have meat and greens to sell. If you don't wish to buy, we will be on our way."

"I will not be spoken to by a peasant."

"He is my voice." Duncan jumped down from the wagon. "If you strike him, you strike me." He sounded exactly like a noble. His hand rested on his sword. "Now, you will buy our meat and greens, or we will leave."

"My lord," the thin man fell to his knees. "I didn't order him to strike. I will have him hanged immediately." The overseer dashed away, and two guards chased after him.

"I have coin in my house." The thin man scurried away.

"We may as well go," Duncan said. "He's not coming back."

They climbed back into the wagon and drove away. Outside the village, Hob threw the last of the venison to the ground. He dropped the overseer's whip in the dust.

Once they were out of sight of the village, Duncan stopped the wagon and insisted on washing the welt on Hob's face.

"I'm sorry. Perhaps I should do the talking."

"I'll talk." Hob said.

"Okay, you're the boss." Duncan walked around to the back of the wagon. "If the trouble gets real, there are spears here. No shields, they'd take up too much space."

They drove until nightfall and made camp. Hob's face ached, but he ignored it and set the fire as usual, keeping it small to preserve their wood.

He couldn't sleep, so he sat in the wagon and stared at the stars.

***

Whispered conversation woke Hob. Someone was approaching the camp. More than one, bandits probably, attracted by the firelight.

Hob slipped out of the wagon and pulled out a spear, then another, and nudged Willow's foot. She'd taken to sleeping under the wagon, claiming it was cooler. Her eyes opened wide. He handed her a spear, then pointed to the tents. She nodded and crawled to the men's tent and scratched on the canvass.

Hob crept out into the darkness and circled round until the whispers were between him and the fire.

"Look at this, didn't even set a watch. It's like they want to be robbed. I didn't think they were merchants."

Duncan walked around the wagon holding his sword. Five men stepped out of the darkness to face him.

"Looks like it's just one light sleeper," a man said, then spat into the dust. "Drop the sword and we'll let you live."

One of the others snickered.

"You really want to die for this wagon?" Duncan pointed his sword at the man doing all the talking.

"There's five of us and one of you." They fanned out to circle Duncan, who put his back to the wagon.

"So, who's first to die?" Duncan grinned at them and waggled his sword.

Hob had used the conversation to sneak up close as the biggest man spoke.

"Kill him boys." He hung back out of the fight and didn't know Hob was there until the spear point came out through his chest. Hob let him drop to the ground. The four remaining men turned to attack Hob. Duncan cut one of them down, then Willow ran her spear through another one. In seconds, the five men were bleeding out into the dust.

"We should have been setting watch." Hob poked the corpses with his spear. "We got lucky this time."

"I didn't think." Duncan stared at the men.

"It doesn't matter. We're alive and they're dead." He wiped the spear point on a body, then searched through their clothes and pouches. "Nothing much useful."

"Let's move camp now, before these are missed." Duncan pointed to the big one. "He was at the village. The thin guy will know something's up when they don't return."

"We bury them." Hob pulled out the shovel from the wagon. "They disappeared. Nothing to do with us."

The sky lighted in the east as Hob tossed the last shovel of dust on the graves.

"Let's go."

Chapter 4

"You can't save them." Sarge watched the faces on the side of the road begin with fear, move to hope, then end in resentment.

Robin frowned. "I wasn't sent north to save anybody. I know that, but not being able to do anything hurts."

"You are doing something."

"No, I'm marching an army through lands on the edge of civil war, looking for someone who might be dead." Robin looked away at the horizon. "They're going to be hungry this winter, if they are lucky. Or maybe they would rather starve than see everything they've worked for fall apart."

Sarge banged his cane on the floor of the wagon. Rud jumped, then reddened and looked away.

"You won't achieve anything by pouting." Sarge snapped. "You got swept up in events and it felt like the world was changing. Now time has slowed and is dragging you down. The adrenaline is gone and you're realizing it wasn't all change for the good."

"How did you deal with it? Going from battle where every second counts to life, where days pass with no change?" Robin turned to look at Sarge.

"Some took to drinking or doing things to get that rush back. Many couldn't fit back in their old lives the way they were."

"What about you?" She looked at him with dark eyes.

"When I was young, I stayed where I could fight and wasn't too worried about why. Slowly, the weight of all the people I'd lost and those I'd killed crushed me. I took up studying war, trying to understand it." Sarge sighed. "I never had a family, no living relatives close enough to care about me. When you called me, I didn't have anyone who I'd call a friend. I'm no model of successful living."

"That sounds so lonely." Robin's voice cracked.

"You don't want to live like that." Sarge tried to find a way around the stone that blocked his heart. "Remember your friends as they were alive. What would they want for you?"

"I can't say." Robin said in a flat voice. "I only see their dead eyes condemning me. In my nightmares, I am the last person standing, alone in the world."

"How much of that is the effect of the broken land here?" Sarge closed his eyes. "How much is not having time to grieve?"

"I try to grieve, to remember Gord and imagine his family's pain. How he tried so hard to be a help to you. I try to think of the times when Gris and I weren't fighting for our lives." Robin's hand moved to the amulet hanging from a chain around her neck. A faint glow shone even in the daylight. It traveled along her arm to her elbow and vanished under the chain mail she wore. "I'm scared, Sarge. I'm scared I'm not good enough to make a difference."

"Aren't we all, lass?"

Robin turned back to the landscape and didn't reply.

***

Robin fell into the trance she'd achieved beneath the tree in the forest. She tried to connect with the land, not just the land they traveled through, but her home.

"Wha'cha doing?" Gord floated in the darkness.

"Thinking." Robin clutched at calm and wrapped it around her like a blanket.

"Bout what?"

"What am I doing here?"

Gord snickered. "Does it matter?"

"Sure it does," Robin said.

"Why?" Gord laughed and vanished.

Sounds from the world dragged at her and she reluctantly swam toward them through the darkness until her head broke the surface.

"Wake up, lass." Sarge knelt beside her, shaking her. "Come back."

"I'm here." Robin looked around, her eyes trying to make sense of the world. Red light lit one side of the sky.

"What's going on?"

"You've been sitting like this all day." Sarge said. "You were scaring me."

"I was talking to the land, just for a few minutes at most."

"I thought I was going to lose you." He tried to move into a more comfortable position. Robin reached out to help, and her muscles cramped. She ignored them and grasped his hands. The black of his hands made hers look white as the full moon, but they were warm and strong.

"Gord, help me get him in his chair."

Rud's brow wrinkled as he took one of Sarge's arm. "I'll help." Robin lifted the other.

"How long was he on the floor?"

"Marshal Hapten come by to say we were camping in the next clear field. The sun was two fingers 'bove the horizon then.

"I'm old, but I'm not dead yet." Sarge adjusted his seat in the chair. "I can hear you."

"Sorry, Sarge." Robin sat at his feet.

"No worries, lass." Sarge patted her head.

They sat like that until the wagon pulled into a field.

Marshal Hapten rode over to them.

"You all right now, Lady Robin?"

"I am thanks."

"Very good. The scouts arranged this spot for us in exchange for help with the harvest tomorrow."

"Good." Robin stood and stretched. "Let me know as soon as our tent is ready."

"Oh, you have a visitor."

"Right." Robin shrugged her mail into position. "Lead me to them."

"This way Lady Robin." She strode into the organized chaos to where an old woman stood waiting with a basket.

"My Lady," the woman tried a stiff curtsey. "I brought some bread for ye, it ain't much, but…"

"Thank you." Robin took the basket and bowed. "You honour me. Marshal, we will host the noon meal tomorrow."

"We can't feed every village." Marshal Hapten said.

"We can feed this one."

"Yes, my Lady, I will speak to the quartermaster." Marshal Hapten saluted.

"I'd better be gettin' home." The old woman bobbed again and left at a surprisingly brisk walk.

"Lady Robin, the tent's ready." Lencely stood at her side.

"Great."

***

Robin rose with the sun and put her mail and dress uniform on. The men and women were already in the fields. She knew nothing about farming, but the harvest looked scanty.

Soldiers stood and saluted her, people from the village bobbed and removed their hats until she'd passed by.

The harvest finished by noon and everyone from youngest to oldest joined the Thousand for a meal. The noise of conversation deafened her, but she smiled. At this moment, in this place, she made a difference.

"Lady Robin, there's some trouble at the gate." She recognized the young soldier. He'd been at the gate when someone shot at her.

"Lead on." Robin followed him to where the guards had stopped a handful of scruffy men.

"You look like bandits," a guard was saying. She wasn't wrong. They wore clothes that were more rags than cloth, and Robin could catch their odour even from this distance.

"What is going on?" Robin demanded. The guards shot to attention.

"These men aren't part of the village, but they want in. They promise to cause trouble if we don't feed them," her young guide said.

"Deserters most likely," another added.

"We're jus' trying to stay alive." One bandit tried an ingratiating smile, exposing a mouth lacking most of its teeth.

"You treat us right, and we'll treat the village right," another tucked a handless arm under the other.

"Guard, fetch a basket with some food for these gentlemen." Robin didn't need to glance over to see the astonished look on the guards' faces. "It is a harvest festival. I don't want to turn anyone away hungry."

The toothless one fell to his knees. "Thank you, great Lady." The others dropped too.

"When the time comes, you will help the village, even if it means your death."

Heads nodded in unison.

"The land hears your promise and will hold you to it."

The basket of food arrived, and the men scurried away into the forest on the far side of the road.

"Why'd you waste good food on the likes of them?" The guard sounded more puzzled than angry.

"They are even poorer than the village. They talk tough, but all of them together couldn't threaten you, and they aren't much threat to the village. Who knows, they may keep their promise."

***

The camp was quiet but for the soft dialogue of the sentries. Robin sat on the floor of the tent and reached for the land. She held Gris' amulet in her hand.

"What are you doing, lass?" Gris said. "You're either hunting or you're not."

"I miss you, Gris."

"Like I told you, grieve and move on. Don't let the dead take over your life."

"Thank you."

"For what?"

"For being you."

"Huh, who else would I be?" Gris laughed and Robin had to laugh with her. She opened her eyes, still laughing quietly, with tears running down her cheeks. Crawling into her bed, Robin pulled the covers over her head and went to sleep.

***

For the next week, they marched north through barren fields and meagre harvests. Robin detached another hundred and had them visit villages and teach them the fae's farming methods. They camped in abandoned fields and marched through empty villages until they reached a city. A man in fine clothes met them at the gate.

"You may camp outside the city, but not enter except for your officers." The man didn't as much as glance at Robin. "They will follow me to meet the lord of this land."

The land nudged Robin. "Hapten, Revont, you will remain here. I'll take Ham and Sargent Temajin along with a squad. We are under the white flag. Let that guide you."

"You?" the man sneered at her. "You aren't to my Lord's tastes."

"Good, then we won't waste time with idle chitchat." Robin held the man's gaze until he dropped his eyes. "I am Robin Fastheart, Shieldmaiden and friend of the king."

"Apologies, my Lady." The man set out at such a fast pace that Robin needed to jog to keep up. Ham and Sargent Temajin had to stretch their legs to stay in place on either side of her. The ten members of the squad had no trouble with the pace, even uphill.

I'm out of shape, and I look ridiculous. Robin slowed down and breathed until her heart rate returned to normal.

"Keep up," the man said.

"No." Robin set out at her pace.

The man stared at her. "Do you know who I am?"

"You haven't introduced yourself, or who your Lord is, so no, I don't know who you are, but I will not be paraded through the streets and made a fool of." Robin kept going. Ham glowered at the man.

"I am Rapustin Lordson. I run this city and I don't have time to waste."

"You won't be wasting time. You'll be acting courteously." Robin let an edge into her voice as she looked around her. If this Lordson was running the city, he wasn't doing an outstanding job of it. People sat in alleys watching listlessly. The shops, if they were open, looked half empty.

"This way then." He walked at such a slow pace that Sarge could have kept up. Robin spent the time looking around. The villagers were in better shape than most of the people here. Many of them coughed and her blood chilled. *Is there plague here?*

"Why are there so many people doing nothing?"

"Lazy people from the countryside. One poor year and they give up. I'd drive them all back to their farms if I had my way." Lordson sniffed and walked faster. "Their parents and grandparents had no trouble working the land and paying their taxes."

Robin hoped the Lord of the city would be more amenable to listening.

They arrived at a fine manor; the grounds were in impeccable condition. Autumn flowers bloomed but, from the front at least, there was no sign of a vegetable garden.

"Your guards will wait here."

Lordson strode through the front door and through the foyer to double doors. He knocked twice, then pushed through the doors. Robin entered the room accompanied by Ham and Sargent Temajin.

"She's here, my Lord."

The Lord looked around, appearing to be a few years older than King Federick.

"Her?" His gaze traveled up and down her body. "Oh well, she'll do." The young Lord heaved a sigh. "Right then. We surrender."

Chapter 5

Hob avoided driving through the next two villages.

"What are we doing here?" Hob said as they sat around a tiny fire set in the middle of the expanse of the plain and the night sky.

"It is your expedition." Duncan said. "I'm just here for support."

"We trust you, Hob," Willow put her hand on his. The others nodded.

"I'm not sure I trust myself. Who am I to be thinking about freeing my people? What can I offer that is better than what they have?"

"You'll figure it out." Willow sighed. "Your lady didn't trust you just because you were there. What you did worked."

"I'm just a peasant."

"You were never just a peasant." Duncan said. "That was clear the first time we met."

"We are within a day or two of my home." Hob said. "I wasn't told I couldn't return, but the expectation was that I would die somewhere far away. The masters may not be happy to see me. My family may not be pleased to see me."

"We'll handle that as we go." Spen said and glanced over at Trab, the youngest man with them. He said nothing, but he blushed. Maybe they were why Willow slept under the wagon.

Hob sighed. "We will stash the spears before we arrive, but close enough to fetch them on foot. I have a spot in mind."

The plain grew rougher, with rocks peeking out of the dust. They didn't need the kerchiefs to keep the dust out of their mouths, but the ride was rougher, tossing them about the wagon. Hob was happy to camp and stay still for a few hours.

Midmorning Hob called for a stop and climbed out of the wagon.

"Come here. You'll all need to be able to find this again." He dug into the dust and found wood, a little more digging, and he unearthed an iron ring. "Stand back." Hob heaved at the ring and pulled what looked like the top of a coffin out of the dust. A gigantic snake slithered out and into the shade of a nearby rock.

"She's never bit me yet." Hob pointed to the ground. "We'll put our spears in here. Look at the rock where the snake is. Walk around it, study it until you can recognize it from any direction. At mid-morning the rock's shadow points to the cache."

"Wouldn't it be safer to open it at night?" Willow asked.

"It isn't supposed to be safe." Hob said. "My grandfather showed me this. There are stashes of weapons all over the plain. I only know a handful of them. They tend to be near rocks that stand out, but they have to be opened at different times of day."

"How long has it been here?" Spen peered into the hollow in the ground, lined with slabs of stone. It held knives, swords, scythes, broken poles from farm implements.

"Since we were a free people." Hob said. "Generations of us stashing what we could, hoping to fight off our oppressors. Back when we had clans, my family was snake clan."

They put the spears and Duncan's sword, along with anything they didn't want taken away, into the hollow, then Hob lowered the top and kicked dust over it. He waved a blanket over it to even out the dust, bowed to the snake, then climbed back on the wagon.

"The next time we stop will be at my home."

***

They rode toward the sun until their shadow moved behind them.

"We've talked about what we are going to do." Hob wiped dust off his face. "It would be safer to sleep with grandmother snake. Remember your part and trust each other. We won't get to make a second mistake."

Hob put a slave face on. Obedient, fawning, eager to please. The others took their parts.

"Master, we are here." Hob said.

Duncan frowned. "I can see that. It will be nice to get away from this fae forsaken plain."

Hob ducked his head to prepare for a blow, but none came. He sighed silently.

The wagon rolled into a square with a manor house built on one side, barns and other building completed three sides of the square.

A man in a white robe strolled out into the square, then spat on the ground. "Peasants around back."

"Sorry, my lord." Duncan spoke flawless Ancan. He turned the wagon in a circle and followed a narrow track to where a tall wall encircled a wide swathe of land, out of sight from the manor.

The crops looked even worse than when he'd left, but that was the least of Hob's worries. Overseers came to meet them.

"What have we here?" A tall, heavily built man sauntered around the wagon.

"Returning slaves from the war." Duncan said. "We didn't enjoy having slaves about, so I was told to return them to their masters and ask a small amount of coin for my effort."

"So they lost," the big man said. "I expected no less, but they were supposed to die doing it."

"The bodies piled up almost to the top of our wall, then the General fled when he learned he could die as easily as peasants."

"The emperor will not be pleased." The overseer didn't sound like he cared.

"Peasants out of the wagon." Duncan shouted. When Hob looked at him too long, Duncan backhanded Hob to the floor of the wagon.

Hob crawled out with the others and stood waiting for orders.

"They've been like this the whole time. Stand around do nothing."

"You have to treat them right." The overseer slashed his whip at Trab. Spen leaned forward, then covered her face with her hands.

"Follow Andrwe here up to the manor. They'll have something for you at the servant's entrance."

"It better include something to drink. This damned dust has parched me." Duncan followed the other overseer.

"Come on then, peasants, I'll show you to your quarters." The overseer laughed and pushed the group into motion, copping a feel from the women and cuffing the men.

They walked to a door in the wall. The big overseer banged on the door.

"Ok, Ok, give a fellow a minute." A fat man opened the door, still adjusting his pants. "Oh, fresh blood." He grinned. "Which one do you want, Perte?'

"Keep it in your pants, or you'll end up worse than a eunuch, Ebbot." Perte slapped the fat man's face. "In." he shoved Hob and the others through the door. They walked through a tunnel to a heavy door barred with steel.

"Try not to die. It would displease the master." The fat one heaved the bar out of place and pulled the door open. They walked through into a warren of huts. Peasants moved about while children ran silently through the streets.

"Welcome home." Perte laughed, then slammed the heavy door shut.

They were immediately swarmed by peasants and children, who roughly pulled their clothes away and left ragged tunics for them to wear.

Hob wandered off to see if his family was still in their hut. The masters would have kept the money promised by the Empire. Peasants weren't allowed coin.

"Hob," his sister screamed and ran away, shouting. It stopped with a slap. His mother waited around the corner.

"So you're alive. I hoped ye'd die and be quit of this world."

"Not yet, ma."

"Yer brother's in the fields. He won't be pleased to see you."

"I don't want his status as the head slave."

"Well, ye might as well go in."

When his brother, Gud, got home, he growled, jumped Hob and pummelled him with his fists until Hob curled on the floor to protect his face.

"You always were weak." Gud sneered. "I bet you hung at the back, wetting yourself for fear."

"Something like that." Hob pushed himself up from the floor and dabbed at the blood on his face. "It's good to see you haven't changed."

"Nothing changes here. We live, we work, we die."
As the lowest ranked slave, Hob was put to work in the latrines, digging out the excrement and hauling it to the fields to be used as manure., the other men from the wagon joined him. Trab, covered with bruises like Hob, Lem who hadn't said two words in all the time Hob knew him. Gren who spat in Hob's direction, and Tad who slapped him on the back.

The field slaves ignored them; the overseers yelled at them to hurry and go away. They split into teams of two, each team digging one of the village latrines each day, and the last team digging out the overseer/guard latrines. Even the Whites tasked with cleaning the master's latrines didn't know what happened, only that they didn't smell like latrines.

Life settled back into the dull routine of life as a peasant.

Soon everyone forgot that he'd ever been away.

***

On the night of the new moon, Gud prodded Hob, and they slipped out of the house. Oddly, one latrine hadn't been used at all that day. Hob jumped in and found finger holes on the side of the hole. He lifted away a slab of rock. Stairs led down into the dark. Hob and Gud stepped in and Gud started down the stairs while Hob replaced the slab. Trailing one hand against the rock, worn smooth by generations of visitors, he followed Gud.

At the bottom was a single candle illuminating a room cut into the rock. Hob stepped into the room. The two oldest peasants sat on carved chairs.

"Welcome back, Hob." The man said.

"Thank you, Grandfather." Hob shrugged and looked at Gud. "I can't say I'm glad to be back."

The old man cackled and slapped his knee. "But yet here you are."

"I paid a visit to Grandmother Snake."

"You think it is time to rise against the Ancans?" The old woman tilted her head.

"Honestly," Hob took a deep breath. "I'm not sure if it will ever be time. I was fortunate to survive one campaign. I don't look forward to a new war."

"Yet," Gud interrupted, "you are here."

"If we wait for the right time, there will never be a rebellion." Hob glanced at his brother. "I think there is going to be no better time than now. Yet the reality is it will be a hard and bloody fight. We can't take half-measures. I have tasted freedom. Many of our people live in Caldera and call themselves the Free."

"Our lives are hard, but we have a life. What you are suggesting will shorten many lives. Not just the men, but women and children." Gud clenched his teeth.

"It will, and if we lose, it will be worse." Hob frowned. "I don't want to mislead anyone about what we're doing."

"And what will we be doing?" Gud asked. "Risking everything on a roll of the bones. It is all or nothing. We break free, or we die."

"Are we not already dead? We live, eat, have children, then we pass to the dust without ever even considering if we should have a dream of something better." Hob spoke directly to Gud.

"If the elders speak in favour, I will not hold back. But the risk starts long before we rise."

"We must consider all you have said and more," the old woman said. "We will call you."

Hob nodded to the elders, then Gud, before walking out. Gud was right behind him. The light behind them went out, and they climbed the stairs in absolute darkness. Hob lifted the slab out and waited for his brother before resetting the stone.

They walked through the quiet streets to the hut they called home.

"This is the best place to look at the stars, where no light intrudes." Gud looked up.

"One day I will take you to the mountains where you can see the entire sky."

***

Duncan drank down the rest of the glass of wine. He sat with the overseers in a rough dining room.

"Can you imagine travelling with them?" He tilted the empty cup, then peered into it. Perte refilled it. "I have to put up with them every day. I can imagine all too well."

"Though I can imagine some compensations." Andwre winked.

"Not with peasants." Duncan shuddered. "You never know who's had her before you."

"I wouldn't mind," Andwre said, "but I don't want to end up like Ebbot." He made a slashing motion at his groin level. "The masters have the first choice of everything. We get a bit of the leftovers if we're lucky."

"But this wine." Duncan took a long drink. "What was I talking about?" He shook his head. "I should be going."

"It's black outside. Take the rest of the bottle with you." Petre handed it to Duncan.

Duncan woke in the morning with a splitting headache and an empty bottle rolling on the floor. He crawled out of bed and made his way downstairs, one hand on the wall to keep him steady.

"There's our new recruit." Perte shouted, and Duncan winced.

"What do you mean, recruit?"

"After all the wine you drank, I was afraid you'd forget, so I had you make your mark on the contract." He held up a paper with an inky thumbprint smeared across it. "Look at your hand. It's covered with ink."

Duncan peered at his hand and the purple smear on it.

"I was that drunk?"

"Drunker, but a contract is a contract." Perte's face hardened. "The master doesn't like people who don't keep their word. He's taking care of your horses and wagon for you while you work."

"How long did I sign on for?"

Andwre came in with a wide grin. "Only a year. The pay is decent, less housing and food expenses."

Duncan groaned.

"Let's get you kitted out," the two overseers dragged Duncan to a room where they gave him pants and a shirt. "You'll need to get used to the whip. Can't have slaves hurt and unable to work, but you can't let them get uppity."

The clothes were itchy, the handle of the whip stuck to his hand, and Duncan vowed to wash it at the first opportunity.

"You'll start at the gate. Master decided if Ebbot liked the peasants so much, he could join them. Don't expect he'll last the day." Perte walked him over to the wall and opened the outside door. "You'll want to keep the outside door closed. It will keep the place cooler. The inside door you keep barred at all times unless someone shows you one of these through this little door here. They put the chip through the hatch. Never put your hand through. Some peasant will take a notion to break your arm. Here is your chip. Black means you can go anywhere except for the main part of the manor. Green is field workers, Red is crafters, Brown is the cleaning crew, you'll spot them by the smell. White works in the manor. Don't mess with the Whites or you'll get the master on your back. The guards stay in the manor, or with the masters."

"Right," Duncan held his head. "I hope I can keep all that straight."

"Don't worry, I'll be back to pound it into you. Just remember the best thing about being an overseer."

"What's that?"

"You're not a peasant."

Chapter 6

"Surrender?" Robin must have heard wrong. "We aren't here to attack anyone."

"Does it matter?" The young Lord flipped a hand. "You are an army camped outside my city. We give up."

Lordson's face behind the young Lord was a study in resignation and disdain.

"Perhaps you should start by introducing yourself." Robin said. "I am Robin Fastheart, Shieldmaiden and friend of the king."

"You can call me Edward."

"My lord!"

"Fine then," Edward rolled his eyes, "Lord Edward of Hemsburg."

"I am not accepting your surrender." Robin had a hard time not rolling her eyes as well. "We are a peaceful force sent by King Federick to aid the Empire as we can and seek an audience with the Emperor."

"You don't have a choice." Edward pouted. "I'm done with this place. You can't return to your army until you accept my surrender. If they want you back, they can come take you and I will surrender to them."

Guards flooded into the chamber. Robin held up a hand to stop Ham or Sargent Temajin from drawing their swords.

"Lock her in a guest room, a nice one, for now." He stalked out of the room.

"Take her to the Green Suite." Lordson frowned. "Remove their weapons and keep them safe."

"I will need to send a message to my people."

"Later." The guards surrounded them.

"Give them your weapons." She ordered Ham and Sargent Temajin as she handed hers over. "We don't want to do anything rash."

They followed the guards to a well-appointed suite and locked in.

"Use a chair to block the door. I don't want unexpected visitors." Robin prowled through the suite. A bath hid behind one door, a small room, probably for a maid or valet behind another.

"I will take the small room. Might as well take the opportunity for a bath as well."

"There may be spy holes, my Lady." Sargent Temajin looked around as if he expected assassins to jump from the walls at any moment.

"I will let you and Ham check. For the time being, we assume we are being listened to at least and probably watched."

"Very good."

The men nodded, and Robin flopped on the small bed in the side room. *What would Sarge say about being captured and forced to accept someone's surrender?* He'd probably laugh and ask what they were really looking for. What did Lord Edward think to gain? Security? Seven hundred soldiers could hold the city for a considerable time, but that would mean he expected an attack soon. Why not just surrender to whoever attacks? The countryside was in rough shape and many farms and villages abandoned. It wouldn't be useful to take it over.

Maybe he didn't want to rule. Lord Edward was young and perhaps impetuous. Yet Robin was younger than he was, and Lordson was doing most of the work as far as she could see. What hidden trap would spring if she accepted his surrender? She didn't want to find out. An itch in the back of her mind wanted her to travel north. She couldn't stop to take over a city from its young Lord.

What would she do if she found the emperor? Would he be willing to resume a throne he'd abandoned for whatever reason?

Robin slipped into sleep with her questions unanswered.

***

A knock on the door woke her, and her eyes snapped open to take in the unfamiliar room and the situation returned with all its weight.

"Pardon, my Lady, but the Lord has asked you to join him for dinner." Sargent Temajin frowned as his fingers drummed on his thigh.

"What resulted from your scan of the suite?"

"We found nothing suspicious."

"Anything else?" Robin sat up.

"A wardrobe full of dresses of different sizes along with some... other things."

"Right. Likely, this isn't the first time the young Lord has tried this." Robin stood up. "I will have a bath and go to dinner in my uniform."

"Do you want to keep in the front of his mind that you have an army at your back?"

"I don't think it is a bad thing. It may be the only thing keeping him behaving."

***

Dinner looked like enough to feed an army, never mind the four seats at the end of the long table. Lord Edward sat at the head of the table, a woman to his left and Lordson beside her. That left the seat to Lord Edward's right for her. She sighed and slid into place. Sargent Temajin and Ham stood behind her.

"You don't need your men." Lord Edward waved his hand. "My aunt will chaperone."

"My men stay." Robin said. "It is tradition. They won't get in the way."

"If they stay, they won't eat. I'm having dinner sent up to them."

Robin stood. "I eat with my men, Lord Edward, or not at all."

"Fine, fine," Lord Edward waved his arms. "Just sit down already."

Robin sat and noted the smirk on Lord Edward's face.

He served her soup, then himself and the other two at the table. The soup had a subtle flavour that had her guessing what the spices were. She'd hardly begun it when servants whisked it away and the Lord filled a plate with the next course. He served himself from the opposite side, then allowed servants to fill plates for Lordson and the still un-introduced chaperone.

Robin pushed her food around on the plate until the servants snatched it up. She observed as he served the next dish, but it was the same thing. Lord Edward frowned as this plate too was taken away.

"You aren't eating much."

"I'm worried about my men outside the city," Robin said, "and I eat little in any case."

"That's why you're so thin. You should eat more."

"So I can fill out the dresses you have in the wardrobe?"

"Those are just in storage." Lordson said. "I will have a seamstress by tomorrow to measure you for a proper dress."

"I don't plan on staying long enough to need a dress."

"We'll see." Lord Edward smirked again. "If you accept my surrender, you'll need a formal gown."

"I won't be accepting any surrender."

"Then you'll be here for a while, and you'll need a formal gown." He laughed as if he'd scored a major victory.

Robin hid a sigh and made it look like she was eating more than a bite or two of each course.

Lord Edward poured her a cup of wine, but she refrained. He pouted. He looked a bit cute with the pout. She was ready to dismiss Temajin and Ham, but her stomach ached like someone stabbed her. Hiding her discomfort, she picked at the cheese placed in front of her, suddenly wanting nothing more than to go to her room and soak in the bath.

Then her mind split. One part stood to the side and observed the dishes on the table, all with the same serving from two sides. *I've been poisoned, or at least drugged.* The other part sipped at the wine and laughed inanely.

From the triumphant smirk on Edward's face, he knew about the poison. He'd probably done this before. *How many times? How many dresses in that wardrobe?* She put a hand on the seated Robin's head.

"I'm sorry, the wine has given me a headache. It's why I don't drink it."

"You look pale. You should go upstairs and rest. But first write a note for your guards outside to take back to your people." Robin scribbled what he dictated on the card a servant put in front of her, then obediently stood and gestured for her men to follow her.

In the hallway to her room, escorted by Edward, she stumbled, and he moved to put an arm around her. Ham swept her up and carried her the rest of the way. Edward kissed her hand before reluctantly letting Ham and Temajin take her into the room.

"That was a true fae's feast." Robin said. The look on Ham and Temajin's faces told her they'd got the message. Ham put her on the bed in the small room.

"What do we do with Lady Robin?" Ham came out into the main room.

"Let her sleep for the moment. That snake." Temajin said.

"I'll sneak out and report to the Marshal." Ham cracked his knuckles. "I'd like to get that SOB alone for a few minutes."

Temajin spoke softly enough that Ham had to lean in to hear. "No, if you make it through, it will mean war, and if you don't, he'll know we've been warned. We should do what they expect us to do."

"But they expect us to eat the poisoned food." Ham looked worried.

"Exactly, but what did they do in the fae story?" Temajin stared at the ceiling, then put a finger to his lips.

"Got it." Ham whispered.

A knock on the door interrupted them.

"Enter." Temajin said. He accepted the plates and snitched a piece of cheese off a plate before closing the door, then spat the cheese out. Ham wedged a chair under the door handle.

He and Ham made eating noises and talked about how good the food was after shoving the food under the immense bed.

They lay down in different parts of the room and played dead.

Robin glided back into the small room and sat down beside her sleeping body.

***

A panel in the wall opened. Robin came alert and merged into her body. Lord Edward slipped through into the room. "Stupid girl. She's not on the big bed. I'll have to move her." He lifted her up and carried her to the large bed, laying her out carefully before going to the wardrobe and ruffling through the dresses. Picking one, he muttered about her lack of figure.

He came back with the dress, then bent over to unbutton her blouse.

Robin's hand shot out to grip his adam's apple, her other put the knife in her hand to his upper thigh.

"Try to speak and you die, fight me, you die. We're going to play twenty questions; you know the game. Nod for yes, shake for no."

"Ham, Sargent, playtime is over. I need you as witnesses."

"Lady Robin." They jumped to their feet.

Edward's eyes widened in fear.

"Sargent, go yell until someone comes, then tell them Lord Edward needs Lordson immediately."

Edward shook his head frantically.

Sargent Temajin returned remarkably quickly with Lordson.

"What is the meaning of thi—" Lordson paled when he saw Robin holding Edward.

"This is a trial. Turn your back to face the Sargent. When I ask a question, you will nod or shake your head."

"Guards!" Lordson squeaked and Sargent Temajin punched him in the gut. "Ham, guard the door."

Ham shut the door and wedged a chair into place, then stood ready.

Robin began questioning. "This drug, it allows you control people." Two nods.

"It is temporary." Edward nodded yes. Lordson shook his head.

"It needs to be renewed." Edward nodded. Lordson didn't move.

"You've been feeding it to women and killing them." Edward shook his head vigorously. Lordson heaved a sigh and nodded.

"You control the women with your voice." Two nods.

"You were going to poison my men." Edward shook his head frantically. Lordson shrugged.

"There is still food under the bed. Do you want to eat some?" Edward shook his head.

"Sargent Temajin, please gag Lord Edward. Ham, if Lordson makes a noise, knock him out."

Once Edward was gagged and bound, Robin stepped back and sat on the bed. "I believe most of the drug is gone."

"Where did you get a knife?" Sargent Temajin asked.

"Stole it from the dinner table." Robin said.

Chapter 7

Sarge grumbled at Lencely and Rud as they helped him to the mess tent. "Why'd she have to go up the hill with just a squad at her back? I don't have a good feeling about this."

"Robin will come through. She always does." Lencely said.

"So far, it only takes once to do for you."

"How have you survived all this time, then?" Rud asked.

"Experience." Sarge resisted the urge to whack the boy with the cane. "She's too young to be looking for treachery everywhere."

"And you do?" Lencely pulled out a chair for Sarge, just about everyone else sat on benches.

"How else would I live so long?" Sarge sat and thumped his cane on the canvas floor of the tent. "I don't mean seeing enemies under every rock, but accepting what my mind and instincts tell me. Deal with what happens, not what you think is going to."

"I guess." Rud sat on the bench across from Sarge while Lencely fetched their meal. "But I'm sure Robin will be fine."

"Don't mind me, I'm just an old man complaining."

"No, you aren't." Rud blushed. "I mean, you aren't just an old man. Everyone listens to you."

"Do they?" As soon as he said the words, Sarge wanted to kick himself. *Am I sore because she didn't come and ask my advice?* He sighed and leaned on his cane. "*I am getting old.*"

Lencely returned with the food, and they dug in.

"Pardon, Master Sargent, but the Marshal would like a word with you when you have finished your meal." The young man was part of the Marshal's staff, but Sarge couldn't recall his name.

"Thank you. I can meet him at the command tent if that is convenient."

"Very good."

Sarge forced himself to eat his meal and chat with the boys. If it was urgent, the Marshal would have said so. No need to spoil the meal. Yet he couldn't help a sigh of relief when they were done.

"I will take the dishes back and catch up to you." Rud stacked them neatly and took off.

Lencely helped Sarge up, and they made their way out of the tent.

"How is the leg?" Sarge asked.

"It still aches now and again, but I have almost no limp." Lencely stood straight as he walked. Rud dashed up to them and walked on Sarge's other side. Lencely frowned but didn't say anything.

They arrived at the command tent and the marshal came over to them carrying a card.

"This arrived about an hour ago, along with the squad who accompanied Robin." He handed it to Sarge.

I am busy with negotiations and won't be back
for several days.

"It doesn't feel like something Robin would say. I don't know her handwriting well, but this doesn't look written by her."

"She had someone else write it for her?"

"No, she knows the importance of clear communication. She'd write her own note and be much clearer about her intentions."

"Exactly what I thought." The marshal took the card back and flicked it with a finger. "The squad leader who delivered it said a servant had given it to him. Which also seemed strange. He decided it was better to let us know than to wait around and possibly make worse problems."

"I think we need to check things out carefully." Sarge settled onto a bench. "But remember, we are under a white flag. We can't be seen to be doing anything hostile."

"Robin said much the same thing as she left with that fellow. I should have gone instead, but I didn't want to argue in front of that man."

"The past is done." Lencely spoke up. "What do we do now?"

The marshal frowned but said nothing.

"We can't act without information." Sarge leaned on his cane. "That is our first requirement."

"I have sent scouts into the city to gather information." Marshal Hapten clenched a fist. "We should have had people in the city as soon as we arrived."

"They are there now. Let's see what it gains us." Sarge fought a sudden urge to rest his eyes. "While we wait, we go over likely scenarios and our reaction to them."

***

The scouts returned, all having similar reports. Lordson, the man who invited their senior officer up the hill, wasn't well liked. Some mumbled about young women vanishing into the manor and never coming out, but Lordson always had some excuse for their absence.

"I don't like this." Marshal Hapten paced in the command tent. "They are rumours, but it makes a pattern."

"I agree." Sarge tapped his cane in place of pacing.

"What are the potential outcomes?" Marshal Hapten asked.

"One, Robin is fine and any action by us will embarrass her." Lencely said. "Sorry, I'm just so used to answering Sarge's questions."

"Continue then." Marshal Hapten waved a hand.

"Two, they are holding Robin hostage, probably to get control of the Thousand for some reason." Rud said.

"Three, this has nothing to do with the Thousand and the guy is just creepy." Lencely clenched his fist, "or it could be a combination of two and three. This guy is after Robin personally, but if it gives him the Thousand, he will take it."

"Good. Whether she's a hostage or a prisoner for a different reason, we can act on the idea that she needs rescue, or support in an escape."

"We could scout out the manor." Lencely brightened. "Rud and I used to explore the castle at home and never got caught."

"And we did the same thing at the king's castle." Rud looked down, red faced. "That was before Robin started teaching us."

"I don't think I want to risk two young boys for such a mission." Marshal Hapten made a slicing motion with his hand. "Lady Robin would have my head."

"It isn't such a bad idea." Sarge tapped his cane faster. "This pair are not just young boys; they've seen battle and death. I think they have a better idea of the risk than you imagine. Besides, if they are off running about the city, doesn't that give us a reason to send people looking for them? And that group would need Lordson's permission to act."

"I still don't think it is a wise idea."

"The boys are my pages, as Lady Robin is my commander. I would go myself, but I'm useless in a fight. Neither of these two are incapable of defending themselves."

"I don't like it." Marshal Hapten stopped pacing to glare at Sarge. "I will take some troops and go up and investigate myself."

"Don't think it is wise to have the highest commanding officer away from the camp at a time like this."

Marshal Hapten started pacing again. "I hate to admit it, but you are right. Even if it was safe, they could take it as hostile intentions. I will send Commander Themson with his hundred. If he agrees, I will allow your pages to accompany him."

***

Lencely ignored the ache in his leg and kept up with Rud, walking beside Commander Themson. His heart banged in his chest, not just because of the climb up the hill. It was easy to talk down in the camp's safety about invading the manor to find Robin, but climbing the steep road to the manor in the dead of night was a whole different thing.

Commander Themson talked his way through the city gate, saying he had an urgent message for Lady Robin. The guards at the gate had let them in and even given directions to Lord Edward's manor.

"You sure about this?" Commander Themson asked them yet again. "I only agreed because Sarge argued for you."

"We're good," Rud said. "We'll be in and out in no time." He led Lencely off up the hill at a jog. It made Lencely's leg hurt more, but he wasn't going to admit that. They crossed the lawn using the shadows of a hedge and trees. They circled the building, looking for an open window, finding one near the back.

They clambered in and crept across the floor to the door. Someone snored loudly in the bed. Easing the door open, they checked the hall and slipped out of the room.

Rud gestured for them to head to the front of the manor where important guests would stay, or be kept. They dodged a couple of guards patrolling while talking about some girl in a green room in the east wing. Lencely looked at Rud and nodded.

Back at the room where they entered, they sneaked through the room and out the window. Rud looked set to dash straight to Commander Themson, but Lencely stopped him.

"We need to be as careful going out as we were going in. If we get caught, they might move her."

Rud nodded, and they rounded the building, hugging the walls until they got to the hedge to take them out to the road.

Once on the road, they dashed back to where Commander Themson would be waiting.

"Green room on the east wing?" The commander scratched his head. "It's good information, but doesn't do us much good if we don't know exactly where it is. I guess this is where we brazen it out. All right folks, we're going to walk up to the door and bang on it until someone answers. We get them to show us to the room and go from there. You lads stay with the main force outside."

"Okay," they said.

***

Someone knocked at the door with a complicated rhythm.

Robin pointed at the door. "Let them in, Ham."

He opened the door and Themson walked in with a squad of soldiers. "Good to see you alive."

"What did the scouts learn?"

"Lot of women have been disappearing. The phony letter they sent put us on high alert. Figured the place to start would be the manor house. I brought my Hundred along for company. We had no trouble from the local guards."

"Good. I want people through the city saying that Lord Edward and Lordson here conspired to drug and attack me while we were under the white banner. I believe the Emperor takes a dim view of that kind of behaviour." Robin took a long breath. "We'll need a magistrate or two for the trial. I don't want the headache of explaining a summary execution. Commander Themson, I'm leaving you in charge. Keep the prisoners under guard and separated."

"Of course, my Lady." Themson saluted, then began giving orders to the soldiers in the room.

Robin yawned. "I will be in the garden, talking with the land. Sargent Temajin and Ham will watch my back."

Chapter 8

Hob paired with Trab in the latrines, but the young man was in a foul mood. Trab complained all day that Spen had refused to see him anymore. She'd been assigned a white chip recently and couldn't be seen consorting with a Brown.

"Would you have her put herself at risk for the sake of your satisfaction?" Hob glanced around and looked for listeners before he straightened and stretched his back. "She is also protecting you. Many people the Whites care about end up in horrible situations."

"I know, but—" Trab dug his wooden shovel into the pile of excrement too hard and it cracked.

"Don't take your frustration out on the tools, or you'll be feeling the lash." Hob put his hand on Trab's shoulder, but the younger man shrugged it off. Hob returned to his work and hauled two buckets up to the pavement, put them on the yoke and headed for the gate. He didn't worry about slopping; the blanks would scrape it up and use it in the tiny gardens they kept hidden from the overseers.

At the gate, he put his chip through the hatch in the gate. The overseer pulled on the chip, almost slamming Hob's face against the wood. Then he released it and opened the gate. Hob carried his burden through the hallway slopping a bit on the floor.

"Hey, I don't want to smell that all day." The overseer jumped up and Hob met his eyes. The overseer hesitated, then Hob turned his back on the man. A flurry of blows pushed him to his knees. Blood ran down until his back itched. When the attack ended, Hob stood and steadied the yoke, then continued on his way to the field.

The overseer at the field was the big, mean one. He laughed at Hob's back, then gave him a red chip.

"Go see the knacker. Can't have our best shit hauler getting sick."

The knacker worked to heal the injured peasants, but wasn't gentle. He stitched up the worst of the wounds, then poured spoiled brandy over them. Hob grit his teeth but didn't make a sound. When it was over, he returned to work, handing in the red chip on the way through the gate. The day wouldn't last forever and the visit to the knackers cost him precious time.

Trab had traded shovels with Hob, leaving him the broken one. He had to be careful not to finish breaking it, forcing him to be slower. They'd be well behind by the time the sun set. Another day.

***

Duncan forced the nausea down after Hob had left. Perte had warned him that newbies were over enthusiastic. Hob handed the red chip in, and Duncan's stomach got worse. He almost apologized to Hob, but anyone who heard, peasant or overseer, would make even more trouble.

An hour later, Trab came through, thankfully not spilling anything on the floor.

This was the slow part of the day, with only the Browns moving in and out of the village, so he expected Trab returning would be the next person he saw.

The shouting outside pulled him to the outer door. He dared not to move any further. Peasants weren't the only ones who got lashes. Trab was swinging the yoke like a club, fighting two overseers. A third lay on the ground with the buckets near him.

Spen huddled away from Trab, holding her face, yelling at him to stop.

Trab screamed like a madman, shouting Spen's name.

A guard showed up from the manor, cursing from the thunderous frown on his face. He waited for his chance and ran Trab through the back; the sword came out his gut. The big peasant looked surprised, then dropped the yoke and fell on his face as the overseers whipped him in a frenzy.

"Why didn't you help?" The guard came over to Duncan, holding the still bloody sword.

"I was told not to leave my post for any reason."

"Not even for a madman attacking overseers?"

"Not even if the wall was burning down around me."

"So what about those poor blighters?" The guard pointed with the sword.

"Not my problem, sir."

The guard laughed and, for a second, Duncan thought he was going to be run through, but the guard used Duncan's shirt to clean his blade.

"I like you." The guard sheathed his sword and walked away.

***

Spen held her face as blood poured between her fingers. It wasn't her fault Trab went mad, but now her face was ruined, and he was dead.

"Go to the knacker and get that dealt with." The overseer at the gate handed her a red chip when she staggered away from the gruesome mess on the ground.

She almost smacked it away, but she'd just had a lesson in what happens to anyone who upset an overseer. Spen didn't remember how she made it to the knacker. Once there, she passed out on the cot while he sewed up the gash on her face. No need to ask if it would scar. She was done as a White.

Spen woke in the dark.

"Lie still." The knacker came over and crouched by her side. "I heard what happened. Don't know what the overseer was thinking, but if it's any comfort, he'll face his own punishment."

"They should all die." Speaking sent tongues of pain through her face.

"They will. Everyone dies, even the masters. It is the one inescapable truth of this world."

Spen almost laughed, but the agony of her face made her suppress it.

"Drink this." The knacker handed her a cup. "It tastes awful, but it will help with the pain."

She obediently drank it down, barely tasting it over the blood still in her mouth.

In the morning, the overseer from the manor came and took away Spen's white chip.

"It's too bad. The master had his eye on you." She tilted Spen's head to get a better look at the injury.

Spen didn't reply, and the overseer frowned.

"Pardon, but I've forbidden her from speaking. It will make her wound worse."

"That bad?" The overseer shrugged. "She'll still be good breeding stock."

"Give her a year or two and she'll have a better chance of surviving childbirth."

"As you say." The overseer shrugged and left.

"You will stay here for a few days until I'm sure it won't fester. Just sleep for now."

Even in her sleep, the pain nagged at her, but by the second day she was restless.

"If you're bored, sew up the holes in those clothes. No need for them to go to waste." He handed her a needle and thread. Spen was no stranger to needlework. Her mother had been a seamstress. She spent that day and the next closing holes in shirt and pants, most caused by a lash. She gripped the needle so tightly her hands shook, but she refused to look away from the evidence of life's cruelty.

On the third day, the overseer returned.

"Why is she still here?"

"I've made her my apprentice."

"Your apprentice? Why?"

"Why not? She has a fine hand with the needle and the rest I'll teach her, and the master will have two knackers instead of one."

So Spen stayed with the knacker and learned about herbs and injuries as peasants came by and even overseers and guards with their bangs, cuts and strains.

One day, when the knacker was out treating a horse for a cut on the leg, the white overseer came running up.

"I need the knacker immediately. The young master has been cut by a knife."

"He's in the stables." Spen still didn't like the feeling of talking with half her face numb.

"No time. You're his apprentice. You come."

Spen gathered needle and thread along with some herbs and scrap cloth, then followed the overseer to the manor where the youngest of the masters sat crying as blood oozed from a slice on his arm.

"She's not the knacker." The boy pouted.

"She is his apprentice." The overseer said nervously.

"If she hurts me, I will cut her with the knife."

"Very well." The overseer put her hands up.

"Young master." Spen kept her eyes on the ground. "You are obviously a strong and courageous man. I will need to stitch up your arm. It will hurt a little." She took a curved needle and ran it through the skin on her own arm. Two tiny droplets of blood formed in the holes. Taking a second needle, she threaded it and put out her hand. "Are you ready, young master?"

"If a peasant can handle it, I can." He put his arm in her hand.

It only took four stitches to close the wound. Each time she put a stitch in him, she ran the other needle through her own arm.

"Father, I cut myself, and the knacker has sewn up the wound. I didn't cry at all."

The master grunted and lifted the boy's arm out of her range of vision. "A tidy enough job, you may go."

Spen put her head to the ground, then gathered her kit and left. The father and son were having a dialogue about what kind of scar it would leave, but she still expected the lash for daring to talk to the young master.

"You did well," the overseer said as she caught up to Spen. "The young master is proud of his wound instead of fearful. You may continue as the knacker's apprentice." She didn't need to say that the alternative to successful treatment would have been dire, and probably fatal.

***

Hob made sure he got the good shovel the day after Trab's death. His new partner was the overseer who had marked Spen, so he got no sympathy when his shovel broke. Breaking a tool was three lashes, delivered by the new overseer at the gate, perhaps with more enthusiasm than necessary. It was part of the punishment, to be demoted to peasant, in his case only for a week.

If he worked hard and was respectful, he might survive. It was a common punishment for overseers to be demoted. It reminded them they were only one step above the peasants.

Later that day, the overseer/peasant walked too closely behind a field worker swinging a pick to break up the hard baked ground. The spike cracked the man's skull. At least he died instantly.

It was a nuisance as it meant he paired up with Gren, who subtly undermined everything. Hob did what he always did. He persevered. Gren would get tired of sharing the punishment for finishing late or he'd find some other thing to be angry about. Anger wasted energy needed to survive. Angry peasants made mistakes that could get them killed.

***

Gren had assumed they would only be peasants for a day or two to gather information, then escape. Days became weeks and nothing happened and the fire in his belly grew hotter until the only thing he thought about was someway of destroying Hob who had betrayed him. Tad told Gren to take a breath and trust Hob. After all, hadn't Hob brought them through the battles of the chasm?

Hob needed to know he wasn't above retribution.

That his sabotage did nothing to perturb Hob only made it worse. So he whispered to the overseer at the field.

"I know where the peasants have a cache of weapons."

"Why should I believe you?" The overseer lashed a peasant who had paused momentarily as if she'd heard the whisper. There was nothing she could do, other than striking Gren dead in front of the overseer. That was a forty lash punishment, few lived through it, and they never left the village again.

The overseer smirked like he'd taken the bait. They were always looking for levers to make the peasant life even less enjoyable, that made them easy to manipulate. The only thing Gren wanted was to be an overseer for a day; somewhere he could find an excuse to lash Hob.

Gren forced himself to hide his satisfaction. He probably wouldn't live through this. The peasants would kill him if the overseers didn't. The overseer was the big one who was the head overseer, like Gud was head peasant.

"Follow me." He led Gren to the stocks and locked him in. "You spoke without permission, peasant."

Through the afternoon heat, Gren plotted more and worse punishments for Hob. His skin dried and burned, his lips cracked, but the fire inside him burned hotter than the sun.

As the day faded into twilight, the overseer returned and let him out of the stocks. "Lead me to this cache."

"First, promise me I can be an overseer for a day, only one day."

"Why should I not strike you dead here?"

"You could, but you will never find the weapons without me. I don't care if I die, I only want revenge."

"If this is a trick, I will strike you dead."

"It is no trick. I will explain on the way. It will be a couple hours' walk."

"Tell me now." The overseer raised his lash.

"Very well. Out in the plain there is a certain rock, beside that rock is the buried cache of weapons."

"There are a lot of rocks out on the plain."

"There are." Gren couldn't keep the smirk from his face. "Think of the reward for locating weapons the peasants have been amassing for years."

"Are you sure you can find it, if it exists?"

"I can find my way to any place I have been, even if only once. It is a gift."

"Lead me, now." The overseer pushed Gren to the ground. "Betray me and I will stake you to an anthill."

They walked out into plains with the sun dropping below the horizon, but Gren didn't slow his pace or falter in his direction. The sensation was like that of rolling up a string, only the string took the shortest path to the target. Each step brought Gren closer to letting the rage in him loose. He didn't hide the wide smile on his face.

The long afternoon in the stocks had dried him out and sapped his energy, but the chill of the evening and the thought of revenge kept him moving. The moon rose ahead of them to turn the plain silver and black.

The moon had climbed high above them by the time they arrived at the rock. Gren tried to picture where the cache was in relation to the rock, but west of the rock was a large area without knowing how far out from the rock to dig.

"I grow weary of this." The overseer slashed Gren with his whip, enough to cause pain, but not enough to open the skin.

"Wait." Gren spoke through gritted teeth. "I can find it. Give me a hundred breaths."

"I will give you fifty."

"Fine." Gren centred himself and closed his eyes. Shuffling this way and that until he stood on the exact spot he had when Hob dug up the cache. He turned until the world lined up with his memory.

"Fifty." The overseer slapped his hand with the lash.

"I know where it is." Gren gasped, he opened his eyes. From where he stood, the cache had only been a long step away *this way*. Gren fell to his knees and scrabbled in the dust. His fingernails broke, but he ignored the pain as a minor inconvenience. He would destroy Hob in this moment, even if Gren didn't live past this hour. Something in the back of his mind said he was forgetting something important, but all he cared about was his vengeance.

He scraped the wood and dug until he found the ring. As he set himself to open the box, the overseer pushed him aside and heaved the lid off. The snake lunged at him and bit his leg. The overseer screamed and lunged at Gren, fastening fingers around his throat even as the venom arrived at his heart. His muscles spasmed and his weight brought both of them to the ground. The spasm tightened the grip of his hands as he died. The overseer fell on top of Gren, still strangling him. Gren tried to loosen the stone like fingers from his throat, but he didn't have the strength. The long day in the sun and lack of water weakened him, and even the heat of his hatred didn't allow him to break free. Gren tried to crawl out from under the dead overseer, but the man's bulk was immovable.

Gren couldn't breathe. *It is all Hob's fault.*

***

Duncan woke to chaos among the overseers. Perte had vanished. Duncan didn't mention one peasant had never checked in at sunset. He'd seen Perte follow Gren out into the plain. The guards followed the trail until the footprints in the sand vanished, then kept on in a straight lined until they reached the road to the north and south. There was no sign of either overseer or peasant.

The masters put out the word there were escaped peasants, one on them dressed as an overseer. He was relieved to hear the report second hand from Andwre. Last thing he wanted was to be connected however loosely to the disappearance.

The loss meant a greater burden on the overseers. They had been short when they 'hired' Duncan. This meant only one overseer at the field and a roving overseer who checked in at the field and the guards' latrine. The overseers didn't go into the village. Duncan was closest to being in the village, and he never went past the barred door. He just monitored the production from the village latrine and reported if it ever lessened. Perte wasn't the warmest of companions, and he'd tricked Duncan into a contract, but Andwre didn't have the same presence as head overseer.

Duncan heaved a sigh of relief in his stuffy hallway in the wall and kept silent.

***

The overseer came to visit Spen. Not that overseers did such things, but she showed up without needing treatment and insisted on talking to Spen.

"Odd that the peasant that got you that mark, and another who vanished, were from the group you came in with."

"What of it?" Spen still didn't like to talk with half her face numb. The sensation of feeling and not feeling the movement of her scar made her queasy.

"You are another, and here you are, apprentice to the knacker, a job many peasants would kill for."

"So?"

"I just think it is odd."

"Many things are odd." Spen shrugged. "It means nothing."

"Did you hear that the overseer who marked you is dead?"

"It means nothing." Spen shrugged again.

A guard came in with a cut from sharpening his sword carelessly. They favoured Spen for stitches since she'd treated the young master. She still realized the depth of her ignorance about knackering. Each new thing she learned revealed five things she didn't. Spen contented herself to spend the days stitching up people and watching the knacker mix herbs and set bones. The human body was a world unto itself and Spen its explorer.

Chapter 9

Hob doubted himself. Was his plan going to fall apart? First Trab and now Gren had strayed from the course. Was it too hard?

He shoveled excrement, no longer smelling it, not worrying how he'd smell to others. A new partner shovelled with him, just as numb and uncaring as Hob.

Carrying the buckets to the field, he thought about how the crops fed them, and they in turn fed the crops, only they took more than they gave, and the soil was dying.

Did it make sense to lead his people to freedom, only to watch them die of starvation when the land finally gave out completely? Hob didn't know. He'd always done the next necessary thing, regardless of risk to himself or others. Would this end as horrifically as the attack on the Calderan wall? Probably, or even worse.

Then one evening Gud took Hob down to the see the elders.

"Your heart is weakening," the old man said.

"I have doubts." Hob hung his head.

"It is too late for doubt." Gud rounded on him, but the old woman stopped him with a raised hand.

"Tell me of these fears."

Hob looked up at the woman.

"You can't face fears you don't name," the old man said.

"What if I fail?" Hob whispered.

"What if you do?" the old woman asked.

"We could all die, Grandmother."

"All of us will die," the old woman smiled. "Some of us sooner than others. But ask yourself this: if the masters kill all of us, who will work the fields for them? We are as necessary as air to their lives. Do they know how to prepare their food, care for their animals, make their clothing? Even they turn to the knacker when they are injured."

"The land is dying," Hob said. "Each year the harvest is smaller, the crops weaker. Even if we win, how will we feed ourselves?

"How indeed?" the old man rapped a knuckle on the arm of his chair. "We were on this land long before the masters came. Have we forgotten everything?"

"Forgotten what?" Hob asked.

"We farm the way the masters tell us, but it isn't our way. If we break away from the masters, we can return to the old ways and nurture the land. Perhaps it will forgive us in time." The old man spread his arms.

"Perhaps?" Gud asked.

"Perhaps we will die tomorrow. Perhaps we will live. We don't know until we've experienced it." The old woman shrugged. "Life is not to be clutched like the masters hoard gold, but held lightly, each day a fresh surprise and a new hope."

"We have communicated with the other elders, and they are in favour. Many will die, but many will live. It will be a new thing for us, to rule ourselves without fear."

"How?" Gud asked.

"Something learned at the wrong time can be fatal." The old man leaned back. "When you sit in this chair, you will understand. Let me just say that we are avatars of the Grandmother and Grandfather."

Hob knelt on the floor and bowed to them. "Grandmother, Grandfather, give me strength."

"You have strength in abundance." The grandmother put her hand on his head. "It is something else you lack. It will come to you when you need it."

"The masters are weakened." The grandfather added his hand, but instead of being heavier, it lightened the weight on his head.

"We need to gather the weapons." Gud said. "We have the ones from Grandmother Snake's den. We need the scorpion and coyote and the others."

"We will tell them," the grandmother said. "But we must hurry. There is danger to the west and the north."

"It is time, well past time," the grandfather rapped his knuckle again. "Arm yourselves."

***

Hob walked through the village. He knocked on certain doors. He talked to those who answered, then moved on. Gud was doing the same thing. The people who answered knocked on their neighbours' doors. Soon the entire village gathered, standing in absolute silence in the space in front of the gate.

Hob didn't need to raise his voice to be heard in the furthest row.

"We rise and reclaim our home and freedom. We will not be peasants, but the Free. Gather the weapons. Any who cannot fight will go to the caves. Otherwise, the first blow will be struck in the field."

The Free dispersed as quietly as they had gathered, leaving Hob, Gud, and a few others standing in the night.

"What about the spies?" Willow asked. "In our village, there were spies who collaborated with the masters."

"I expect them to choose, and some will go to the masters in fear, not knowing they aid our plans. Any who side with the masters will die. I expect the masters will kill them to keep them from revealing they know what we do."

"But the people in the fields..." she said.

"They accept what they risk." Gud said. "Trust Hob."

Hob looked at him in surprise.

A man ran up and whispered. "We have been betrayed. I heard our neighbours arguing, then it went silent. I found a tunnel heading toward the manor."

"Good, it begins." Hob said. "There are wheels among wheels. Show me this tunnel." Hob and Gud followed the man to a house near the wall. The man showed them the floor pulled up and a square of darkness.

Hob knelt to investigate the hole. A grunt came from behind him.

"He pulled a knife and intended on stabbing you in the back." Gud stood with a bloody knife over the man who had dropped a sliver of blade.

"I suspected as much. Spies wouldn't argue so loudly. Light a lamp and let's investigate the 'tunnel.'"

They lit a lamp and climbed carefully into the hole. A tunnel, shored up with scraps of wood, curved under the wall and came up under a bush outside the wall. A shadow flitted up the path toward the manor.

"The fire is lit." Hob said. "Now to feed it."

***

"Overseer." A guard shook Duncan awake. "You know how to fight?"

"Of course." Duncan rolled out of bed. He followed the guard to a section of the manor he hadn't been to yet. They gave him a crappy sword and a rusty buckler. "We must guard the masters with our lives. You and the other overseers will go to the field tomorrow. The peasants plan an uprising. We must kill it before it bears fruit."

"It will be good to swing a blade again." Duncan tested the balance of the sword.

"The blade will be more than the peasants have. The tool shed is kept locked. You will face unarmed peasants, along with the other overseers."

"As you say, sir." Duncan nodded.

"Go now. I woke the head overseer, but I'm putting you in charge. None of them can do anything but flail their whips."

Duncan joined the overseers, who were smacking their whips in anticipation.

"We kill the instigators quickly, then show their bodies to the rest of the peasants." Duncan hoisted the sword. "The uprising will be done by breakfast time."

The overseers laughed and followed Duncan out to the fields as the eastern sky was brightening.

The chill air made Duncan think wistfully of his uniform with its thick cloth.

"How will the blighters get out here for us to kill them?" Andwre asked. "We should burn their village down around their ears."

"Are you going to work the fields in their place?" Duncan asked. "We should think about joining the peasants. Then we'll be at the top of the heap."

The others stared at him like he'd grown a second head.

Andwre slashed at him with the whip, Duncan sidestepped the blow and ran him through the heart. Three of the overseers fled screaming, the other three attacked. They were no match for Duncan. They got in each other's way and swung their whips like they were maces.

Duncan looked at the bodies. "Too bad, I didn't mind some of you." He hoisted the sword and headed toward the village gate. He hoisted the bar out of place and pulled the door open.

Hob stood in the gap, holding some ragged clothes. "You'll want to look like a peasant today." Duncan stripped and put on the rags. Hob handed him his sword and picked up the spear, leaning against the wall.

"Where is everyone?" Duncan waved a hand at the empty village.

"Outside breaking into the tool shed, or in a safe place."

"We'd better join the crowd." Duncan swept his sword through a couple of cuts. "Damn, it's good to have my sword back."

***

Spen was organizing the herbs when the overseer crashed into the room, holding her whip, ready to slash. Spen threw the herbs she held into the woman's face.

"You knew, you little minx." The woman screamed and tried to whip Spen, but a paroxysm of coughing shook her. "What did you do to me?"

"That herb is very dangerous to breathe."

The overseer gasped for air, but blood poured out of her mouth and eyes. She collapsed on the floor and thrashed for a moment before lying still. Spen backed out of the room and dropped the curtain. It would take a while for the powder to settle so she could clean it up.

"You all right?" The knacker asked.

"Fine." Spen shrugged and touched her scar. "We'll be busy today."

Chapter 10

Lord Allin watched Henry chop wood on a small farm north of Ancapolis. No one would have guessed this sunburnt, calloused man was the Emperor of Ancan, or that he was the Duke of Fhayde, emissary to the emperor.

The guards would have attracted too much attention, so Allin had sent them home to the Marques. Given the state of the Empire, the man would need them. Allin, Henry, Rebecca, Magpie traveled as a man, his son and daughter, and daughter-in-law. A poor family fleeing the chaos in the capital they blended in with the other refugees from the city. Allin let his beard grow out, as he was probably the most recognizable of the four of them.

Henry stood up and stretched his back. His third wife, now known as Rebecca, brought him a cup of water from the pump.

"Thank you, Sister." Henry drank the water, then returned to his wood splitting. In a chair on the porch of the small farmhouse, Magpie did mending at an almost miraculous speed. More than one farmwife had commented on what a hard worker she was. The farmers were more likely to comment on the fact that she rarely spoke.

Speedier travelers talked about how the fire in Ancapolis had burned for three days until it left hardly one wooden building standing. Troops marched through the city, but it hadn't yet come to open fighting. Few would stay for the inevitable.

Allin didn't think they were much safer on the road. Smaller nobles were jealously guarding their holdings. He'd seen the result of more than one battle as they walked.

As a result, they walked a crooked line to avoid coming too close to noble estates. The villages were polite to whatever forces marched through, and glad to see them go.

"We need to travel faster." Rebecca stood beside Allin. "We need to get north before the winter rains settle in."

"We're going as fast as we can without drawing unwanted attention." Allin shook his head. "We'd need to buy a horse and cart, and it isn't safe to be seen to have that much money."

"Then we need to take the main road. It would halve the distance we travel."

"That has its risks, too."

"I know." Rebecca sighed. "I feel my homeland calling me."

"At least you are walking in the right direction." Allin tried not to worry about the invasion of Fhayde. There was nothing he could do from here.

Henry finished the wood-splitting and the farmer's wife gave them a sack of stale bread and old cheese. There was even a piece of smoked meat buried in the bottom, probably from a poached deer.

They headed out since there was at least another hour or two of sunlight.

"Rebecca would like to travel more directly. I want to hear what you think."

"I'm not in a hurry to get anywhere." Henry scratched his head. Magpie stood on tiptoes to whisper in his ear. "Magpie says since I don't have a destination, it doesn't matter how fast or slow we get there."

"Then I guess the next time we cross the main road; we'll take it for a while. Remember, we are at the bottom of the ladder. We get out of the way of anyone we meet. Better to wait at the side of the road than get a beating because we didn't move fast enough."

"Sounds fine." Henry scratched again. "The only thing I miss is the baths."

"If we pass by a creek or pond," Rebecca said. "I wouldn't mind a bath myself."

The main road was busy, but it was people on horses, or with carriages, the occasional wagon pulled by oxen. It was easiest to walk on the green verge and stay out of the way.

They stopped for the night and feasted on the bread and cheese. Henry ate the smoked meat as it was too strong for Magpie or Rebecca. The morning started out beautiful and sunny, but clouds built up in the northeast and by noon they were walking through a downpour. Except for the farm carts, they had the road to themselves as the wealthy took shelter at the waystations.

"Might as well keep walking," Henry said. "We're already wet and we'd only get cold if we stopped."

Personally, Allin would have liked to take shelter in a barn, but along the main road, the farms were larger and less welcoming. Dogs barked at passersby, even in the rain.

Toward the evening, they crossed a small bridge with a faint trail off to the right.

"Let's see if this takes us to a place to camp.' Allin turned onto the track. It wound down to the creek and ended at a little clearing next to a pond. "Looks like as likely a place as any."

"There's wood. We could have a fire." Rebecca clapped in delight.

"I'm guessing that is why it is there." Allin took his flint and steel out of his pouch, and under the shelter of a spruce tree, he lit a fire and added wood to it.

"I'm going to bathe in the pond." Henry stripped off his clothes and walked into the water. Magpie followed him and Rebecca shrugged and joined the two playing in the pond.

"I will gather more wood." Allin stood and brushed off his legs. He had to go farther than he thought to find wood. Obviously, someone had stashed wood for themselves.

As he returned to the campsite, he heard screams and thought the play had got out of hand, but a voice he didn't recognize cursed and yelled for them to shut up.

Allin put his bundle down and picked up a branch which might make a decent club. He crept through the brush, years of hunting and stalking making him silent.

"Okay ladies, out of the water, hands to the side. We don't want you hiding anything from us." The comment brought a laugh from at least two others.

Allin moved close enough to see what was happening. Three men in rough clothes were ogling Rebecca and Magpie, while Henry fumed.

"Come slow and easy." The leader hefted a rusty short sword. "You are too valuable to kill, but that don't mean I won't hurt you if you act up."

Henry walked out of the water uncaring about his nakedness, His eyes told Allin he was going to attack the leader.

The other two only had eyes for the women, so Allin stepped into the clearing and whacked the closest one with his makeshift club. It snapped without so much as dazing the man, though it distracted the leader. Henry planted a punch to the man's short ribs, doubling him over, then struck a massive blow to the side of the leader's neck, dropping him to the ground. He snatched up the man's sword and crouched at the ready.

Allin's man drew his sword and spun to face Allin. Allin stepped in close and kicked the side of the bandit's knee. Henry's sword slashing through the man's throat cut the scream off.

The third bandit ran off shouting. Rebecca picked up a knife from the sheath on the unconscious leader and threw it at the fleeing man. It hit hilt first, but it was enough to make him stumble at full speed into a tree. The crack of his neck breaking was audible even at a distance.

"Get dressed." Alin kicked out the fire. "We need to get out of here now. Who knows if someone was close enough to hear that shouting?"

"We should take the swords." Henry hefted the rusty blade.

"Too visible, but take the knives and sheathes." Rebecca dressed quickly, then trotted over to retrieve the knife from the man lying crooked against the tree. She took his blade as well. By the time she returned, Magpie and Henry had dressed and Allin had the knife from the man he'd killed.

"Quiet now. We go back to the road and walk all night if we must." Allin picked up the sack with the now soggy bread, dropped the knife in and headed for the road. Magpie and Rebecca were close behind, with Henry at the rear, still holding the sword.

When they reached the road, Henry dropped the sword in the tall grass.

The rain let up toward the morning, and they staggered into a village.

"Oh dear, you look like drowned rats." A big woman stood with her hands on her hips. "Come in and warm up some by the fire." She led them into an inn and shooed them over near the fire. The heat loosened Allin's cramped muscles.

"A penny each for broth and a crust of bread. Can't afford to give it away." Allin dug into his pouch and pulled out four coins by touch and handed them to the woman.

"Ain't never seen a coin like this one." She held a copper coin from Fhayde.

"Don't recall where I got it from." Allin searched for another penny.

"No matter, a penny's a penny." She put the coins into the pocket of her apron.

The four of them sat on a bench by the fire. Soon steam rose from their clothes. The woman returned with four bowls and a plate with bread crusts on it.

They ate the bread dipped into the broth, warming their insides as much as the fire warmed their skin. When they were done, Allin stood and groaned.

"We thank you for your kindness, but we had better get moving while we can."

"Surely you can rest some more." The woman waved at the fire. "T'ain't anyone here to bother you."

"We're travelling to pay our respects to a family." Allin shrugged. "A little damp is easier than my family's wrath."

They walked through the village, the woman's stare itching on Allin's back until they rounded the corner and were out of sight.

After another day of walking under grey clouds, Allin was comfortable enough to camp in a tiny clearing to the side of the road.

He took first watch, leaning against a tree. Killing the bandit didn't bother him. He'd hunted enough bandits. If the word got around about the dead bandits, the woman didn't seem like the type to not gossip about her visitors. It could mean trouble. Nothing they could do but keep on walking.

The next day dawned clear and sunny, and they made good time. There were no more problems until they arrived at a gate across the road. People travelling through showed a carved wood plaque.

"Ye need a pass to travel through." The guard at the gate barely glanced at them.

"How do you get a pass?" Allin asked. "We're travelling to pay our respects to an aged uncle before he dies."

"Hoping for an inheritance, huh?" The guard laughed. "For you good people, it is silver for a pass for the family. Don't be thinking of walking around and getting in without paying. Everyone from the beggars up have passes. You won't make it a day."

"Father, maybe you should dip into my dowry." Rebecca held onto Allin's arm.

"I'd hate to do that; it is poor enough as it is."

"We need to see our good uncle."

Allin sighed and dug through his purse to find an Ancan silver, which he handed over to the guard in exchange for a plaque.

"Hope you make it in time." Guard winked at them as they passed through the gate.

"Good thinking to talk about your dowry." Allin said, when they were an hour away from the gate. "It gave me a reason to have a silver coin. I just hope things go smoother from here on."

Chapter 11

Robin connected with the land, but it was more fractured than before, as if the actions of Lord Edward made it worse, or perhaps the distress of the land affected Lord Edward. It didn't matter either way. Lord Edward would face judgement, and if that helped heal the land, so be it.

She stood up and checked for Ham and Sargent Temajin. They were comfortingly close at hand.

"I'm going down the hill to sleep in my tent." Robin yawned. "Sargent Temajin, inform Commander Themson. He is only to call me for a dire emergency."

"As you wish, Lady Robin." He saluted and struck out across the lawn toward the manor.

"Let's get a move on before you have to carry me." Robin walked to the road and down the hill. She entered her tent and collapsed on the bed, barely taking time to kick her boots off.

***

The sun shone from high in the sky when she woke. She changed her uniform and headed out to the mess tent, stomach growling.

"Ah, Lady Robin." Marshal Hapten waved her over. "You get a good rest?"

"I did, but I have the feeling it is a prelude to a lot more work."

"You'd be right about that." The marshal laughed. "You've stirred up a hornets' nest."

"Not my intention." Robin tucked into the meal Ham put in front of her before sitting down to his own meal. "But I wasn't about to allow an attempt to poison me pass for convenience's sake. Though poison may be the wrong word. It was a mind control drug."

"You are fortunate to come out of it so well."

"I appear to have a resistance to drugs and poisons, but the results were strange."

"Morning, Robin." Sarge sat beside her opposite Ham. "Though it may be generous to suggest it is still morning."

"I didn't get much rest last night."

"Neither did I." He cupped his hands around a cup of tea. "I worried about you, lass."

"I was a bit worried myself." Robin admitted. "It was only my being a shieldmaiden that kept me from being drugged and who knows what else."

"Be careful. In the stories, the shieldmaidens can die as easy as the next person." Sarge scowled.

"I don't plan to die." Robin pushed her plate away. "But it is my work to live in danger. I don't like it any more than you."

"Living in danger doesn't mean courting danger." Sarge rapped his cane on the table. "You are our chief commanding officer; you shouldn't be meeting people without a suitable guard."

"And who's to say that a suitable guard wouldn't have all been drugged too?" Robin wanted to bang the table, but restrained herself. "So far, our journey has been a picnic compared to what is coming. You don't think I'm not scared? I'm not even old enough to be a knight and here I am commanding a Thousand in enemy territory. I'm making it up as I go, because the land is broken and sick, and it is giving me no help."

"Robin–" Sarge reached for her hand, but Robin stood and stalked away.

She was being a fool, but she couldn't stop her feet. There weren't any trees near this camp, so she went back to her tent and plopped down on the floor. *What do you want from me?*

The land gave her no answer. Just the steady tug north.

She pounded her hands on the floor in frustration.

I don't want to die because you won't talk to me.

She sank into the dark. The Ancan general came and sneered at her.

"You think you're special, but you're just lucky."

"You're one to talk." Robin said.

"If your companion wasn't there, I would have carried you with me into death."

"That wasn't luck. Sargent Temajin was doing his job. He was there to watch my back."

"You were lucky up that hill. You could have been used and discarded like all the rest. Your luck is going to fail and you will die."

"I will die doing my duty, unlike you who disobeyed his emperor."

The general faded away, sneer intact.

Robin opened her eyes and at first wondered if she'd gone blind or got stuck in the vision. All she could see was darkness. Then her eyes adjusted and she realized it was late at night.

She hung her head and fought the tears unsuccessfully.

"Lady Robin, are you all right?" Ham's voice came through the canvass.

"Yes, no, I don't know." She drew in a shuddering breath. "Do you believe in luck?"

"I won't say I don't." Ham said, "But the luckiest people are the ones who are always ready to take advantage of the situation. Having a plan is better than luck, but you work with what you have."

"Ham, should I have gone up the hill with just you and Sargent Temajin?"

"It's not my place to say," Ham said. "But he might have reconsidered if you'd brought a full hundred with you, but maybe not. He thought he could manipulate you because you're a young girl. That was a mistake. Would he have tried the same thing on Marshal Hapten? Who knows? It doesn't matter."

"It does matter." Robin stood up and walked out of the tent. "Is Sarge still awake?"

"I expect so." Ham shrugged. "He doesn't seem to sleep much."

"I need to talk to him." She headed for his tent.

"Sarge?" she called through the canvass. "Sarge, are you there? I'm coming in." Robin pushed through the door and wished she had light to see better. A soft, green glow filled the room. Lencely and Rud slept on their bedrolls. Sarge lay on his cot. At first, she didn't see any movement and her heart stopped, then she saw him breathing, but very shallow. She shook Sarge's shoulder, and he moved limply.

"Ham, get the medic. Sarge is sick."

***

"How is he?" Robin's voice trembled. She couldn't remember ever being this scared.

"I've never had someone this old in my care before." Dr. Vinud held Sarge's wrist. "I can say that his heart is weak. If he wakes, I have some herbs I can try. Sorry, I can't be more positive."

"I should have stayed and listened to him. Now what will I do?" She sank to her knees beside Sarge and took his hand. It lay cool and limp in hers. "Prepare those herbs. I will watch until he wakes."

"I will." The doctor put a hand on her shoulder for an instant before he left the tent.

"Robin, we should have known." Lencely stood in a corner, his face wet. Rud sat staring at his feet.

"It isn't your fault." Robin said. "I was the one who upset him."

"Not your fault either, Robin." Rud looked up through red eyes. "Let us stay with him. One of us will always be awake. He wouldn't want you to stop your work because of him."

"I will take a shift too." Robin said. "Thank you." She left the tent, and for a moment, wanted to run into the darkness and disappear. That would be against everything Sarge had taught her. Instead, she walked to the command tent to meet Marshal Hapten and Commander Paychen.

"He is resting, but the doctor isn't sure he'll wake up. Lencely and Rud are with him. Right now, there is nothing we can do for him."

"If it is any help, Sarge wasn't mad at you. He was angry with himself."

"He was right." Robin said. "I need to think like a commander. More than my life is at stake here." She shook herself and scrubbed her eyes. "We have the trial tomorrow; I have a feeling it is important to healing this city. Marshal Hapten, I want you to sit on a tribunal with two city magistrates. We'll hope he hasn't drugged half the city. I'm fairly confident that Lordson is under Lord Edward's influence and a few of the guard. If we remove Lord Edward, those should regain their full senses."

"That sounds like a good plan." Marshal Hapten sighed and rubbed her eyes. "We can't appear to be convicting him before the trial."

"Right." Robin clenched her fist. "Commander Paychen, you will be the accuser. I will brief you on my testimony and we'll get Ham and Sargent Temajin to do so as well."

"Very good, Lady Robin." Commander Paychen saluted.

Robin went over everything that happened from the moment she started off with Lordson to when Commander Themson entered. He asked a few pointed questions and shook his head when she described how her consciousness had split.

"That's beyond me," he said. "We have plenty to go on, even without that."

"You doubt my word?" Robin frowned.

"No, but I have to keep in mind how it will appear to the tribunal."

"Right." Robin took a deep breath. "I am going to try to sleep. You should as well."

***

The trial convened three days later. Lordson insisted on defending himself and Lord Edward. The city magistrates were upset about having to decide on the case, but when Marshal Hapten told them the trial would go on with or without them, they agreed to sit on the tribunal. A table had been placed in a large yard so the crowd could watch the proceedings.

Commander Paychen opened by explaining the charges.

"We aren't here to decide if Lord Edward's actions were murderous, but rather whether they broke the truce of the white banner." He ran through the order of events as Robin, Ham, and Sarge Temajin stated.

Lordson stood up. "Lord Edward invited Lady Robin for a pleasant meal, and they have turned it into a farcical accusation of drugs and poison. It isn't us who is pushing the so-called truce they unilaterally declared. You will note that all their witnesses are people under Lady Robin's authority who can be ordered to lie for her."

The witnesses took the stand and told their story. Marshal Hapten ordered each of them to speak only the truth. The magistrates took their oath following that.

Lordson challenged each of them about whether they'd lie for Robin. When they said no, he commented, of course they were commanded to speak so. Marshal Hapten was livid. One magistrate looked like she was buying the line, the other had sunk into a lethargic coma.

When it was Robin's turn to testify, she swore by the land she would tell the truth and only the truth. Commander Paychen ran Robin through the story and introduced the note as evidence.

Lordson stalked forward to ask his questions.

"Can you prove you are telling the truth?"

"No more than you can, but my oath as a shieldmaiden demands the truth."

"So, this isn't a plot to take the city?" Lordson sneered.

Robin laughed. "I wouldn't take the city if you gave it to me. Remember, Lord Edward offered it. It is so badly run there is sickness in the poor people. You've lost so many farms you cannot feed yourself, never mind the people."

"Ours is a great city, second only to the capital." Lordson turned purple.

"The capital that burned to the ground." Robin leaned back and peered at him.

"This is all a plot against Lord Edward and me."

"You have nothing I want." Robin glared at him. "But I have something you want."

"And what would that be?"

"Access to food. Obviously you don't mind if your people starve, but I expect you prefer to eat heartily."

"Just admit you planned all this." Lordson caught her eye and held it.

The desire to agree with him grew in her. She couldn't look away from his eyes. So she responded with her own magic, denying him what he wanted.

"No."

"Unless you have more questions," Marshal Hapten emphasized 'questions,' "Let us move on."

Lordson called witnesses, who one after the other told the identical story about what had happened, swearing that Lord Edward was a kind and generous young ruler.

Commander Paychen pointed out again and again that the witnesses stating word for word the same thing was suspicious. Lordson glowered at him and responded that since they all saw the same events, it stood to reason that they would have the same testimony.

Robin frowned when Edward told the same story, with the addition that she'd invited him to her room and attempted to drug her own men. "The person running things is Lordson, not Lord Edward."

"We'll see when he takes the stand." Commander Paychen said.

"I have made my case." Lordson announced. "There is no proof of any kind that there was a plot against Lady Robin. All the testimony is by people ordered to lie for her."

"The same could be said for your witnesses." Commander Paychen countered.

The tribunal sat and argued for an hour, Marshal Hapten wanting to convict Lord Edward, the magistrate wanting to convict Robin. The man in the lethargic slumber, finally overturned the table.

"Everyone is lying. They always lie. Decide with a trial by battle. Let each side choose their champion and let's be done with it. Battle to the death."

"I will fight for us." Robin said. "I won't put anyone else at risk, besides if they use poison, it's less likely to work on me."

"Here is our champion." A gigantic man, bigger than Ham, stepped forward carrying two massive hammers. Guards pushed the crowd back and laid down a large circle of rope.

"I would ask the magistrates to examine the weapons for suitability before the fight." Commander Paychen stated, glaring at Lordson.

The champion put the hammers on the table in front of the tribunal. Marshal Hapten frowned, but could find nothing to object to. The magistrates barely looked at them before giving their approval.

Robin took one hammer at random, struggling to lift it.

The champion laughed and twirled the hammer easily. "I'm going to enjoy crushing you, little girl."

"I'm not in this for fun." Robin hefted the enormous weapon. "May the land judge between us."

"The land is going to drink your blood." He charged forward, swinging the hammer high over his head. It moved much slower than a sword, but the weight slowed Robin too. She swung enough to dodge to the side. The champion followed, calling her names, telling her what he'd like to do with her body. Robin fought silently, always a hair's breadth from disaster. Then his maul grazed her arm, leaving a bloody streak from shoulder to elbow.

"Give up and I'll end you quickly." The champion leered at her. Robin ran her finger in her blood and painted runes on her face, dodging by leaving her hammer behind. The champion picked up her weapon and laughed.

"What are you going to do now, little girl?"

"Leave the hammer on the ground." The once lethargic magistrate yelled.

"Why? She left it behind." The champion whirled both hammers.

"Those are the rules. The duel must be fought with the weapon you chose, or fists. Nothing else is allowed."

"Fine." The champion dropped the hammer, then smashed the handle with his hammer. "Let her fight with that."

The magistrate sighed. "Okay then, have it your way. The gods will judge you."

Robin danced back to the edge of the dueling ground while the champion and magistrate argued. She couldn't use her knife and fists would do little against the giant, yet a buzzing ran through her body.

When the champion approached swinging the hammer in a figure eight, she watched his timing. He was quick, but he couldn't move the massive weapon like a sword or a spear. She had a good sense of his style, which was brute force with a dash of dexterity. It was the dexterity that worried her.

The champion charged, trying to pin her against the boundary. She ran straight at him and when he looped the hammer up to crush her; she slid past as his weapon whistled above her head. That gave her the chance to pick up the broken hammer, using her momentum to spin and throw it.

The throw was weak, but it put off his timing. She pulled a loose piece from the handle and held it like a knife.

"You're going to fight me with a toothpick?"

Robin grinned. "You're forgetting something, little man."

"What?" he leered at her. "I'm going to break your knee, then the other knee, crush you little by little."

"This is a trial by duel, and you're fighting for a rapist and a panderer."

"That doesn't matter. They could be the devil himself and I would still kill you." He charged at her; hammer held ready. Robin danced aside, and he almost stepped out of bounds.

"Careful, little man."

He charged again, this time sweeping the hammer close to the ground. Robin jumped over it, then darted inside his swing as he continued around, jumping on his back and stabbing the small piece of wood as hard as she could into the side of his neck. The champion roared and threw her off his back. Robin rolled to her feet as he ran at her, blood oozing from the scratch on his neck.

The buzzing in her grew, and he appeared to move slower. His taunts stopped and he growled as he gave up any finesse and smashed the hammer into the stony ground. A piece of stone caught the side of her knee, and she stumbled close to her broken weapon. The champion shouted in triumph and swung his hammer high over his head, then brought it down so fast it whistled through the air.

Something took hold of Robin and moved her like a puppet. She charged inside his reach and stabbed upward with the longer piece of handle, sticking it in his eye. The grip on her actions vanished.

The champion screamed and reached with both hands to pull it out. Robin danced back and grabbed her hammer and hit his kneecap. He slashed at her with the broken handle. She ducked just far enough back to let it scrape across her uniform, then jumped in and hit his other knee. The champion grabbed wildly for her as he fell and caught her leg, so she shortened up on the hammer and smashed his elbow.

She hit the ground hard and staggered to her feet. The champion lunged for her with his other hand, and Robin dodged by a hair's breadth. Rolling toward his blind side, she lunged with the hammer and caught him behind the ear, denting his skull, but he still swatted her and sent her tumbling across the yard. She lost the hammer, and it slid out of bounds.

Robin turned to look and didn't have time to dodge as he impossibly scrambled toward her. No space to go backwards or time to go sideways to get out of his path. She jumped as high as she could and landed with both feet on the back of his neck, driving him into the ground. Running away, she put the width of the court between them and gasped for air. The crowd looked to be in pandemonium, but she couldn't hear it over her thudding heart.

Her back twinged and Robin spun to see a man stepping into the circle to stab at her with a knife. She drove the heel of her hand into the man's nose. He dropped to the ground, and she grabbed his knife, moving away from the crowd.

"Kill her," Lordson yelled, "kill them all."

The guards charged at Robin, and the buzzing became a roar. They froze in place as she ran between them and rammed the knife into Lordson's neck.

The world snapped back to regular speed, and she staggered to the side and fell to her knees. The blow she expected never landed. She turned to see what was happening. The guards had fallen, clutching their heads. Lord Edward, sword raised over his head to strike her down, fell back and cracked his skull on the pavement.

"Judgement has been given." Marshal Hapten yelled. The magistrate who had sided with Lordson held her head in her hands and was shrieking in pain.

The other magistrate jumped on the table. "Don't anger the gods any further. It is bad enough that our lord broke the truce. Don't make it worse."

Robin closed her eyes, suddenly exhausted, and passed out.

Chapter 12

Hob stood outside the manor with a crowd of peasants behind him armed with picks, shovels, ancient swords, or even just bits of sharpened wood.

"Our brothers and sisters are sweeping the craft section and the barn. We are left with the manor."

"We should just burn them out," a man behind him said.

"If need be, we will do that." Hob didn't turn around. "But there is much in the manor we can put to use, not the least the stores of food."

"Right, they're going to let us walk in and take everything."

"Who knows if we don't try." Hob turned to face the mob behind him. "I am going to try to parley with the masters. If they will leave quietly, we allow them to live. If they attack under the white flag crush them completely, they don't deserve to live. Try not to light any fires, but don't waste time fighting something lit by the masters. Use windows, doors, climb to the second floor, overwhelm them with your numbers. Some of you are going to die today, but you will die free."

"I will walk forward with you." Duncan sheathed his sword and helped tie the whitest cloth they could find to the tip of Hob's spear.

They walked toward the manor, holding up the white flag.

"We want to parley." Hob shouted.

"Go to hell." Arrows flew at them, which Duncan knocked away with his sword.

"I knew I should have brought my armour."

"Last chance to talk." Hob shouted. "We will allow you to leave alive with what you can carry."

Two guards walked out, swords in hand. "Fine then, we'll talk."

Hob stood and waited for them to get close.

"Leave now and never come back, and you and the masters may live."

"How can we trust you?" One pointed his sword at Hob.

"We are here, willing to talk." Hob pointed to the white flag. "Parley under the white flag is sacred. The gods will curse any who break the peace."

"You are peasants, what do you know of parleys?" The guard waved his sword.

"I commanded the army through the gorge to Caldera. Twice I spoke with my enemies and came away unscathed. The second time we came to peace that benefited all of us."

"Should have just killed you when we had the chance," the second guard said and lunged at Hob.

Hob lowered the spear and caught the guard in the neck where his chain mail protected him. The spear didn't cut him, but he fell on his back. Hob ran the spear through the guard's face into his brain.

The first guard attacked Duncan.

"You shouldn't mistake bullying peasants as battle experience." Duncan batted the sword aside and lunged, taking the guard in the eye. The man dropped lifelessly.

More arrows flew at them, but the mob of peasants charged into the fray, some heading for the door, others smashing windows and climbing into the house. Shouts and screams came from inside and the arrows stopped.

Hob stripped the guard he killed and donned the chain mail. Duncan shrugged and followed suit. Once done, they headed into the chaos of the manor. A group of peasants had a guard pinned to a wall with wooden poles, while another chopped at him with a shovel. Hob reached over with the spear and caught the guard in the throat. This one wasn't wearing chain.

"Take the weapons and continue," Hob ordered them

Within an hour, all the fighting was done. The manor had been trashed, but not burnt. The food stores had been raided, but most remained salvageable.

"Take the bodies out with the broken furniture and burn them." Hob tried not to notice the small size of some bodies. If only they'd listened, they'd all be alive and heading somewhere safe, or as safe as this world allowed.

Hob walked through the craft building into the barn. The grain storage was much lower than he'd hoped.

A heavy weight landed on his shoulders, and something slammed into his back. He rolled away and came up with his spear at the ready. "Cursed peasant," the guard spat and circled around Hob, knife held in a low grip in the centre of his body. This guard wore a breastplate and helmet. He batted Hob's lunges to the side, ducked in and slashed. The chain stopped the blade, but it only covered his torso and was larger than it should have been.

A knife slash caught Hob's cheek, sending chill pain through him.

"Let me take a horse and I won't kill you." The guard stood at the ready, unfazed by Hob's spear. Hob fended off two more lunges before someone heard the fight and shouted. The barn flooded with peasants who piled on the guard and wrestled for the helmet. The guard rolled and stabbed and slashed, but the sheer weight of bodies held him down. When the helmet came off, he didn't last long. Hob picked up the helmet and tried it on. It was too small, so he handed it to someone else. The peasants stripped the body, passing the armour and mail around. Some dragged the guard outside.

"Check upstairs for anymore. No one escapes."

"You better get that sewn up," one peasant told him. Hob walked over to the knacker's shop.

"Just a few minutes." Spen handed him a cloth. "Put pressure on the cut." She sewed up a peasant's arm that was sliced from elbow to wrist. Many others sat with bandages on.

"The knacker is busy." Spen adjusted Hob's face so she could reach it. "It isn't deep; you're lucky." She stitched it up, ignoring Hob's wince at each pass of the needle.

Hob called for the peasants to gather. Out of the hundred men who had fought, fifty of them were injured and twenty were dead. The women fared better since they followed behind to clean up anyone left breathing.

They spent the next week burying their fallen, and tending the fire, burning the bodies of the masters, guards and overseers. Duncan had hunters out on the plain as scouts. "Someone sees the smoke. We could be in trouble."

Hob met with Duncan, Gud and the elders, who'd come into the sunlight for the first time in years.

"We're just started." Hob said. "If we stop here, the masters will build an army and come for us. We will have to face an army eventually, but we aren't ready. Hunters take the bows and collect arrows. If you have a sword, Duncan will show you how not to cut off your own leg. Lem will train the rest on spears. Four soldiers with spears can kill any guard."

They trained until the scouts reported people coming three days after the battle.

"Get ready, bows to the right, swords and spears to the left. Don't attack until I tell you."

Hob walked out to get a closer look at the people. The approaching peasants threw their hands up and begged for mercy.

"There are no masters here." Hob told them. "Join us or keep walking."

Over the next week, more peasants arrived. Some had heard about the uprising and rose themselves. The cost of victory was higher than Hob's group. As the numbers swelled, Hob grew worried that their food would run out.

"I will lead an army to defeat the masters in other villages where the rebellion has failed." Hob called for volunteers. Half of them, about four hundred men and women, stepped forward. "Gud, you're in command here. You'll need to have scouts out and work the fields. Keep your weapons close. If the trouble is too big, retreat to the caves. We should probably make sure we stock them up. Some will need to return to their own villages to work the crops we can't feed everybody here.

"Why did we fight if we were just going to be working in the fields again?" One newcomer complained.

"Who else will work them?" Hob said. "But there are no overseers, no whips, and we keep what we grow. Free doesn't mean no work to do." Most of those staying behind nodded their heads. "If you don't want to work, then pick up a weapon and follow me to fight."

The army left the next morning, Hob walking at the front, carrying his spear. The rest of the peasants trailed after him in a disorderly line. Duncan drove the wagon at the rear of the nascent army.

The villages between them and the mountain had freed themselves, so the army marched to the next village to the north. They found the village burned to the ground, and the manor filled with bodies of both peasants and masters.

"We bury the dead, but collect the armour and the weapons. We will need them." They found a horse running free in the field and hitched it to a wagon that had escaped the flames. "Any weapons we don't carry, go in the wagon."

They trained in the morning and marched through the afternoon to the next village. This village hadn't rebelled, but the masters gave up immediately. Many of the army wanted to kill them, but Hob insisted they be given the chance to walk away, carrying what they could. Hob found a room full of maps and poured over them with Duncan.

"The Free hold this." Hob put his hand over a small corner of the plain. "Let's make copies of the maps and divide the army into four to free more of our people faster. We'll meet in a month at Westburg, the master's city on the edge of the plain."

Over the next week, Hob and his hundred meandered north while one group freed the east and one the west. By the end of the week, Hob's group had ballooned again, the villages grew larger, many of them had already rebelled, and when Hob's army arrived, the tide turned against the masters.

The second week saw them arriving to empty manor houses and peasants not sure what to do. Some still had overseers in control, but mostly everyone from master to overseer had fled, taking horses and wagonloads of goods. Rarely did they take any food. The peasant's anger burned hotter as they learned just how much the masters took of what they worked for.

Hob organized the mob into groups of fifty and asked them to appoint a leader. They trained more and sent out groups to visit villages. Progress slowed to a crawl as the mob grew. Women, children, elders all wanted to be part of what was happening. Finding people to stay and work the land became difficult.

They arrived at Westburg to discover a vast army surrounding the walled city. Hob took control. His council grew to ten people who each commanded more than a thousand peasant soldiers, plus the others who joined them to cook and heal.

"We don't have time to wait for the city to give up." Hob pointed to the map with the city on the edge. "Word will have gone west, and the emperor is going to send an army to stop us. We don't want to be caught between the city and an army."

"We could surround the city and cut off all supplies going in. Send the fleeing masters somewhere else." Tad, a past-guard before he'd been demoted for being too friendly with the master's daughter.

"Surrounding the city is good, but the more people they have inside, the faster they will run out of food." Pok argued. She was the oldest commander, but had no trouble keeping up. Pok had come from the north, where most of the villages rebelled early on and sent people to join Hob's army.

"Find the tunnels," Tad said. "There's never been a peasant village without tunnels past the walls."

"Easier said than done." Pok shook her head. "The exits will be close to the walls, within bow range."

Everyone looked at Hob.

"It's your army," Duncan said. "Your decision."

"We surround the city. No one leaves, but the masters can go in. They'll assume we're simple and still afraid of them. If there are tunnels, they go both ways, watch for people coming out." Hob shook his head. "It isn't my army, we are all part of it down to the greenest new Free."

"Someone needs to be at the top." Tad shrugged. "I led the revolt in my village because I had a beef with the masters. It is your army because it is your vision."

"Very well," Hob sighed and pulled the map to him. "Pok you take the north of the city. The river runs through the city. See if you can move it."

"You want me to move the river?" Her eyebrows vanished into the wrinkles on her forehead.

"Think of it as an irrigation project. Tad, you set up checkpoints around the outside of the army. We need hunters and people going for food, and anyone who decides to go home to pass, but not to the west."

He handed out tasks to each of the commanders, from keeping scouts to the west to guarding the other three sides of the city.

Though many peasants left to return to their villages, disillusioned with life in the army and failing to find a life free of responsibility, more arrived with wagons of food looted from the masters. Traders looked at the sea of peasants and quietly turned around, except for an enterprising few who sold goods in return for favours owed.

A man was brought to the command tent, claiming to be from inside the city.

"Name's Leckod." He tugged at his tunic, as if he wasn't used to wearing it. "The people on the inside are ready to revolt. There is so little to go around."

"You're saying they need a spark. Tell them to take the city for their own. I have no idea how to run a city."

Leckod stared at Hob like he'd grown a second head. "Run the city, peas—, people aren't ready for that."

"Take the word back or don't." Hob pointed to the city gates. "Get them open for us and we'll do the rest."

Leckod was guided away. One of Tad's scouts stayed close to watch how he returned to the city. He entered after knocking on a small gate in the north wall.

"Don't trust him." Pok spat to the side.

"Doesn't mean he's not useful." Hob stared at the map. "We need to make some noise, let people know we're here. A riot on the north side of the city would help."

"How are we going to start a riot inside the gate?" Tad asked.

"Not inside, outside. We need volunteers. If it looks like discipline is falling apart, they will attack and try to get at the dam on the river. We draw them out, then circle them and crush them. If we can get people in the city, it will be ours within the day." Hob tapped on the west gate. "The emperor is going to send an army. We feed the empire. He'll want us broken and back under the yoke."

"I have an idea." Duncan grinned.

Chapter 13

Robin woke in a tent beside Sarge. "How long was I out?" She sat up and the world tilted around her.

"Most of a day," Lencely said. "Lucky you. A delegation from the city guilds came and asked Marshal Hapten to take control of the city. Seems most of the important people lost their minds when Lordson died."

"I hope she said no."

"She's still negotiating. Doesn't want to leave chaos behind us."

"I'd better get up and find out what she's thinking." Robin stood, then fell back on the bed. "On second thought, ask her to send someone to brief me"

Commander Themson showed up a couple of hours later.

"You should rest. We thought we were going to have two people in comas." He held up a hand. "But as long as you stay in bed, the medic said we could let you know what was going on."

"Fine." Robin sat crossed legged on the bed. "Report."

"Marshal Hapten suggests she detach a hundred to help get the city back running the way it should. She's insisting it is an advisory capacity. We've already been working through the slums, working on hygiene. Some of the old farmers might go back to the farm with our support. The guilds have set up a committee to negotiate with us, and Marshal Hapten's hoping they'll take on running the city. They have the connections and, more to the point, none of them were drugged by Lordson."

"Don't tell me. They're insulted because they weren't important enough to subvert." Robin rolled her eyes.

"Pretty much. Marshal's playing on that to get them to feel important by leading the restoration."

"People, I'll never understand them." Robin shrugged and stretched her back. "Marshal Hapten takes command of the hundreds we've sent out, and runs them from the city. It will be easier for them to report to the city instead of runners chasing a moving target. We should send some people east. According to Lord Huddroc, the eastern plain grows a lot of the food for the cities of the empire. If they are facing the same issues as the landowners and farmers we've met, it could be disastrous."

"You aren't going." Sargent Temajin entered the tent. "The peasants there are slaves under the nobility. System has been going since before the empire. It will not change soon, if ever. They sent a lot of the troublemakers on that suicide attack on Vilscape, according to the guilds. They weren't happy about being forced to fund the army."

"What will happen now that they lost?" Robin asked.

"Beats me. Nobody's heard anything from the army since they crossed the pass. We know they were turned back at Vilscape, but no details." Commander Themson said. "They marched through the southeast to get to the pass. Maybe they stayed there."

"Okay, I have a feel for the situation. We aren't going to be able to free the peasants and achieve our goal." Robin sighed and rubbed her eyes. "I'm going to sit with Sarge for a bit, then I'll go back to bed. I don't want to mess up Marshal Hapten's work."

"The deal was you stay in bed." Commander Themson reminded her. "We need you on your feet and healthy, for morale, if nothing else. We're stuck here until you're ready to take command again."

"Then move my bed closer to his. I need to talk to him."

"As long as you're in bed." Sargent Temajin shook a finger at her.

They lifted the bed and Robin in it and moved it next to Sarge's.

"Remember, you need to rest." Commander Themson stood and cracked his back.

"I will rest better after talking to him."

"There is nothing to say he can hear you." The commander put a hand on Robin's shoulder. "He's older than anyone the medic has ever known. It is possible he may never wake up."

"All the more reason to make things right." Robin reached over and took Sarge's hand. "You're dismissed." The two saluted and left the tent.

"Sarge, I don't know what happened. We went from talking every night to barely seeing each other. I know you are worried about me, but I want you to concentrate on getting better." She scrubbed tears from her eyes. "You are right. I wasn't thinking like a commander. I need you to teach me more, so you have to wake up."

She put his hand back on his bed and lay down, asleep, before she realized it.

***

"You said the drug cause you to split." The medic took her pulse. "I'm concerned the drug has affected your body."

"I'm just tired."

"More than tired." The medic put a hand on her forehead. "You were breathing slower than your Sargent there. If it had been anyone else, I doubt you would have survived the stress you put on your system."

"Right. I need to rest. But I also need to be up to date with what is going on," Robin pleaded.

"Last thing you need is to take any command at all."

"I won't, but I need to be able to step into command when I'm ready without a lot of catching up to do. Just an hour a day. Commander Themson and Sargent Temajin won't let me push myself."

"I will discuss it with the marshal at the briefing tonight."

"Thank you." Robin had to push back tears of relief. *I'm weaker than I thought.*

Robin spent most of the days for the next week playing cards with Lencely and Rud. She'd asked about Ham, but neither would say anything. They kept her briefings to exactly one hour, but she made the best of it.

When she wasn't sleeping or playing cards, Robin talked to Sarge. The more she talked, the more she realized how much of a shell she'd built around herself. As she talked, she peeled the shell back, layer by layer, talking about how she knew now she didn't have to single-handedly save the empire, nor the land. Robin wasn't sure what she was going to do, but it had to change.

At the end of the week, she was given permission to take short walks about the tent, gradually building her strength. Another week and she could walk to the mess tent to eat. She looked for Ham but didn't see him.

"Sargent Temajin, I need to talk to Ham. I'm worried about him, and it is distracting me."

"Ham is furious that you fought the trial yourself. He sees it as his job." Sargent Temajin frowned. "Unless you give him a direct order, he won't come here. Says he doesn't want to argue with you."

"Ham wouldn't have survived the fight." Robin said. "It almost killed me."

"That's exactly his point. He should have been allowed to put his life on the line to preserve yours. It is his role."

"I see." Robin didn't like what she saw in herself. It was back to not listening and taking everything on herself. It wasn't healthy for her, nor the Thousand. "Bring him my regards and ask him, when he is ready, to visit so I can apologize."

"I will do that."

That night, she talked to Sarge about Ham.

"What should I do? I took his reason for being with me away from him and didn't even stop to think about it. If I believed in the trial by combat, Ham would have won as I did. I didn't believe in Ham, and I don't know if he'll ever forgive me."

At the end of the second week, the medic allowed her to start training with the sword. She couldn't do a fraction of her old routine.

Then Ham showed up.

"Doc says a bit of a tongue lashing won't kill you." Ham glowered at her, arms crossed. "Ye keep jumping into the middle of things. You're the only shieldmaiden we have. If something happens to you…" He trailed off.

"You're right." Robin almost laughed at the expression on Ham's face. "I wasn't thinking about anything but my anger. I should have trusted you."

"Damn right you should have." Ham shouted at her. "What's the worst thing that happens if I die? We pay retribution for losing the case. If you die, we're lost, everything is done and we might as well go home, if we're allowed to."

"You're right." Robin didn't feel like laughing anymore. "I would like you to take on training me. I'm weaker than a kitten, and need to be stronger just to walk around."

"Train you?" Ham's brow furrowed.

"I messed up, Ham. Now I'm paying for it. I want your help."

"Don't expect me to go easy on ye."

"If I was allowed to give orders, I would order you not to take it easy at all. A little dose of reality may be just the medicine I need."

"Tomorrow, at the training yard." Ham met her eyes. "You do exactly what I say, nothing more, or I'm done."

"Deal."

***

Half the camp found some excuse to loiter around the training yard. Robin sighed; she'd survive the humiliation of being weak. She had to be weak before she could be strong again.

The basic trainee workout made her exhausted, but she kept her word to Ham and didn't do any training outside of his supervision.

Her memory of the rhythm of the exercises improved and within a week, she could get through the entire hour of training without resting. Ham increased it gradually as she recovered more quickly, but starting from the beginning again forced her to pare her style down to the minimum needed to survive. She hadn't realized how much energy she wasted until she had none to spare.

With the training, she started attending the command meetings. Robin sat and listened, getting a feel for what was going on. The city was striving to recover and the word from the outlying farms was hopeful that the fae's methods of growing food would work.

They were discussing whether to send a team east to assess the situation when Robin spoke up for the first time. "I don't think we need to worry about the east for now."

"Why not?" Commander Paychen asked.

"I'm not sure, just a feeling that things are going the way they should be. I'm not getting any sense I need to travel that way.

"The land is telling you this?" He frowned.

"No, at least not as certainly as it has told me other things. I still feel the tug north. There is something we need to do there. I don't know what it is yet."

"I think we still should send scouts to the east. I'm not comfortable having no information at all about what is going on."

"Understandable." Robin nodded her head. "What do you suggest?"

When everyone around the table stared at her, Robin realized again how much she had got used to pushing her own agenda.

"When we set out, I said I expected my commanders to take care of day-to-day details. I'd forgotten that. You know your job. I am going to stop trying to do it for you."

"I think send two squads. Enough to protect themselves from bandits and such, but not so much as to intimidate the power structure on the plains." Commander Paychen leaned forward.

"If I may make a suggestion, send someone who is a top-notch negotiator." Robin stared into the distance. "I have a hunch it will be useful."

"And how much leeway do you think we should give them?" Marshal Hapten asked.

"Whatever they need, subject to the agreement of the crown." Robin tapped the table with her fingers. "Peace with the plains will settle our eastern flank."

"I suggest sending Commander Themson. He's shown a lot of initiative and solid thinking." Marshal Hapten looked over at him.

"I'm honoured by your trust." He stood up. "I will put my squads together and be ready tomorrow to head out."

***

Ham brought in Lencely and Rud to help with the training. Robin was shocked to discover that she had to struggle to keep up with Lencely. Her ability to read her opponents improved, and she surprised Lencely with a couple of touches she shouldn't have been able to manage.

Her strength began to return more quickly, and her appetite became voracious. Every night she talked to Sarge about what she'd been doing and learning. It was almost like back when she was just Sarge's squire and no one special.

Commander Paychen suggested it was time to move his five hundred north. The network between the hundreds and Marshal Hapten had solidified. The reports said that Marques Povost and Baron Timost had reached out to Fhayde to broker a peace in exchange for aid.

Robin stayed out of most of the discussion, only contributing when she felt nudged to.

A month after the duel with Lord Edward's champion, Lencely and Rud packed up her tent, and they rode on the wagon north, with Sarge sleeping beside them. That was the only time Robin had put her foot down. She needed Sarge with her. The medic was travelling with them and decided it wouldn't make the ancient man any worse. Lencely and Rud took turns with Robin feeding him broth as they travelled.

***

Commander Themson led his twenty soldiers east through the mixed farm and forest land. As they walked, half the thousand marched north toward Ancanopolis. *Keep your head on your task, Bodan.*

After a week of living off the land, or the generousity of small farms, he had them moving the way he wanted. They moved in half squads to be less intimidating to the people they met, but also to lessen the danger of the entire group being ambushed. He insisted on using first names.

"Someone hears you calling me commander, I become the prime target for any archers. We keep it loose and informal; you all know who I am."

"Aye, Bodan," the squad responded.

They moved by leap-frogging the half squads to keep from getting too focussed on one direction. As they travelled, they noted the forests becoming thinner and farther apart. When they came to a spot where no more forest could be seen, Bodan called his people in.

"This is where it gets tricky. There may be fighting on the plains, and we don't want to get caught up in it. Stay alert, but don't get jumpy. Just because you can see to the horizon, doesn't mean there aren't hiding spots and people watching us."

"You tell us not to be jumpy, then warn us that people may watch us from behind some bush."

"Exactly, someone steps out. I don't want them skewered before we can talk to them."

They didn't see anyone before they encountered a track through the sparse vegetation.

"We head north, even odds a village is in that direction."

"Bodan, I can scout farther ahead," Sylve had been a member of his squad back when he hunted bandits in the northern forest.

"Okay, but stay doubly alert. I don't want to be finding your body if the wrong people see you."

"Nice of you to worry." Sylve grinned. "But I plan on living long enough to tell stories to scare my grandkids."

"You'll need kids first." Bodan laughed and watched her vanish into the thin brush. He set a stiff pace for the rest of the regulars. None of them could keep up with Sylve.

One thing he hadn't counted on was the lack of game on the plains. They saw a few snakes and lizards sunning themselves, and found tracks of small animals, but didn't see any larger animals. They had to munch on their emergency rations, which limited their useful time before they needed send a squad back west to hunt.

Sylve returned with a frown on her face.

"There is a village ahead about a half day's march. Aren't many men or healthy women, but they are singing in the fields. No one looked to be keeping watch."

"Thoughts?" Bodan rubbed his beard.

"I think it looks like a place that has sent its fighters off and doesn't think it has anything to fear. I suggest we swing around it. Something's making me nervous."

"Very well, we'll keep our distance. We'll move west a half day and have scouts monitor the village for trouble."

They moved in silence around the village, but there was no issue. None of the scouts reported being spotted. Bodan kept them on high alert, anyway. A day north of the village, he let his soldiers relax.

Then a scout dashed up to Bodan.

"Bodan, Sylve wants you to come a look at something. It will take a day to get there."

"Right, Nascup, keep the squads moving north. The maps show a city about a week north at a hard march. We will head in that direction after I observe what is going on there."

Bodan pushed the nerves in his stomach away. "Move with wide sweep scouts and double lead scouts. Camp within sight of the city and we'll find you."

He followed Sher northwest at a bruising pace. Neither of them said anything. He would see what Sylve wanted him to soon enough.

Sher allowed a rest at sunset, then started out again under the stars. They rested twice through the night. By the time the sun rose behind them, Sher slowed the pace and moved from cover to cover with almost as much skill as Sylve. They arrived at a slight ridge, and she wormed her way up to the top where Sylve was scanning the plains.

"What is this about?" Bodan crawled up the slope to lie beside the women.

Sylve pointed out onto the plain.

"See that movement out there?" She pointed east.

"Yes, what am I looking at?"

"An army, Bodan, and not a small one. They are marching in loose order like they haven't a care in the world." Sylve didn't sound happy.

"Which means they are inexperienced."

"Or they control the plains and really have nothing to worry about."

"Any idea where they are headed?"

"Northeast toward that city, Westburg, I think it is."

"Right, and I just sent the squad to view the city. I think we'd better catch up and make plans. Last thing we want is to be in the middle of a fight without knowing whose side we're on."

The three of them returned to the squad, aiming to intercept them before they arrived at the city. They could see the walls of the city in the distance when they caught up to Nascup and the others.

"New plan." Bodan said. "There is an enormous army moving east of us, heading for Westburg. We don't want them between us and the thousand. Drink up and eat your fill. I'm going to take a half squad and run north to the road leading west from the city. The rest of you head back to Hemsburg and report on the situation."

They loped north, alternating running with walking instead of taking breaks.

He got closer to the wall. An immense army surrounded the city. The others would report the army to Lady Robin. He wanted to see what happened with the battle.

Chapter 14

Allin worried that they'd had no trouble since they'd passed the gate. At each village, soldiers checked their travel permit, then let them pass. It felt like a storm was gathering, but he couldn't say what it was.

Henry, Magpie, and Rebecca simply enjoyed the peace and safety of the travel.

"It's been several weeks," Allin said. "We will arrive in Dordnom tomorrow. It's the last big city before we get to Rebecca's home."

"We've been fine so far," Henry said. "Lots of work and we've been able to sleep in barns more than out in the weather."

"The winter rains will start any day." Rebecca stared north. "We'll be happy for the shelter then."

"So, what do we do when we reach the city?" Allin asked. "Do we pass through quickly, or should we stock up for the last bit of travel north?"

"I wouldn't say the last bit," Rebecca chewed her lip. "We have almost as far to go as we've already come. We'll need proper gear for the winter. It should be safe enough to spend a little of the reserve you have on proper equipment and food. There won't be a lot of farms north of here. It is mostly mining and forestry from here north."

"As long as we spread out the purchases, it shouldn't be an issue." Henry held Magpie's hand. "I have nowhere to be in any rush."

Dordnom was a walled city with sprawling development outside the wall. It wasn't slums, as the roads were clean and the houses in good repair, but it wasn't wealthy either. They found a hostel to stay in exchange for work and Magpie was soon in demand for her sewing.

"I didn't know that baking bread could be so exhausting." Allin flopped on the bed in their room. "My arms are shaking from kneading the dough."

"I've spotted merchants who carry what we need." Rebecca sat with her back to the wall. "Warm clothes and oilskin cloaks. Dried meat and fruit that doesn't weigh too much. We'll want to travel with a caravan if we can. There are bandits in the forests. They take a toll to pass through, but just the four of us alone could be in trouble."

Henry was out cleaning ditches, and Magpie sewed in the back room of the hostel.

"What's your home like?" Allin asked.

"Lots of hunting and fishing, mining, of course. We aren't a cultured people, though we have our stories and myths. Life is work, so we carry our colour in our clothes and music. We hold storytellers in high regard." Rebecca played with the hem of her shirt.

"Yet you ended up in the emperor's harem."

"The empire took over in my grandfather's time. It was a gradual thing. An ambassador from the empire, then an embassy. They pushed trade with the empire, and, of course, had their own guilds for the job. Without quite realizing it, we'd sold ourselves to the empire. When they demanded I join the harem, father knew it was about keeping a hostage for our continued good behaviour. Not long after that, the nobles decided we'd be best served if we joined the empire as a province instead of being our own people."

"Sounds like a familiar story, giving away identity in place of safety. In the beginning, that was Fhayde's relationship with Caldera, but it developed over the years into something more equal. We had the fae's farming and forestry techniques and could teach them to Caldera in exchange for more independence."

"Independence is one thing we don't have." Rebecca said bitterly. "The empire demands obedience from its vassals, and we were no different from the plains to the east or the people along the coast. As long as we acknowledge the empire's rule, their legions would keep us safe."

"So what happened?"

"The planned invasion of Fhayde happened. They moved legions south, leaving our borders open to raiders. All our fighting men were in the legions and had marched south. The perception of strength has always held the clans to the north back. Once in a generation or so, some leader would try to invade and get pushed back. But we have no strength to push back anymore, and the clans are getting more aggressive every year. With the defeat of the empire, there is no reason for them to hold back any longer." Rebecca closed her eyes and sighed. "To be honest, I don't know that the clans would be any worse than the empire, but my home would become a battleground for some general trying to make a name for themselves. General Ordamy didn't play palace politics like the other generals, but he runs his province as a country to itself with only a token nod to the empire. With the capital gone, there is nothing to stop him from declaring himself emperor of his own kingdom, then pushing north to expand his lands. We've lost so many to the legions already, another war would destroy us." She sighed and stared at the floor.

"What do you hope to achieve by travelling north?"

"Perhaps I can use my position as third wife to negotiate some kind of peace between the clans and what is left of the empire. I am also my father's daughter, and that still carries some weight in the north."

***

Henry wielded his shovel, keeping a steady rhythm. He'd learned the secret of pacing himself. He could read and write, but somehow physical labour suited him better. The further the task from sitting on the golden throne, the more it suited him. A coin glinted in the ditch, and he put it in his pouch. There were never very many coins, but they belonged to him.

A chill settled into the air, and it began spitting rain. Henry kept clearing the ditch. If the rain got heavier, it could cause a flash flood. That would be a much bigger mess to clean up. He'd arrived at the corner when it began to pour. The icy rain soaked him, stealing warmth from his muscles. Before long he was shivering and couldn't see the end of his outstretched arm.

"Get out of the rain, idiot." The raspy voice was barely audible over the crash of falling water. Henry followed the sound to where a roof provided shelter. "Ye may as well come in. It will be awhile 'for it clears again." An old woman sat in a chair, knitting. "Hate rainy season, 'll have mushrooms growing between m'toes by spring."

Henry sat on the wood floor and stared out at the screen of water. It got rainy in the capital, but nothing like this. In his palace, he'd be drinking mulled wine and his harem would be fighting to provide him with warmth. He didn't miss the constant power struggles in the palace. His wives, his servants, his generals all of them had a plan for him, but no one asked if he wanted to be used.

"Ye must be new here." The old woman pointed with a knitting needle. "That view will drive you crazy soon enough."

"Don't mind." Henry turned to face the woman. "I'm Henry."

"Pleased t'meetcha, Henry." The old woman cackled. "Call me Su, it ain't me name, but everyone calls me that."

"Why don't they use your real name?"

"'Cause I don't tell 'em." Su laughed again. "Names have power, Henry. Ye should be careful who ye give yer name to."

"I will remember that." Henry's lips twisted. *What would she think if I told her I have twenty names and hated all but one?*

"The rain will stop in a few minutes, you'll want to run back to yer rooms, it'll be on and off for a week 'fore it settles in proper, then y'll be stuck, so make sure ye can stand the people around ye."

Sure enough, the rain let up and Henry scrambled through the drizzle to get back to the hostel.

He agreed with Su. Names had power. The name Henry set him free.

***

The onset of the rain caused problems for Allin. Henry and Magpie spent most of their time together, meaning he had to deal with the increasingly depressed Rebecca.

"I'd forgot how the rain affects me. Even in my father's house with plenty to do, I'd get sluggish. Here, I'm bound to go stir crazy."

"How long do they last?" Allin asked.

"About two months." Rebecca slumped against the wall, sitting on her mat. "Should have known we wouldn't make it in time."

"What happens while it rains?"

"Nothing. Being out in the rain too long can drive you mad. Everyone sits at home waiting for the breaks in the weather so they can get outside for a few minutes. Farmers build their barns attached to the house, so they can do their chores without going into the rain. I'm told even the animals go into a stupor through the rainy season."

"What did you do in the palace?" Allin put his elbows on his knees and gazed at her.

"There was always some plot or other to keep me busy, and the rains aren't as heavy, so it is possible to get out and breathe more often." Rebecca sighed. "Never thought I'd miss the palace."

Chapter 15

Hob watched Duncan's riot start by the north gate. Some of Pok's people got into an argument with Tad's. Fortunately, most of the rioters dropped their weapons and fought with fists. The noise was unbearable as it echoed off the stone walls of the city.

He worried that their enthusiasm for the riot would encircle the city and pull in all the thousands of Free soldiers. After a couple of their few tents caught fire, he was rethinking the plan. Would the city people buy the ruse? The ruckus lasted for an hour before the city gates were thrown open and a disciplined column of two hundred soldiers started into the fray, lashing out at anyone in their way. The rioters broke and ran, leaving a gap in the circle. Other Free moved away. The column marched into the gap, filled with the certainty of their superiority. Not until the soldiers to either side of the riot closed in behind them did they think to stop.

When those fleeing picked up weapons and turned on them, the city soldiers formed into a square, and held their position, still disciplined.

Hob climbed on a wagon and waved for silence. The Free stopped their yelling and cursing and faced the soldiers silently, with weapons ready.

"Surrender your arms and armour and we will let you return to the city." Hob shouted.

"Peasants." One soldier spat in Hob's direction. "No guts. We will march back to the city and take our weapons and armour with us."

"Look again. Even if it takes ten of us to kill one of you, you won't survive back to the gate."

"You have sticks and old steel. We're invulnerable to the likes of you, even if you have twenty times more than our number."

"Then you will die." Hob waved at the surrounding host of Free. Archers jumped onto the wagons and fired into the crowd of city soldiers. The soldiers laughed and blocked the arrows with their shields. They didn't see the silent attackers until the Free overran them. Here and there a soldier stood and fought, but most were pulled to the ground as peasants held their arms and legs, then tore off their helmet to stab their eyes.

Within a few minutes, all the soldiers lay on the ground motionless as the Free stripped them of their armour and weapons. Arrows rained down from the wall, but the battle was too far out of range for them to be anything but a nuisance.

Soon the stand-off resumed.

Hob had hoped others would try to come out to rescue their men, but there hadn't been time. Maybe he should have talked longer. That night the Free walked the battlefield recovering arrows and whatever else they found. Others moved the bodies of the city soldiers to outside the gate and left them. The city gates stayed closed, and vultures and other scavengers pecked at the bodies.

The peasants took to singing songs they had chanted for generations in the fields, but with the words changed to reflect their new freedom. In shifts, they sang all night all around the city.

The river flooded the west side of the plain outside the city.

"The rains are starting to the north." Pok said. "Soon the roads will be impassable."

"Any who want to leave may do so." Hob looked around at his commanders. "We don't have enough food to feed all of us through the winter, and we need the fields planted properly for the spring all across the plains or our people will starve in the summer."

"We are the Free." Pok saluted him. "We will meet at the end of the rains and take the city."

"We are the Free." Hob returned the salute.

***

The horde reduced to a thousand at the north, west and east gates and smaller groups wherever there were small doors. The muddy plain made it easier to keep the city closed in. Then the diverted river burst its banks and returned to its original path. It swept the debris the defenders had piled there to keep the Free from entering through the river channel and roared through the city, bursting out the south river gate carrying bodies and trash with it.

"I have a plan." Tad came to Hob's tent. "It is crazy enough to catch them by surprise."

"Sounds interesting," Hob said. "Explain."

"I have twenty volunteers who know how to swim. We will enter through the river gate."

"It is crazy. The rain is getting to you. Twenty wouldn't be enough to achieve anything."

"We have to do something."

"Why?" Hob shrugged. "They are as bored as us. Why give them something to do?"

"We need to communicate with the peasants inside the city. If we can get them to act, then we can take the place. The defenders know there is no way for us to break the stalemate. They'll hang on until someone comes to drive us away. There is no way for us to break the city, but the peasants inside can. They might be hungry enough to rebel." Duncan rubbed his chin.

"Twenty would be enough to talk to the peasants and get them to riot. We can get to the gate in the chaos and open it." Tad winked at Duncan.

"Twenty-one volunteers." Duncan leaned forward. "The river is high, so they think it is impregnable."

"Fine," Hob sighed, "next time the rains grow heavier, get to the wall. I think you are rain crazed, but you have the right to try. I will have the soldiers ready to act at a moment's notice."

***

Duncan regretted joining the insane plan, but he would not back out now.

"Remember, swim on a diagonal with the current, get to shore and get out of the water. There is a bridge across the river on the main road up to the keep. We'll meet there. The land go with you." Tad dove into the river, followed, one by one, until Duncan took up the rear.

He was already so chilled that the river didn't feel any colder. Tad had figured three seconds to get under the wall, if there was no grill left. It was so black that he couldn't tell which way was up. He let the current take him where it would until the water roiled up on the inside of the wall and spat him out onto the cobblestones. He lay there gasping like a landed fish until he had the strength to stand and head toward the main bridge.

Tad and five other soldiers met him under the bridge.

"There may be others, but we have to move now." Tad pointed up. "Already been one group walk across the bridge, maybe changing the guard on the walls?"

"You need to find the peasants and convince them to rebel." Duncan pointed to the wall of the city, barely visible through the rain. "I can't open the gate, but I can open a door."

"We should stick together; our strength is in numbers." Tad shook his head. "Let's get that door open, then find the peasants."

"Suits me." Duncan crept up onto the bridge and crossed to the west side of the river. The others followed him. The streets were a maze, and it took far too long to find the small door. They could just make out the guards leaning against the wall for whatever shelter it gave them. Duncan walked through the rain listening to the guards complain.

"I don't get enough food for this duty," one said.

"More than you'd get if you didn't take guard duty," the other said.

"True, the masters have all the good stuff."

"Not sure if there is any good stuff left."

Duncan grabbed the one closest to him and smashed his head against the stone wall. Two other Free held the man's arms. It took three blows before the guard slumped to the ground. Tad had the other guard down. No one moved in the small courtyard.

"Okay, we're good for now." Tad lifted the bar out of the way and pulled the door open. "Nich, run to Hob and tell him the small door is open. We can get lots of people inside before they can react. The others, move those guards, strip their weapons and armour. Stand here like you are on guard." Two of them took up the guard's position. Duncan claimed one sword.

"Not as good as mine, but it will do." He took up watch at one entry to the courtyard, Tad at the other.

An old man walked around the corner, head down. Duncan was on him immediately. "Silence or you die."

The man shrugged. "Might as well be dead. Haven't eaten in days. I don't know you." He peered through the rain, then shrugged again. "Need to get home to my Molly." He pushed Duncan's sword away. "I promised we'd die together." The man shuffled off into the rain. Duncan followed until he opened a door and stepped in.

The door in the wall opened and Nich slipped back into the city, pushing the door wide to allow a steady stream of men and women to enter, carrying swords and spears. They melted into the rain, heading into the city. Hob handed Duncan his sword. "Thought you'd like your own."

They left the two guarding the door as more and more Free flooded into the city.

"Let's head to the keep." Hob led the way through the maze to the main street. It zigzagged through the city until it reached a large courtyard with heavy gates leading into the keep. This wall was the height of two men with iron spikes set along the top.

"The map must be new." Hob pointed to the courtyard. "Barring secret tunnels, those gates are the only way in or out of the keep."

"What about over the wall?"

"We'll try that if we need to."

An alarm bell interrupted him. "That's the signal the gates are open." A roar drowned out the bell.

"They are on their way." Hob leaned against the wall. "I hope they will follow my instructions."

Soon, men and women flooded the courtyard. Some carried a huge beam. They charged forward and crashed into the gate. It shook but held steady. They backed off and ran again into the gate. After the third time, it bowed inward. On the fourth, one gate tilted on broken hinges. Spears jabbed out through the gap. The Free grabbed the spears and pulled on them while the soldiers with the ram hit the gate one more time, bursting through. The beam rammed into the wall of armoured soldiers, breaking their line.

"The keep is broken. Food, the masters have food." A mob of peasants pushed through the Free to get to the gate and through it.

"Food." The chant echoed off the walls of the courtyard.

"Back up, let them through." Hob yelled, and the order was passed along until the city peasants could stream into the keep unimpeded. Screams and shouts came from the inside of the keep.

"The city is ours." Hob said, but he didn't look happy about it. After an hour or two, the keep fell silent. "Time for us to check it out."

Duncan followed him through the gate, sword at the ready. Bodies littered the path, both guards and peasant, farther in, masters' corpses also lay on the ground.

"We won." Duncan said.

"We didn't lose." Hob looked around. "But I don't know if this counts as winning."

Chapter 16

The rain started on the second day of marching. Robin shivered in the wagon, but Ham didn't want her marching in the wet and muck yet. Instead, she did her exercises as best she could, then wrapped up in a blanket under an oilskin cloak. Sarge lay on a cot under a tiny tent with one of the boys always with him.

"Robin, your turn to sit with Sarge." Lencely crawled out of the tent, making a face at the rain. She handed him the blanket and oilskin and entered the tent. There wasn't room for anything but sitting by the cot and watching Sarge.

"It's still raining. Our escort says it will rain for two months. I don't know if I can handle two months of this, but I know you'd tell me I don't have much of a choice." Robin snorted. "I'm told it gets worse as we travel north. I'm getting stronger and faster, slowly."

Robin talked to Sarge through the hours until they stopped and made camp. While Rud supervised Sarge's tent and him being moved to it, Robin and Lencely trained under Ham's watchful eye.

"'Tis no use knowing what your enemy is going to do if you haven't the strength to counter it." Ham shook his head. To prove his point, he picked up a training sword and chased Robin around the training yard. He ignored Robin's attempts to parry and pushed through them.

"Maybe I should go back to wearing a weighted pack again."

"I don't think it would kill you now." Ham nodded slowly. "But if you lag, you'll take it off again."

"So I can march with the others?"

"I'll be watching, so if you fall behind, it's back on the wagon."

"I'll build up to it slowly." Robin stretched out the kinks from training, then headed to the quartermaster to pick up a pack she could load with sand or gravel.

The extra weight shocked her and it was less than half of what she once wore everywhere but the bath and bed. *How did I survive for years wearing this?* Lencely and Rud took turns running around the perimeter of the camp with her. As they travelled north, she grew used to running on slick mud and rocks. The wet didn't bother her until she stopped, then she had to change to dry clothes to keep from shivering.

While they marched, Robin ran up and down the line, carrying messages from the lead to the rearguard.

By the time they arrived in Acanopolis, she felt almost normal. The city looked empty, with the burnt buildings cleared away and only the occasional fire blackened stone edifice still there.

The bureaucracy had been sending messages back and forth between Commander Paychen and the palace guard. They'd been allowed to camp in an open field on the outskirts of the city under the agreement that they'd supply their own needs. Wagons arrived, escorted by Baron Timost's soldiers, on a weekly basis. Once bandits attacked, trying to steal the food and supplies. The Ancan soldiers had annihilated the bandits, leaving a couple alive to warn that robbery wouldn't be tolerated.

"Marshal Hapten sends her respects," the squad leader said to Robin. "She has sent a report on the situation in the city."

> Lady Robin,
> The city is calm. We have been working with the farmers to get the winter grain planted. It is late, but the elders think it worth the effort. Most of the farmers have returned to their land to the point where there is a labour shortage in the city. The guild has a council running the city, and they are paying the people to keep the streets clean. Healers have been busy with

minor illnesses, but with the crowding gone, nothing serious has come up.

I received a report from Commander Themson's people. A large army moved on Westburg and surrounded the city. An army that size may decide to move west toward the capital, so keep watch for trouble.

Bandits have been a minor irritation, but most are worse off than the farmers they attempt to steal from. I have reached out to some along the road the wagons travel in an attempt to get them to find legitimate ways to maintain themselves. A few are working with foresters to cut lumber to rebuild the capital. I have negotiated for wood to build semi-permanent buildings to last the winter rains. The first shipment will arrive with this report.

"We should start with barracks for the soldiers." Robin said.

"That will take a lot of wood and most of the winter to build." Commander Paychen frowned. "We'd be better to build storage and administrative buildings first."

"It might be wise to build something we can sell to the city when we are ready to move on." Commander Hacet said. "We can convert barracks to warehouses easily enough, then it won't matter that they take most of the rainy season to build.

"True." Commander Paychen looked at Robin. "What will you have us do?"

Robin scanned the faces in the tent. "If we are building something to become warehouses, we will need to build in offices. That will give us the admin space. We'll get the soldiers to start on the foundations for a warehouse. That will get supplies and admin out of the rain, but give the men and women some incentive to work. I can't imagine a campaign in this rain, but we'll keep an eye out just in case."

"Very good." Commander Paychen nodded and looked at the list in his hand. "Next, we have the request by the palace to provide some demonstration battles for the arena."

"It would help with keeping the men and women sharp, so long as it is clear they are with training weapons. I'll not have unnecessary blood shed for entertainment." Robin said. "I'd keep it to four squads at a time. It will work the squad leader's abilities and keep things from getting out of hand. Sargent Temajin can help with the organizing and I can act as a judge occasionally along with the Commanders of whichever hundreds are involved."

"Works for me." Commander Paychen grimaced. "Anything to keep me from needing to run the thing, and it will keep the soldiers busy, along with the building project. We should get through the winter with no trouble."

***

The court was held in the office of the newly constructed warehouse. Robin, Commander Paychen and Commander Hacet sat as the tribunal.

"I didn't mean it to go so far." Eric sat red-faced. "It wasn't like she wanted to stop."

"How can our daughter get married?" The trader waved his hands dramatically. "It has brought shame on our family. He should be hung, and suitable reparations paid."

His daughter's face whitened at the mention of hanging. She opened her mouth, but her father glared at her.

"You're saying that sex before marriage is the same as rape." Commander Paychen steepled his fingers. "But you only suggest hanging our man. What of your daughter? There is no suggestion of force here."

"I will discipline my daughter and you shall discipline your man."

"If you're going to hang Eric, you'll have to hang me too." The girl jumped up. "It is as much my fault as his. Father, you are more concerned about your reputation and money than about my honor. You were looking to sell me to some fat old man as soon as I was of age."

"No one will have you now." The father stood up and raised his hand to strike her.

"Hold." Robin rapped the table. "I will not stand for any violence in my court."

"She's my daughter and mine to do with as I please."

"The moment you brought the rape charges against our soldier and brought your daughter into this court, she became my concern." Robin pointed at him. "Sit down or I will have you removed."

"You can't do that."

"I can and will. You can take your case to the guild and see what they say about it." Robin said. "My inquiries suggest they would do little more than impose a fine since there was no force involved."

The father reddened and stepped toward his daughter.

"Ham." Robin said, and the big man stood up to move between the girl and her father.

"Sit down." Commander Paychen leaned toward the man. "This is a court, not your back room."

The girl ran to Eric's side. "I don't want to go home. I want to stay with Eric."

"But you are not of age to be married and I will not allow such a relationship in the camp." Robin sighed and looked at her. "If you were of age, it might be a different matter."

"I will be of age in a month; I'd rather spend it locked up here than with my father, whose only concern is his purse and his pride."

"That is not up to me." Robin frowned. "Though I understand your feelings."

"I will stay with her, to protect her honour for the month." The mother stood up.

"Sit down, woma—"

She swatted the husband on the back of the head. "Don't you 'woman' me, Horold, I'm no meeping bride to be ordered around by the nose. A month without me may remind you who built up the trading business you are so proud of." She turned to face Robin. "I see you bending over backwards to be fair, and I approve, but I do not wish to put Merle through her father's 'discipline'. She can work for her board, then in a month the children will get married, and I will return home."

Eric and Merle turned red as they looked at each other, but nodded.

Robin sighed and looked at the two commanders. They shrugged their shoulders. "It's up to you," Commander Paychen said. "I expect Commander Hacet to keep Eric busy enough to stay out of trouble."

"Very well, Merle and her mother will bunk with me. They can work at whatever suits them." Robin met Merle's eyes.

"I can help cook." Merle smiled brightly at Eric, then at Robin.

"I will as well," Merle's mother smiled grimly at Robin. "I taught her to use a knife myself. She'll be no trouble."

"Now the only thing to do is explain the sentence to the rest of the camp. I want no more such trials." Commander Paychen stood. "We're adjourned."

That evening, as she readied for bed, Merle sang the praises of her Eric. She'd clearly set her cap for him, and he, not being much older than her, fell for her, hook, line, and sinker.

Merle's mother, Fabell, rolled her eyes at Robin and winked. "She's a good girl, a solid head on her shoulders. They'll be fine."

***

"Lady Robin, you're needed at the amphitheatre, bring your kit." A young Fhayde man on horseback controlled his mount's fidgets with casual skill. Robin dashed into her room, snatched up the satchel, and ran back to mount the horse behind the young man.

"Ham!" she yelled, "I'm headed for the arena, emergency."

The big man waved at her. "I'll be seeing you there in a few minutes. Don't fall off the horse."

Robin held onto the rider with one arm and her satchel with the other. They arrived at the arena, and Robin was off the horse before it came to a stop. A woman waited for her and guided her to where a man lay with a bloodied bandage around his head.

He was breathing, but his eyes were half open and not responding. She took off the bandage and gasped. A channel, oozing blood, ran from his temple to the back of his skull. Not until she put her hands on either side of his head did she recognize Eric. He looked older somehow.

Eric's brain was swelling and would kill him soon if nothing was done. Robin closed her eyes and reached for the healing power that occasionally came to her when she needed it. *Intention is everything.* Robin set herself and determined she'd save this young man, as much for Merle as his own sake. The land fought her, some animosity blocking her.

"I don't care what little thing you have against this man." Robin stretched her mind's hand and gripped the land to shake it. "I will heal him."

"He isn't worth it." Sarge said. "You are going to exhaust yourself for someone who couldn't keep it in his pants.

"He is worth it." Robin gave the land another shake. "I judged him for myself and saw foolishness, but no malice. If you want my aid, you will help me."

"Drop it, lass, you're risking your own life here. You are too important for this."

"This is who I am."

"You aren't the only person to speak to me." Sarge stepped forward with his hand raised.

"Then the others can find your precious emperor and heal you. If this man dies, then we are done. I will head home and find another quest."

Sarge sagged and faded into darkness. Power flowed through her and burned her from the inside, but she used it to repair the damage to the skull, then relieve the pressure on the brain. She was repairing the blood vessels when Gord showed up.

"That's enough. Killing yourself won't do no one any good."

Robin opened her eyes to find herself sprawled on the floor.

"What happened?" Eric sat up to look around. "Last thing I remember was arriving here."

"That Ancan brute tried to crush your skull."

"Ancan brute?" Robin sat up slowly and winced at the pounding in her head.

"Some guy who wanted to spar with one of us." The woman soldier frowned. "He'd set his sights on Eric from the beginning."

"Sounds like someone I should talk to." Robin stood up and the world tilted under her, but she kept to her feet. "Let's see if this brute is still here."

The woman led her out to the arena where a big Ancan guard was taunting the Fhayde soldiers. "That would be him."

Robin stalked over to the man.

"Let me see your weapon."

The man made a move to drop his pants, but the soldiers around growled at him and he shrugged. "She asked."

"This one." Ham took the practice sword from the man and passed it to Robin.

"This has been weighted." Robin scowled. "Ham, arrest this man. We will ask his superior officer to form a tribunal for his judgement."

"You can't do that. I'm an Ancan, you can't touch me."

"Is that what you were told?" Robin stepped up close to him. "Well, allow me to enlighten you. I signed an agreement with the palace, which put my soldiers under the guard's jurisdiction as long as I, or one of my officers, is a member of the tribunal."

"So what?"

"The reverse is also true." Robin met and held his gaze. "I have jurisdiction when it comes to combat with my soldiers, especially when it involves an illegal weapon."

"You can't prove it is mine. You're trying to frame me."

"I have several hundred witnesses that will attest that this is the very weapon you used on my man. His blood is still fresh on it."

"What is going on?" Another Ancan strolled over to them.

"Hi, Captain, these idiots think they can arrest me," the big man laughed.

"Shut up, Hunce." The captain scowled. "You were told to cooperate with the Fhayde people."

"Do you wish to sit on the tribunal, or should I speak to your superior?"

"I will sit on your tribunal." The captain grimaced. "Who do you want as a third?"

"The commander of the hundred my man belongs to is present." Robin pointed to Commander Hacet.

"Fine, what are the charges?" the captain asked.

"Using an altered weapon, deliberately trying to injure my man during an exhibition match."

"The condition of the man?"

"Lucky to be alive." Robin said. "He has no memory of the incident. His skull was crushed in. I was able to repair the skull and save his life. You are welcome to speak to him and examine the wound."

Hunce turned grey.

"Funny how your man is more concerned that my man survived than he was to have injured him so."

"It's a frame up, Captain."

"I ordered you to shut up," the captain said. "Do I need to have you gagged?" He pointed to a woman sitting with the

Fhayde. "You, tell me what happened. Only what you saw for yourself, no assumptions."

"Yes, sir." The woman saluted. "Hunce, as you called him, came over after our practice sparring and wanted to have a friendly sparring match. Try his style against ours. He picked out Eric and challenged him. Eric accepted. Since Hunce didn't have a helmet, we offered him one of ours, but he rejected it. Eric was going to spar without a helm, but the commander ordered him to wear his." She walked over and picked up the helm. "Here is his helmet." She handed it to the captain.

He rapped on the metal helm. "Good quality. It should have protected him against any normal blow." The captain passed it to Robin.

She ran a figure along where it was creased. "You're right. Even a weighted sword shouldn't be able to do such damage." Robin passed it to Commander Hacet and held up Hunce's sword, then passed it to the captain.

He examined it closely, then dropped it before stepping back. "It's cursed." The captain pointed to a mark on the blade of the sword, but refused to touch it.

"A cursed blade." Robin picked it up and peered at the mark. "I see, meant to kill a specific man." She hefted it. "No need to weight it too. Perhaps the sword was already weighted."

"I warned you about that." The captain shouted at Hunce. "What did I tell you? You don't mess with your weapons. Where did you get the curse done?"

"Captain, you aren't siding with these foreigners?"

"I don't care about the foreigners, but wielding a cursed weapon is a hanging offence." The captain turned to Robin. "If your man had died, the mark would have vanished. As long as the sword exists, it is a danger to your man."

"Do you need the sword as evidence?"

"Hell, no. We'll have to call a priest here to have the curse removed. Do it wrong and your man could still die."

"I will bow to your greater knowledge." Robin put the sword on the ground.

"Camad, fetch a priest on the double," the captain bellowed, making Robin jump. "What is the punishment for the weighted sword and the injury to your man?"

"Since the man is alive, I would have asked for him to be imprisoned. But from what you said, this is a deliberate murder attempt. That's a capital charge."

"We are agreed then." The captain glowered at the sword.

"I didn't know the thing was cursed." Hunce said.

"How could you not?" The captain replied. "Who were you working for? Help me out and I will argue for five years heavy labour instead of the noose."

"He'll kill me." Hunce wailed.

"You're going to die anyway, you fool."

"I can guess who it was." Robin said. "Eric fell in love with a certain merchant's daughter, a girl named Merle.

"Oh great, the head of the guild." The captain rubbed his temples. "This is beyond me. I will have to bring it to my superior."

"Perhaps we shouldn't be too quick to remove the curse. I can imagine it would be useful evidence against this guildmaster." Robin picked up the sword and peered at it again. "I would hate to destroy the curse and allow him to deny its existence.

"No worries about that. The priests will attest to the curse. They are the ones who insist that it be death to wield one."

"And what punishment for creating it, or paying for its creation?"

"Death." The captain's voice had no give to it. "It matters not who you are."

Chapter 17

Hob frowned at the delegation led by Leckod. They met with him in a room in the manor, looking more comfortable with the luxury than him.

"What do you have in mind for the administrators?" Leckod frowned.

"The same as everyone else. There are no peasants or overseers, or administrators if you like, just the Free. We work together for the good of everyone." Hob repeated the message again.

"The peasants won't know what to do if they are not told."

"They will learn." Hob frowned. "We are the Free. You are welcome to contribute to the work, but there will be no preferential treatment. If you are unhappy with this, you are welcome to leave the city with all you can carry."

"We will take a master's horse and carriage."

"You will take what you can carry with your own strength. Horses and carriages belong to the Free."

"You mean they belong to you." Leckod puffed up.

"I own only what I can carry." Hob shook his head. "I lead the army, but that doesn't make me a master. You may coordinate the work, but that doesn't make you a master."

"We will leave, and you will wish for our guidance within a week." Leckod turned and stormed off.

"Any who wish to stay and be free are welcome, any who wish to leave may do so. The Free will not allow any masters to rule us again."

About half of the delegation followed Leckod as the others looked at each other.

"We will work with you." A woman put her hands on her hips and met Hob's eyes. "But we won't let anyone treat us different."

"If there are problems, we will solve them."

The problems took more work to solve than Hob expected. The overseers who left took whatever they could raid from the masters' manor. They took with them the all those who thought they should be the new masters. The larger challenge was the Free who didn't want to work equally with the past overseers.

"Ain't nobody telling me how to do my job." A Free stuck her jaw out.

"What are they saying?" Hob asked.

"They's asking how much weaving I've done and saying they need blankets more than fine cloth."

"Are they right?" Hob muffled a sigh. "We need blankets and warm clothes at this moment. There will be a time when we need fine cloth. And how can we know how to pass out your work if we don't know how much you have completed?"

"They's just gonna take my work?"

"No, you share you work and share the food we have. What good is weaving if it sits in a room and never gets touched? What if the farmers decided they were keeping all the food they grew? We need to share and take care of each other. If we don't, we are no better than the masters."

Hob spent his days talking to one group or another who thought someone else was getting a better deal. His throat ached from the talking. It had been easier with the Browns. He gave an order, and everyone jumped to it, but it was he who had insisted that everyone was equal. That meant no more orders until the people understood the reason behind it.

The word had spread that Westburg had fallen to the Free, and many showed up out of curiosity and boredom. At least most were smart enough to bring food with them and didn't mind working on the city security. Blacksmiths rebuilt the gates to place in the north and south river gates. The city was cleaned and prepared for the spring.

"We will need to be ready to fight." Hob talked to the council elected by the Free in the city once they saw that some organization was needed. "The masters won't sit around now that we've taken one of their cities."

"We beat the masters once. We can beat them again." Helga, a past overseer, made a fist.

"We can, but it will take work." Hob sighed. "Anyone who wants to fight needs to train and be willing to follow the plan of battle. There will be thousands of soldiers. We will need to be soldiers ourselves to win."

Fortunately, Duncan had some understanding of the tactics of defending a city and explained them to Hob. They made sense. Keep the gates closed, control the food and water. Throw things off the wall at the invaders. They'd already made substantial piles of rubble from clearing the roads and tearing down dangerous buildings. The manor house became a meeting place for resolving arguments. They took armour and weapons from the armoury and dispersed them to those who volunteered to walk the walls.

Pok showed up to check in, and Hob took her up to the walls.

"I'm impressed. I expected to show up in the spring and find you still camped in the mud."

"We will need the army." Hob pointed west. "The masters won't relax with us running the city."

"Can we beat them?"

"We win or we die." Hob shrugged. "But if we have the numbers, we will push them back. We will parley with them before we fight. An army that outnumbers theirs ten to one will help to convince them to talk."

"I have an idea about that." Pok grinned. "What if they thought they were only fighting the Free in the city? Then we show up and surround them, trapping 'em between us and the walls?"

"If we can work it right. You'd all have to show up at the same time."

"Leave that to me." Pok said. "We been talking through the winter. We'll have a couple weeks between the end of the rains and the spring planting season. Let the people work off their energy from the winter."

"As long as they don't expect battles and mayhem every year." Hob shuddered. "We should build for peace."

"First, we need to teach the masters that we're serious, and that we can get along without them." Pok waved a hand to the west.

"And they still can't do without us." Hob said. "Let's get out of the rain."

***

The rain finally stopped.

The people of Westburg stood outside, staring at the blue sky and laughing. Not their first spring, but the first that they didn't get whipped for stopping to enjoy it.

Hob encouraged them all to celebrate, joining the line dancing through the labyrinthian streets. The celebration lasted all day and long into the night.

The next day started with rain, but the excitement of a new beginning lasted as they returned to work, planting crops outside the city, cutting lumber. The rain grew less frequent until they expected the blue sky and warm sun.

Working hard for their own good was a far cry from slaving for the masters.

The good feelings lasted until the scouts reported an army approaching from the west.

"We planned for this." Hob shouted to the crowd of worried Free. "If any of you want to leave, you can run to the east. You have time to reach safety. The army will be here in a week." Not one person moved.

"Time to finish up our work to prepare for the battle." Helga said. "The good news is a wagon train of food and other supplies just arrived, so we won't need to go to short rations for the siege."

The crowd cheered, then dissipated.

"The people on the walls are in armour and the messenger system is in place." Hob rubbed the back of his neck. "The most dangerous part is going to be getting them to talk to us and take us seriously. The word has gone out to the hordes. They know their part."

"So do the people here," Helga said. "They have a taste of freedom, and they won't give it up easily. We got rid of the weak already. Not one person in Westburg is going to let the city fall easily."

"You're right, I just hope we are strong enough. The road to victory is paved with blood."

The river gates were checked and reinforced one more time, the stashes of rubble on the walls topped up. Young people ran back and forth carrying messages. Elders counted bandages prepared them for the knackers to use. The Free sang the songs of their revolution. Old forbidden words to tunes sung in fields for generations.

As the army grew closer, their scouts checked the gates but ran from rocks that thudded into the dried earth beside them. The week the scouts had reported passed, but finally, on the western road, the watchers on the wall saw the first banners of the approaching army.

"How many people did the scouts say there were?" Duncan peered west.

"They guessed between three and five thousand." Hob said. "They should be here before the evening, but if was their commander, I'd camp early and march in the morning with the sun behind them."

In the morning, the approaching army circled the city, setting most of their people at each gate. They flew colourful banners in the morning light.

Chapter 18

Robin looked at the judges as they deliberated in the city square. The trial had been open to everyone and bets changed hands daily. She suspected bribes had been at least attempted and possibly successful. The trial of the master of the trader's guild for the purchase of a cursed weapon had been a grand show. Hunce's sword lying on the judges' table, cleansed of its curse by the priests, was the only solid fact. The head priest sat as a judge and his face thundered his disapproval for the entire proceedings. He'd made it clear he thought the guild master and family should have already met the noose and the flame.

A well-dressed attorney stood to speak. "My client admits to hiring a guard to teach the young Fhayde man a lesson, but there was no intention of killing him and certainly no procurement of an illegal weapon, cursed or not. We have already heard that the man, Hunce, has been disciplined before for tampering with his weapons. The sword was cursed. I do not doubt the word of the priesthood, but there is no proof that he was involved in the curse."

The man was right. They hadn't proved beyond any doubt the guild master had been directly involved in the sword's cursing. Hunce had died in his cell, the priest suggesting the breaking of the curse had rebounded on the caster. Robin had her doubts, not only about the death in the cell, but about the righteousness of the priest. The head priest's bloodthirsty ways had forced the other judges to be more moderate or give up on the pretense of a trial. Even Marshal Hapten looked like she'd bitten into a rotten fruit whenever the man spoke.

Robin had awakened one morning in the rain as they unloaded wagons into the warehouse/barracks with the decision made to call the thousand together. She'd sent a message back with the wagon and the Marshal and Commander Revont with her five hundred arrived just after the rain stopped.

Having the full thousand at her command gave her bargaining power with the palace bureaucracy, who tried to pin the whole mess on the Fhayden troops. The camp had a wall and a gate, not tall enough to be threatening, but enough to keep people from wandering in and out without permission.

The practice skirmishes continued at the arena and grew in size and complexity. Commanders of one hundred were set against each other. The audiences grew and rumour was that fortunes were won and lost betting on the outcome.

The captain of the guard who had arrested Hunce took his turn to talk. "The guild master has admitted to interfering in an agreement between the palace and Fhayden army, who have been nothing but helpful through winter. It is astonishing that only one member of their troops fell for a local woman. I need not remind you of the problems we've had with the city guard over the past year. Notwithstanding the curse, he suborned a guard to cause harm to someone under the authority of a person with a contract with the palace. This must not go unpunished."

The judges turned to deliberate.

"The man who bought it is dead from his own curse." One judge, a member of the guilds, said.

"We don't know that. All we are certain is that he is conveniently dead. If one guard could be bribed, why not two?" The head priest glared in the captain's direction.

"No proof of that, either." Marshal Hapten. "We must deal with the facts at hand. One, this Hunce had a cursed sword. Two, he is dead. Three, the guild master denies involvement with the curse, but admits to interfering with Hunce to get back at Eric."

"Interfering with a palace contract is a serious matter." A bureaucrat insisted. "But sadly, it is not a capital crime."

"There'd be mighty few left if it were." The first judge rolled his eyes.

"The reputation of the guard is at stake if anyone can bribe a guard. It should be an offense for the one making the bribe and the guard accepting it." The Guard General said.

"We can recommend that in our judgement." The priest made a note.

"Without proof of involvement with the curse, the noose is off the table." The bureaucrat winced and looked at the head priest.

"I am alone seeing guilt in the man, yet I'm but one on the panel." The priest sighed and slammed his hand on the table. "I won't see the man go guilt free."

"I agree." Marshal Hapten said. "What punishments do we have at hand?"

"He interfered with a contract, that rates a suspension of his licence to trade." The bureaucrat cracked his knuckles. "He can't be guild master without a license, but that is only a suspension for a year at most. Then he'll be back like nothing had happened. There are reports of rebellion in the east. Some people showed up in the rain and tried to sell was what clearly plundered from the nobility. Perhaps we should send him to find out the truth and resolve the situation."

"I like the notion, keep him busy and out of trouble. Don't give him any command of the forces we send. I suspect it is some minor uprising. The nobility have been in charge out there for generations. It shouldn't take more than a few thousand soldiers." The Guard General chortled. "Kill two birds with one stone."

"And if it is more than a small uprising?" Marshal Hapten frowned. "I don't trust him as far as I could throw him."

"If it is more serious, I doubt we will see the guild master again." The head priest smiled.

"Don't sound so much like you hope it is a bigger problem," the Guard General said. "I don't want to send three thousand good soldiers into a bear trap."

"Perhaps the Marshal and her forces will accompany them in a supervisory role. You are, after all, impossible to bribe."

"I will need to speak to Lady Robin, but I am not averse to a march to shake the rust off the thousand. We would expect you to supply us for the duration of the campaign. Of course, we will be a separate command. We won't fight unless attacked, but we can be part of a show of strength."

Robin wanted to jump up and object, but couldn't interrupt the deliberations of the judges. The idea of marching as a show of strength under the white banner didn't feel right, but she didn't have any solid argument against it. Embarrassing the marshal would be a bad idea.

The Guard General stood to give the verdict.

"Guild master Haffmon has been found guilty of interfering in a contract between the palace and the Fhayden army. The punishment is twofold. First, we suspend his license to trade for a year. Second, we send him with a force of arms to the eastern plains. He is to negotiate a resolution to the situation, whatever it may be."

Haffmon turned white and opened his mouth to speak. His lawyer tugged on his arm and whispered in his ear. They argued fiercely for a minute or two before Haffmon shrugged and leaned back.

"My client accepts the judgment of the court and will put all his efforts to resolving the issue in the east."

***

"Sorry," Marshal Hapten looked at her feet. "I got a bit carried away." The lamp made a small circle of light in the command room in the barracks. The smell of fresh wood still filled the air.

"We will deal with the situation." Robin said. "At least we are a separate command, not under the Ancan Guard. I would like to leave a hundred behind to secure our supply line. It is already too long for my liking."

"I don't think that will be an issue, and it will keep us from returning to find they have taken our camp over in our absence."

They chose ten volunteers from each hundred and left Commander Paychen in command of the mixed hundred.

Eric and Merle, now properly married, stayed with the commander in Ancanopolis. Fabell went back to take over the business while her husband was under suspension.

"Keep an eye on him. He's trouble through and through."

"If he is so awful, why stay married to him?" Robin asked.

"Business." Fabel shrugged." I have the connections, but he's a man and people don't start out assuming they can cheat him. He started getting too big for his britches when they went and made him guild master."

"I'll watch him, and Commander Paychen is going to keep things tight while we're gone. Maybe give him a hand with the logistics. Someone is going to need to reopen trade with Fhayde and Caldera."

"You sound sure they will be interested in trading."

"We have an excess of food but lack some other items. Trade will be good for all involved."

"You make it sound like it will be more than the empire and Fhayde."

"The empire, as it was, is gone," Robin said. "You'd do well to work on trade connections with other parts of the empire and not assume that it will work as it always has."

"I will take your words to heart. To be honest, the Empire has been cracking for years."

"Take care of yourself. Trade will be more important than armies in the years to come."

***

Bodan crawled out of the shelter they'd cobbled together just before the rains hit. They had eked out food by stealing from the encampment around the city who didn't have an effective sentry line. Going in and out of the camp was almost too easy. Life had become much harder when the city fell. Bodan had been in shock watching the gates open and the Free, as they called themselves, flooding in. Later, people had walked out with heavy bags and walked west. There was no fire, no ransack of the city as far as they could learn.

When the rains stopped the Free planted fields near the city. A few came to visit the city, dressed in the same ramshackle way as the Free.

"They are gathering the army again." Sylve looked exhausted. "But they are hanging back from the city. It is like they are waiting for a signal."

"They're waiting for an attack by the Ancans to the west. They've turned the entire city into a trap." Bodan peered at the city in the distance. "We are going to pack up and head out to meet up with Lady Robin and the thousand. We don't want the Free discovering our cozy hideout here."

"As if." Sylve snorted.

"There will be as many at least as were here before the rain. The chance is too high that someone will just stumble on us, and it will trap us here so we can't report. I will go ahead; you wait here and bring the others as they arrive back from their sweeps. Something is itching at me to get a move on."

***

Robin took a long time with Sarge. He had a room with Lencely and Rud in the warehouse. The first room to be occupied. It was small, only holding his bed and a cot for the boys.

"I can't risk bringing you with me. You stay here and get well." Robin's voice caught. A part of her didn't believe he'd ever wake up, but as long as he breathed, she, Lencely and Rud would make sure he was cared for. "If you need me, call and I swear by the land, I will come as fast as I am able."

"We'll stay with him." Lencely brushed his hand along the blanket and tugged it straight.

"You two are my heroes." Robin hugged Lencely and Rud, then left before the tears found their way out of her eyes.

"I'm ready." Robin took a long breath as she walked out to join Marshal Hapten.

"I wish everyone else was." Marshal Hapten sighed. "Let's inspect the troops while we wait for the Guard to arrive."

The soldiers all wore their brown uniforms, each with a white cloth on their left arm. Some had pikes and the others spear and shield.

"This has been a longer stay than any of us expected." Robin spoke as Sarge taught her to be heard by the farthest row. "I appreciate each and every one of you. Your dedication to peace and the willingness to help this broken land. I don't make many promises, but I promise I will do my best to get you back to your homes before the next rainy season."

The army cheered, and Robin smiled. For this moment, she knew where she belonged.

The guard arrived with the tramp of feet and the shouts of commanders.

"Let's get on the road, the finest thousand in Fhayde or the empire."

They marched out behind the last of the Ancan guard. Fortunately, the road wasn't dry enough to kick up a lot of dust.

The worst part of the march was Haffmon's carriage. He insisted on riding in the vanguard in a carriage pulled by two matched horses that had never pulled for more than an hour at a time. When it was the thousand's turn to lead the march, he never so much as put his head out the door. The issue was the carriage was made for city streets and kept breaking. They spent as much time repairing the thing as they did marching. Robin let Marshal Hapten meet with the other commanders. She ate with her thousand and marched with them as much as she could. She no longer noticed the weighted pack and didn't fall into bed, exhausted, at the end of the day. Ham drove a wagon with the supply train. Sargent Temajin helped with logistics. She was content to have the time to herself. When she wasn't checking on her people, Robin spent time feeling out what the land wanted. The sense she got was of waiting. It wasn't as fractured as before the rains, but it had no direction. The faint tug north still had her looking to her left as they marched, but it held no more pull than that.

The scouts reported Westburg was shut up tight. There was no activity outside the city, but fields were freshly planted. Some scouts had rocks thrown at them, but no other sign of hostility.

Robin ordered her own scouts out to check farther east. Things seemed far too peaceful for a city taken over by the ravaging horde the survivors described.

Something else was going on. The land wasn't interested in the east, as if it had vanished from existence. It nagged at her about going north, but gave no reason for it.

They finally arrived. The carriage had given out entirely and Haffmon had to ride with the supply chain or on horseback. After the first morning on horseback, he'd retreated to the wagons. When they stopped early, short of the city, Robin got an earful about how Haffmon could make a fortune using the wagons as the basis for a better carriage.

"It isn't my technology to sell." She told him. "The Fhayde have used such wagons for generations."

"My dear girl, never turn down a chance for a sale. We could make a fortune."

"Master Haffmon, I'm not interested in making a fortune. The wagons are not mine to sell."

Early morning, the columns of the army marched in order, the Fhayden thousand at the rear, but that meant Robin could check in with Ham and Sargent Temajin.

"That blighter was all about buying the wagon from me." Ham complained and made a face. "Wouldn't hear any sense. He could go down to Fhayde and buy a dozen for what he was offering."

"Hint that you might be willing to let one go." Robin rubbed her eyes. "It will let us monitor him and probably stop him from trying to steal one."

"Yes, Lady Robin." Ham saluted and cleared his throat. "I think you're ready to return to full duty. I doubt there is anyone in this army who could land a touch on you."

"I will try to honour your trust in me."

"Try?" Ham raised his eyebrows.

"Circumstances may dictate putting myself in danger, but I will not do it foolishly."

"Good enough, Lady Robin." Ham nodded. "Now I suggest you and Sargent Temajin catch up to the vanguard and fly our banner. Maybe whoever's in that city will want to talk before they fight."

The lead of the column was the commanders and their honour guards. Robin was outnumbered with just Sargent Temajin. At his insistence, she had put on her full armour and carried her helmet at her waist, and she appreciated it as the other commanders wore fancy armour and had people carrying their personal, as well as the regimental, colours. Marshal Hapten wore her brown tunic over the same armour the others in the thousand wore. The difference was she didn't carry a spear or shield.

"Bout time you got here." She rolled her eyes. "You'd think this crew was going to kick down the gates and sack the city without the help of the army."

"Excuse me, Lady Robin, one of our scouts wants to report. It appears to be urgent." Sargent Temajin saluted her.

"Go take their report, Sargent."

"Yes, Lady Robin." He jogged off to the side, where a scout in dirty browns waited for him.

"Someone on the wall." One commander pointed. A second later, a white banner flew from the western gate. "Guess they want to talk."

Chapter 19

Allin stepped outside and immediately wondered what was wrong. Then he realized it wasn't raining. Citizens moved through the streets with an extra bounce in their step and a smile on their face. He could understand why. The months of constant rainfall had been oppressive. The last few weeks were a blur of staring at the wall and repeating old conversations.

He ran back into the hostel. "Rain's stopped, for now anyway."

Rebecca came outside and stretched. "Finally. I can go spend some of my dowry."

"Be careful." He handed her a purse. "Have a reasonable story for the foreign coinage."

"I'm going to say I'm from near the border and this is my grandfather's stash from raiding in Fhayde."

"The dating system is different in Fhayde than in the Empire, so you should be all right."

Rebecca grinned and vanished into the crowds out enjoying the respite. Allin decided to walk around and shake the cobwebs from his head. Henry and Magpie would have heard by now as well. The celebration was hardly quiet.

He explored the streets near the hostel until a few raindrops fell and he headed back.

A man blocked his way. "You look like a fine citizen." He played with a knife. "By that I mean rich."

"Hardly." Allin laughed and spread his arms. "Look closer and you'll see threadbare cloth. I once was a man of means, but in the past years, I've slept in more fields than beds."

"No matter, I'll take what you have."

An arm reached around Allin's neck from behind. He reacted instinctively, pushing the elbow up and ducking under the arm, shooting his elbow back to connect solidly. The man with the knife jumped forward, Allin batted the blade aside with his arm, protected by the heavy jacket, and punched the attacker in the throat.

The two men lay in the mud, choking and gasping. Allin kicked the knife into a flooded ditch and headed for the hostel. The rain made it hard to tell if he was followed, but he didn't see anyone between where the men lay and the hostel.

"Where were you?" Rebecca asked. Henry leaned against the wall and arm around Magpie.

"Just stretching my legs." *They'll just worry if I tell them about the attempted robbery.*

"I did pretty well, if I have to say it myself." Rebecca pulled out oilskin cloaks and sweaters that looked too thin to be warm from a worn-looking pack.

"Boots will have to wait until we can try on boots from a vendor."

"Your coat is torn." Magpie came and poked at it. "No, it looks cut."

"I ran into a couple of lads who thought I looked rich. The knife must have cut my jacket after all." Allin peered at the sleeve.

"This could be trouble, if they remember your face." Rebecca said.

"More likely to remember my clothes. I'll wear something other than my jacket and shave." He sighed and shook his head. "I hate shaving."

"It will only be for a week. I used to shave my grandfather, so if you don't trust your own hand." Rebecca gave him a half grin.

"Let's try it." Allin ran his finger through his beard. "I was thinking it needed a trim, anyway."

The shave went with no bloodshed, but Allin's face felt cold and foreign. Rebecca cut away some of his hair as well.

Magpie stitched up the jacket, and he buried it in the bottom of the pack Rebecca had bought. He tried on one sweater and was amazed that it wasn't itchy.

"Royal wool." Rebecca ran her fingers across the sweater she'd claimed. "He thought he was cheating me, but this is so rare outside of my country that he didn't know what he had. It is warm and comfortable in all weather."

Magpie provided a coat that was too big and had seen much better days. She'd repaired it from the lost and found, but no one wanted it. It cut the wind better than it looked. She'd relined it from another couple that weren't worth saving. She had quietly earned almost as much coin as Rebecca had spent, but since hers was in local currency, it was safer to spend.

The next day, there was another break in the rain. Allin stayed at the hostel trying to get used to his unfamiliar face while Rebecca and Henry went shopping for better boots. The ones they'd got from the guards were already worn, and the trek north had them falling to pieces.

They came back before the rain started again. Rebecca had gone out again to do her own provisioning.

"The shave is a new look." The host leaned against the door.

"I'd promised my daughter to shave when the rains stopped." Allin rubbed his chin.

"Too bad, that was a grand beard you had."

"It will grow back." Allin looked away and leaned his head against the wall.

"Right." The host left and Allin stared at the empty doorway. Something about the man didn't ring true. He was always starting personal conversations and Allin was careful to be non-committal in his responses. What worried Allin was who the man talked with.

The others came back and went through the purchases. Henry bought another worn backpack and they put everything they planned to keep in one or the other.

"We'll leave tomorrow." Rebecca said and sighed. "It will be good to be out of this place. The north is calling me."

"It will be good to be on the road again." Henry groaned. "I think I got soft this winter."

"It looks good on you." Magpie poked him and giggled. She's really coming out of her shell. This winter has been good for her.

They headed north from the hostel, and Allin enjoyed the sunshine, though the air was still chill. The passing people ignored them, intent on their own errands.

"Well, well." A familiar voice interrupted Allin's thoughts. "A little birdy told me you'd come this way. I never forget a pair of boots."

Allin looked around and saw the would-be thief standing in their way.

"Against the wall." He ordered and searched the crowd for other men.

"Guild business, folks." The thief drawled. "Hurry along and we won't bother you."

The busy street emptied except for five men holding clubs and the thief with a new knife.

"This is how it works." The man said. "You give us everything you are carrying, including that royal wool stuff my birdie talked about, and we'll let the three of you go peacefully on your way. You," he pointed at Allin, "owe me."

The men moved forward in casual teamwork, four of them aimed for Allin. The other one leered at Magpie. "It's a pity to let you go. You'd be worth something. Don't waste time now or you'll go to the market." The man with the knife spoke like he was telling them to hurry and order tea.

An icy rain fell and turned the men into shadows. Allin grabbed at the closest one, twisting the club from his hand and elbowing his temple. A club hit his shoulder and Allin snatched at it. *If it is swinging from there, then the man should be here.* He smashed the arm holding the club and blocked a blow from another. Blows and screams came from behind Allin, but he couldn't do anything but try to stay alive long enough to help them. It had been a long time since he trained with clubs, but his muscles remembered.

He clobbered the man shouting about his arm, and he went silent. A shadow came at him, then another from the left. He stepped into the man on the left swatting the club aside and walloped his collar bone. The crack sounded over the falling of the rain. *The other man should be... here.* His club connected with something hard and was followed by cursing.

The rain stopped as suddenly as it had started. Six men lay on the cobbles and a seventh stumbled away until a rock hit his head and dropped him to the ground.

"Everyone all right?" Allin asked.

"Used to hunt squirrels with rocks." Rebecca handed him an oilskin cloak. "Grandfather hated it, said I should use the bow."

"I am out of shape." Henry had a hand on his arm where it had been cut. Magpie used the knife lying beside her to cut a bandage from one other thieves' shirt, then bound up the wound. She shrugged on the cloak Rebecca handed her.

Rebecca already had a cloak on and passed one to Henry. "We need to get away from here. Good thing he warned us to be ready."

From the looks of the attackers, several, at least, wouldn't be waking up. The knife man's neck hung at a sickening angle.

They headed north at the fastest pace that wouldn't look suspicious. Evening had arrived by the time they made the north gate of the city. The guards checked Allin's travel chip and waved them through.

"Hope you have gills. The rains ain't done yet."

"Thanks for the warning." Magpie replied. The gates closed behind them.

"There looks to be a barn that way." Rebecca pointed and they hustled toward it, arriving just as the rain resumed. The derelict barn provided minimal shelter, but in the morning, they were off again north.

This road wasn't as well maintained as the one into the city, but they made good time. Coaches and people on horseback passed them, but none looked at them twice. After three days without trouble, Allin relaxed. It took another week to reach the village by the gate leading to the forest. By then, the rains had slowed to an occasional shower.

"We're heading north for a funeral." Allin said. "Here's our pass."

"Sorry, we aren't letting anyone out. You can wait in the village or go back to Dordnom. Orders of the Emperor."

Chapter 20

A group of soldiers in brown uniforms who flew a white banner stood beside the colourful troops. Hob's heart banged painfully. He pointed at them and asked Duncan, "Am I seeing right?"

"You are; those are my people."

"Put out the white banner." Hob ordered. "Let's see if they're truly ready to talk." He looked over the west gate at the approaching army. At Vilscape, he'd been the one to stare up at a high wall and wonder how they'd get past it. Now he worried he wouldn't be able to hold it.

"No Calderan would dishonour the white banner. I don't know why they would be here, but we can ask them."

"You and me, Pok and two others you choose. We'll be careful. I don't trust the Empire, though I would like to trust the brown uniforms."

"It is better to be cautious to no purpose than reckless and regret it later." Pok said.

They waited as the army approached, then someone in gleaming armour rode forward.

"Hello, the wall," the person yelled. "We're ready to parley. Shall we say the commanders and an honour guard of twenty?"

"Very well, no weapons present."

"Of course."

"In one hour, midway between the gate and your vanguard."

The hour passed quicker than Hob imagined. They put together the honour guard and had Pok, Tad, Duncan, and Hob as the commanders.

The gate opened.

"Keep the gate open but watch for treachery. If there is treachery, close the gate and wait for the hordes."

Hob and the others walked out to where the others already waited. Their commanders wore shiny armour, except for the browns. He could see that scabbards were empty; the meeting ground was out of reach of all but the most desperate bowshot. His gut began to unknot. Maybe they would honour the white banner even with the Free. Lord Huddroc had even before Hob knew what it meant.

"Welcome." The man from the horse said heartily. "I am Thadonix, General of the Guard of Ancanopolis. My companions, Major Fanyx, Major Sarigal, and Ser Haffmon, negotiator appointed by the palace. Oh, and Lady Robin from Fhayde."

Lady Robin stood with the browns. She had a giant of a man, along with a man wearing odd stripes on his uniform.

"I am Hob, this is Pok, Tad, and Duncan."

"Let us sit down and discuss what is before us. Thadonix gestured to a table.

What kind of people carried tables and chairs with their army? Hob sat with Duncan on one side and Pok on the other. Tad sat beside Pok.

Lady Robin sat across from him with the nobles on either side of her.

"The Free hold the city." Hob waved behind him. "We hold the entire plains. All the masters and their servants who wished to flee have. We will grow our food and trade it with you at Westburg."

"You are peasants," the man introduced as Ser Haffmon sneered. "We don't negotiate with peasants. We are the Empire."

"Now, Ser Haffmon, no need to be rude." Thadonix turned to the man.

"What's the use?" Haffmon said. "Kill them all."

The two majors flipped the table, pulling swords fastened to its underside, and jumped toward Hob and his friends.

"Stop! I will not allow treachery." Thadonix pulled one man back who turned and stabbed the General in the throat.

"Ham, Sargent." Lady Robin shouted and kicked the man closest to Hob in the back of the knee. Hob rolled out of the chair and faced the twenty soldiers who made up the honour guard. Somehow, they carried short swords. One slashed at Lady Robin. She parried with her armoured arm, wrenched the sword from him and slashed his throat. "Hob, get your people back to the gate."

He stood stunned for a second, before ordering his people to flee, leaving Lady Robin to dance between him and the traitors with her sword.

***

Robin's blood boiled as she cut down one treacherous bastard after the other, but she, Ham and Sargent Temajin were outnumbered almost five to one, and neither one wore armour. She'd clapped her helmet on as she jumped on the table to protect Hob.

"I'll take the majors; you get the rest." She handed her sword to Ham and broke a soldier's arm to take his sword to toss to Sargent Temajin. Smashed in a throat to take another as Major Fanyx bowled into her, trying to take her down. She spun away and clanged the sword into Major Sarigal's helmet. The woman staggered to the side and tangled with a soldier trying to get to Sargent Temajin.

Robin turned to deal with Major Fanyx. They exchanged enough blows to tell her he was a very competent swordsman and used to fighting in armour. She had to trust to Ham and Sargent Temajin to protect her back and didn't have time to waste with the major. He lunged at her, and she batted his sword to the side. Jumped toward him and kicked high, catching the man under his chin. Something snapped, and he fell to the ground.

Ham was fending off three men as Sargent Temajin traded blows with Major Sarigal. Robin formed a triangle with Ham and the Sargent.

"Move toward the gate." Robin twisted a sword from a soldier and used hers to cut his hand off. "I don't know who to trust among the Ancans."

They were going to lose the fight; it was only a matter of how many they took with them. Suddenly, a roar sounded behind them. The major broke off and ran, followed by the remaining soldiers. Hundreds of the Free surrounded them.

"We need to get you back to the city." Hob said. "They will attack any moment."

"They will have other things to worry about soon enough," Sargent Temajin gasped, holding his side. "There are about fifty thousand Free surrounding the Ancans and us. I don't expect they will be in a forgiving mood."

"Back to the gate." Robin ordered them. "MARSHAL TO ME!" The shout in Fhayden tore at her throat, but she could only hope the marshal heard and understood.

They retreated to the gate as the Ancan army moved forward to attack. A column dashed around their left flank and made a line between the Ancans and the Free retreating to the city gate.

She wanted to shout for them to defend themselves, but her throat wouldn't even let her whisper.

The Ancans clashed with the thousand, but there was nothing Robin could do but blink the tears away and watch the heroism of the Fhaydens.

Just as they reached the gate, a deafening roar sounded and Free poured in an endless wave to swallow the Ancans and the thousand.

As the gates closed them in, Robin looked for Ham and didn't see him. Then the bar banged into place and Robin dropped to her knees.

***

Hob hurried to Lady Robin's side; sure she was injured. She had to be after such a battle, but she had her face in her hands, weeping. He could understand a wound, but not the tears. He signalled for the knackers to aid a brown, who stood holding a bloody hand to his side.

"These are friends. They stood with us against treachery. Care for them as you would our own." Hob ran for the stairs to the wall. Duncan followed him and a part of Hob relaxed.

"Pok and Tad?" He asked, and Duncan shook his head.

They reached the top, and Hob gazed out at a scene from hell. Thousands of Free surrounded the suddenly panicked Ancan army.

"Send a message. They aren't to pursue on the road."

"Some of the treacherous bastards will escape."

"They will tell of the Free so numerous that we covered the land. The next general will think twice before attacking. I want scouts out along the border of the plains from south to north. There is no law that says an army must march on a road."

"Maybe some of the thousand, the browns, will escape too." Duncan didn't sound like he believed it.

"Perhaps, but they had enemies all around. We will sing of their courage and honour."

"That won't help the dead." Duncan kicked the wall.

"It will comfort the living."

"Maybe someday." Duncan waved over a wall guard. "Orders are not to pursue, and if possible, spare anyone in a brown uniform." The guard nodded and clattered down the stairs.

"Should have thought of that." Hob forced himself not to turn away from the battle. The Ancans had rallied and organized themselves into squares and retreated foot by foot. He couldn't see any brown uniforms. The fighting raged until mid-afternoon. Hob swallowed back nausea at the number of people dying out on the plain because a few Ancans wouldn't talk to the Free.

Downstairs the gates opened, and a line of wounded hobbled or were carried into the courtyard. The knackers went to work, among them Lady Robin, who tended to the worst injured.

"I gave orders to spare your soldiers wherever possible." Hob reported to her.

"Thank you." She straightened and met Hob's gaze. "I could not stand for treachery. I broke my peace for your sake. It is good to know it was the right decision."

Hob scanned the wounded. Most were the Free, but there were a few Ancans and even fewer browns. "Thank you for your help with the healing. The knackers do what they can, but there is only so much we know. The masters kept a lot of knowledge from us."

"I can pass on what I know later." She moved to the next patient. "You talk like you know the regulars."

"That is what you call the browns. I learned much from Lord Huddroc."

"You were at Vilscape?" Lady Robin didn't look up. "That explains a lot. I heard a member of the invading army brokered a peace. You know something about that?"

"Lord Huddroc was kind enough to give me credit for the peace, but his people were the ones to come to our aid."

She tied a bandage and moved to the next. "It must have been hell."

"Fewer than one in ten survived, but they live free in Vilscape. I can hear their singing in my heart."

"The battle at the border got hairy for an hour or two, but we worked out a peace." Robin shook her head.

"Yet you are here." Hob fetched more bandages. When he returned, Lady Robin was bowed over a woman in brown. Green light leaked between her fingers.

"She might make it. The cut reached her stomach. I've done what I can." She scanned the courtyard. "Looks like I've done what I can here. I'd like to check the battlefield."

"I will send some people with you." Hob talked to Duncan, who put a squad together and followed her out the gates. He met with the leaders of the horde.

160

"I don't think it is over. The masters don't see us as human. We will need to teach them the meaning of our freedom."

"Why should we teach? Just kill them as they come." Hvoc, Pok's second in command, said.

"If we want peace, we need to build peace. It isn't enough to become like the masters." Hob sighed. "I could have stayed happily in Vilscape, but freedom for only a few of our people wasn't enough. Now we are all free, but that means nothing if we can't live in peace with our neighbours. Not all of them are like the masters. Two of the commanders tried to stop the treachery. One of them died and the other spent the afternoon healing our people. "

"I will seek to understand." Hvoc saluted. "You said something earlier about patrolling the border."

"Yes, we will need to protect what we have gained. It is a strange thing to talk about war and peace in the same breath." Hob shrugged.

"Now that there is more travel between villages, the patrols shouldn't be a problem. It will be good training for the young." Another new leader, Gan, stood. "I can see we must work to become a people."

"That may be a harder task than freeing us from the masters."

***

Robin walked across the battlefield. Others stripped armour and weapons from the fallen, while some checked for wounded who needed to be taken to the courtyard. She looked for friends. There weren't as many in brown uniforms as she'd feared, and few she recognized by name. Ham wasn't there, nor were any of the commanders. It was as if they had strolled off the battlefield and vanished. It made her heart ache less, though now she worried what would become of the thousand. They'd defied the charge and bought a few precious seconds for her and the Free to escape.

She didn't know what to do next. Part of her wanted to stay and help the Free, but there was still the tug north and the desire to find her thousand. Another part wanted to return to Caldera and be normal. The biggest part wanted to find Sarge. Separation from him pained her even knowing he was unconscious and didn't know where she was.

"You are Calderan," she turned to Duncan. "You met Hob at Vilscape?"

"His first parley." Duncan stared to the south. "He wandered around at the base of the wall, like he didn't think anyone would attack him. I climbed down a rope and invited him for a meal. He had a pleasant chat with Lord Huddroc. Turns out that made such an impression on him, he surrendered to get help for his people. Never met anyone like him. Says exactly what he means, but he's no innocent. I think he still blames himself for the deaths at the end. It made this look like a party. There was a riot in the canyon and people ran away, straight into the wall, then on top of each other, trying to escape until they reached to the top of the wall. We'd left, but Hob came looking for us with a white cloth and surrendered so we could work together to save as many of his people as we could."

"Sounds like an extraordinary man. I can see why you follow him." As the sun lowered, the Free made camp and burned the dead. Robin sought a quiet place away from the smoke.

Sarge came to her in the dark.

"What have you accomplished?"

"I have kept the honour of the white banner. Treachery is never a solution." Robin replied.

"Pfah, the Ancans will come back with more soldiers. You think the peasants can hang around here? There are fields to be planted, assuming there is anything left to plant."

"Tell me one time that treachery won a clean victory?"

Sarge grunted but didn't reply.

"What do I do next?" Robin stood beside Sarge, but her hands floated through his. "What do you want from me?"

"If you don't know by now, then we're all doomed." Sarge faded into the black.

"That one is troubled." An old woman appeared. "They fear the healing that is necessary."

"Why would one fear healing?"

"If healing meant losing a leg or a heart, wouldn't you be afraid?"

"I can imagine losing a leg, I've seen too many with one leg. But I can't see losing a heart and living."

"When you can understand that, you will know what to do." The old woman nodded at Robin and vanished.

Robin opened her eyes to deep night with people holding torches around her

"They were worried." Duncan said. "You weren't responding."

"It's all right. I was talking with the land."

Duncan's eyes widened, and the people holding the torches stepped back.

"It is part of who I am. The land takes a long time to say anything" Robin sighed and stretched. "Right now, it knows what is needed, but it is afraid."

"What can the land be afraid of?"

"That's what I need to find out."

Chapter 21

Marshal Hapten limped to make the rounds of her people. More of them survived than she had any right to expect. They huddled in a makeshift camp in the sparse woods within sight of the city walls.

"Marshal," Commander Revont stood and saluted. "You should be resting."

"Resting will wait, Commander, report."

"The scouts are out to find stragglers, but casualties are at one hundred three. Of them, thirty-seven are walking wounded. There are still one hundred fifty who are missing. Lady Robin and Sargent Temajin were seen entering the city and few of our people were carried there."

"Very good, someone was watching out for us." Marshal Hapten shifted to find a position where her knee didn't ache.

"How did you know that ordering shields only would keep us out of the worst of the fighting?"

"I didn't, but it felt like the order Lady Robin would have given. Honestly, I didn't expect to survive."

"Neither did I, but I wasn't going to draw sword on my allies, and the horde seemed to ignore anyone with no sword or spear in their hand. Strange."

"Strange indeed, but very welcome" Marshal Hapten wandered through the makeshift camp. They only had the food they carried on them, but everyone shared. It made for a scant meal. Most of the conversations were about how lucky they were to be alive.

In the morning, the troops gathered.

"We are at a crossroads." Marshal Hapten said. "The Ancans have shown that some of them won't honour the white banner. I'm certain we are being vilified at this moment by those who would have committed murder under truce. Some of us saw Lady Robin jump to the defense of the truce, though greatly outnumbered. Her last order to me was to move to her banner. We followed that order and bought her time to be rescued by the city people."

"How do we know she isn't being held hostage? She was guarded by a squad of the city people day and night." Commander Themson stepped forward. He was gaunt from the winter watching the city, as were the rest of the people he had with him, but he didn't look weak.

"If she is a hostage, it is better than the death she would have eventually found with the Ancans. We know she is alive, for now that is enough."

Commander Themson saluted and stepped back.

"Now we need to decide what to do next. We are probably not welcome in this land, but we have companions who are waiting for our return. We have lost all our supplies and the men and women who worked for the quartermaster. All we can do is pray for their safety." Marshal Hapten held up her hand. "Any attempt at rescue would mean breaking the truce we have worked so hard to keep. Now we must decide what to do next."

"Do we retreat to Fhayde? It will be a long and difficult march with no guarantee the Ancans won't turn against us. Do we follow Lady Robin, and march up to knock on that gate?" Marshal Hapten couldn't repress the wince at the pain from her leg. "I give you one hour to think and decide for each for themselves what they will do. There is no shame in either choice. Dismissed."

Marshal Hapten limped to a log and sat with her leg up. She sighed and undid the straps holding the greave in place. Even through the padded trousers, she could see the swelling. It was just a bruise but blasted uncomfortable. *Is the pain making me weak? Should I have given the order to retreat? I want to be done with this, but I can't just abandon Lady Robin.*

Her thoughts swirled for the hour, then she loosely strapped the greave back on and walked to meet her people.

"My soldiers, let me tell you now that I burst with pride for every one of you. I will not give you an order, rather those who wish to go home, stand to my right, those who wish to stay, to my left." The marshal stood with a blank face as the men and women of the thousand stared at her, then one man walked to her right, then a stream of people, fewer moved to her left. Finally, they formed two groups. One man stood in the centre, Commander Themson.

"Commander." She couldn't give him an order. "Speak what is on your mind."

"I don't like either option. One man can do what many cannot. I would see how our people are being treated by the Ancans and warn Commander Paychen."

"Very well." Marshal Hapten sighed. "I would ask that you take a few volunteers with you. Commander Revont, please take command of those returning home. It is my decision. I'm ordering you and all those who stay with you to return home with all speed. Warn the duke's heir that this Haffmon is treacherous and dangerous. Warn Marques Povost and Baron Timost if you have the chance. March with shields at the ready and swords loose in your scabbards. If you are attacked, defend yourselves, but do not be the first to draw blood."

Commander Revont saluted and walked over to the right. "Commanders meet me in one hour. We march in two, make yourselves ready. Dismissed." She returned to Marshal Hapten's side. "Are you sure you want to stay?"

"Not at all." Marshal Hapten took her tunic off and handed it to Commander Revont. "We're about the same size. I'm promoting you to Marshal. I suggest you stay on the border between the forest and the plains."

"I will take care of your people until you get home." Marshal Revont saluted and left.

Commander Themson had five people with him. Marshal Hapten waved him over. "Take care. I don't give you any orders. Do what you must."

Commander nodded and waved his half-squad to follow him.

The marshal hobbled over to the last group.

"Let's form up, commanders behind me." The group of about two hundred fell into line.

"We brought the worst injured with us." Commander Betrice saluted.

"Good thinking." Marshal Hapten borrowed a spear and used it as a walking stick. "Let's go while I can still move."

The march wound through the light forest to the plain, where soldiers from the horde surrounding the city met them.

"What are you after?" A person Marshal Hapten assumed had some command authority came over to them.

"We are Lady Robin's troops." Marshal Hapten tried to straighten, but her blasted knee was on the verge of giving out.

"We will escort you to the gate." The man waved and a loose line formed around them. It took another two hours to reach the gate because Marshal Hapten couldn't walk any faster. But Lady Robin, surrounded by city soldiers, came out to meet them.

"Is this all that's left?" Her face paled.

"I've sent about five hundred home with Marshal Revont. There are some still missing."

"You sent them home?" Lady Robin frowned.

"Yes, it is no longer safe for any Fhayden. After the Ancan treachery and our defiance, I expect they will be safer heading home. I told them to stay on the border between plain and forest. What you see here are the wounded and dead, and those who refused to leave you behind."

"I'm not sure if I'm furious or relieved." Lady Robin's frown deepened. "It makes sense to send most of the thousand home, but why didn't you send the wounded with them?"

"They have a long march through territory they don't know, and which might be hostile. I thought they'd get better care here."

"In that case, we'd better get to work." Robin knelt and put her hands on Marshal Hapten's knee. "You've got some nasty bruising and dead blood. You might want to look away for this, and it is probably going to hurt." She stabbed her knife into the worst of the swelling. Black blood poured out and Marshal Hapten swallowed, but kept her eyes on her knee until the blood flowed red and Robin bandaged it. "You don't happen to have my kit on you?"

"Someone is carrying it, and your sword and knife." Marshal Hapten sighed as the ache subsided and the more urgent pain of the knife wound took over.

"Let's get you into the city. If it gets too much, hitch a ride on a stretcher."

"I'd rather—"

"That's an order Marshal." Robin's voice had no give in it.

"Yes, my Lady." Marshal Hapten sighed. Part of her wanted to lie down immediately, but there were worse off than her.

"Lady Robin, someone has run to get the knackers. We will help carry the stretchers to meet them."

"Thank you."

They marched, limped or were carried through the gate where pallets had been set up, or maybe they'd been there already. The knackers looked weary, but they helped with the wounded.

"Someone find who is carrying Lady Robin's kit and get it to her." Marshal Hapten sat down with her leg out straight in front of her. A knacker put rolled blankets under her knee and ankle. "Thank you."

She watched Lady Robin and the knackers at work. By the evening, they had moved the wounded inside a warehouse where there were other people being treated. Sargent Temajin was there, but she didn't see Ham. Those covered with a sheet were carried somewhere else.

"Sargent," Marshal Hapten limped over to sit by his side. "Did Ham make it out?"

"No, we were hoping he was with you. Lady Robin said he wasn't with the dead out on the plain."

"I hope he is safe somewhere."

"Perhaps Commander Themson will find him. He's taken a half-squad to see about freeing any Fhayden prisoners and warn Commander Paychen. He used to hunt the northern forest. If anyone can pull it off, it will be him."

"And when were you going to inform me?" Lady Robin stood behind them.

"I didn't want to talk in front of the city soldiers."

"They are the Free, and they are our allies. Is there anything else you've held back?" Her voice grew colder and Marshal Hapten would swear her eyes were glowing.

"Honestly, I don't think so, but with my knee, I might have missed something. Talk to Commander Betrice."

"Very well, Marshal. You are relieved of duty until I clear you. I want you focused on healing."

"Yes, my Lady." Marshal Hapten saluted. *Damn, I should have gone home with the rest. Right, and died on the way.* The argument carried on in her head as Lady Robin nodded sharply and walked away.

✳✳✳

Robin stalked away from the courtyard, angry at herself for treating Marshal Hapten so harshly. It wasn't the Marshal's fault Ham was still missing. She hated to think of what would happen to Sarge if Haffmon took the camp prisoner. That, too, wasn't Marshal Hapten's issue. She'd followed Robin's order the best she could and more of the thousand survived than Robin had expected.

But she missed the thousand. She felt diminished, which was stupid and only added to her bad mood. The connection to the land defined her importance, not how many soldiers she had at her beck and call. She dismissed the thought from her mind. She needed to find Hob and get help for the soldiers heading home. That was a long march without supplies. When she asked about Hob, the person led her through a maze of streets to a manor. The richness of the building contrasted starkly with the grey tenements that made up most of what she'd walked through.

Hob was in a meeting with his commanders, but he called her in. The room had an ornate table and chairs, tapestries hung on the wall.

"We were just discussing how many people we need to keep the city if the masters attack again."

"We had about two thousand at Vilscape, but we had the geography to help us. Here it is easy to circle the city outside of bow shot and wait. The question may not be how many people you need, but what supplies you can lay in to keep the people fed." Robin reminded herself of the map and discussions that felt they were from a different lifetime.

"We counted on hunger to weaken the defense," Duncan said, "but if we get hit by a large enough army, supplies will be an issue. Perhaps instead of how many we need, we should be thinking about what the minimum is that can hold the city for in case of a siege."

"You need guards at every possible exit to the outside, including watching the wall for ropes. Many sieges are decided by treason, at least that's what Sarge said. Preferably multiply the number of people on the wall and at the gates by three to keep from wearing out your people. Until there is an attack, you don't need as many people, and you can work on training. Plant gardens where there are flowers and grass. See if there is a safe supply of water. You can't count on the river. They could taint it or dam it up."

"Thank you, Lady Robin. That sounds much like Duncan's advice. He also suggested having straw men to make the enemy think there are more people than we have." Hob smiled wryly. "I have fought my share of straw men. We planned to set the gate on fire and burn out the straw men."

"You will want a response to fire in the city." Duncan said.

"Hob, I have a favour to ask," Robin took a breath. "Most of my people are marching south along the border. If you could send a guide, it will make their march faster."

Hob looked around the room. One commander spoke up. "We have people from that region in our horde to send. Water will be the main issue. Our people will know of the wells and springs. I will see to it now." He walked out without Hob's permission or a salute. Robin reminded herself that chains of command would look very different in the Free than what she was used to.

"My people who are healthy are available to train anyone who wants basic knowledge of spear, bow, sword. Maybe I'm presumptuous, but it will help to keep them busy and out of trouble."

"I will let them know." Hob glanced around the room but said nothing further. Robin was sure every commander would pass on the offer before sunset.

"What is the likelihood of an attack?" A commander asked.

"What do they get from taking the city?" Robin asked.

"It is the trading hub between the capital and the plains," Duncan said. "It was our position in the negotiations, before they were cut short."

"That's right." Robin could have kicked herself for forgetting. "I think it depends on how hungry the Ancans get. Their farms aren't doing well, and the harvest wasn't great. If you make food into too big a stick, they will put together a big enough army to take the city or at least destroy it. Sarge thought the entire war with Fhayde was about food."

"Who is this Sarge you talk about? I heard the name at Vilscape."

"He is a ancient warrior from another world. Sarge has already taught all of us a great deal. He is my Master Sargent, the person who lets me know when I'm making a mistake."

"That would be like Willow for me. I will send and see if she will come." Hob rubbed his eyes. "There is so much to learn, and I feel we don't have a lot of time."

"You already have a command structure, and it looks to be decentralized, so if a commander goes down, the entire horde isn't thrown into confusion. That's good. You look like you know some basic strategy and tactics. Passing that along is important."

"See, I didn't understand most of what you said. I look at what needs to be done, then think of how to do it." Hob shook his head.

"You understand the concepts, if not the words." Robin smiled. "Now I will excuse myself. I need to talk to my troops about what we will do the next few days."

"I thought you ran your army like the masters. The people at the top make the decisions and everyone else follows them."

"That is a weak chain of command. Better to have people who know what needs to be done and decide based on that. That's what you have. If you are attacked again, take out the people in the fancy armour." Robin saluted and went to find her people.

Chapter 22

"Going to the village is a better idea for now." Allin headed back down the road from the gate. "We don't want to return to the city and run into our friends."

They found a crowd of people at the inn either complaining about the prices or offering outrageous amounts for a room.

"Let's see if we can find a barn." Henry grimaced. "It will be quieter."

On the fourth try, they found a tiny run-down farm outside of town who were willing to let them stay in the barn in exchange for work. They were an elderly couple who, after getting past the initial suspicions, were welcoming.

Magpie mended clothes for the couple while Henry tackled cleaning the barn. Rebecca helped plant the vegetable garden which, aside from chickens, was the last remnant of a once prosperous farm. The neighbours heard about Magpie's work and began bringing clothes to be sewn. Some of them helped seed the small field and one arranged to pasture cattle on the larger field.

Allin spent his time listening to the reminiscences of the old couple. Their children had gone to the city years ago and aside from an occasional letter they couldn't read, heard nothing. When Allin told them he could read, they brought out a stack of letters for him to read, some dating back decades.

They worked their way through years of joy and struggle until it was the grandchildren writing and the letters were further apart. The rains had stopped altogether, and the sun shone brightly. Magpie and Rebecca went to the marker in the villages to sell eggs and buy a bit of meat.

When the sun was close to setting and they hadn't got back, Allin and Henry worried and headed out to the market. They found Rebecca beaten and unconscious in the ditch.

"Damn, we should have gone with them." Henry smacked his fist into his leg. He picked up Rebecca and carried her back to the farm. The old couple was frantic. A man in a cloak and a mask had dropped off a note for Allin, telling he'd be watching to be sure they passed the note on.

Allin glanced at the note. 'Come to the cemetery by high moon with your money, all of it, or the girl dies.'

Henry put Rebecca on the bed, and the woman went into the kitchen, then into the room holding Rebecca

"Etta's a witch, she'll put your friend to rights." The old man smiled proudly.

After an uncomfortably long time, Etta came out of the room holding a dish of water and placed it on the table. Her breath rippled the water for an instant and Etta peered intently into the dish. She didn't move, didn't even breathe.

"Dear Magpie is not injured, but she's surrounded by men. Don't believe them when they tell you they have her to exchange." Etta rubbed her neck. "Scrying takes so much out of me these days."

"Sit down a moment." The old man led Etta to the chair.

"They're going to kill you and take the money, then sell Magpie. They are furious with you."

"How many men?"

"Maybe a dozen?" Etta gave Henry a tiny bag on a string. "Follow your heart and you'll find her."

"There are axes in the barn which would make suitable weapons." Henry stood up and put the bag around his neck.

"Been a while since I swung an axe." Allin pushed himself to his feet and sighed. "We may not survive this."

"Don't care." Henry growled.

"Let's get those axes, but we need a plan."

"We'll plan on the way."

"What about the watcher?" Allin stepped into the dark barn and a cold blade connected with his throat. He put his left hand up to protect the big artery and spun to the right "Trap."

"Now you tell me." Henry said.

Allin continued his spin under the knife arm, forcing it straight, then slamming it with his elbow. The crack echoed in the barn. The man's scream was cut off by his own knife. Allin crouched with his back to the wall, expecting another attack. But all he heard was Henry grunt.

"Only the two of them, both dead. We'll clean them up later." Henry said. "I should have gone in first. I expect I see better in the dark."

"I'll remember that the next time I'm going to walk into a trap."

Henry chuckled, handing an axe to Allin. "You good to go?"

Allin cut the cloth from his shirt and bandaged his hand. "Am now, you?"

"Let's find Magpie." Henry led the way out into the less dark of the quarter moon. He had a bandage around his leg but carried two axes. "This way, I can feel her fear." They left the road and walked across fields and through a woodlot, with Henry moving unhesitating through every obstacle. Allin stumbled along after him. He'd worry about his hand later. It didn't feel like any tendons had been cut. He hoped.

In the village, they wound through back alleys until Henry stopped at a door. He nodded toward it and pointed up to where the moon shone down on them.

***

Magpie sat, gagged, tied hand and foot in the corner of the room. A single candle provided light. Other than securing her in the corner, they ignored her, four of them playing cards, muttering curses or whispering triumph. Something in the air made her nose run, so she struggled to breathe.

The leader came in. "Stay sharp. We're heading to the cemetery. We have crossbows this time; they won't get close, the guards better stay bribed, or I'll take them out too."

"Careful boss, the contract says we don't touch the guards."

"The emperor can shove his contract. He needs us as much as we need him."

"For now."

The leader just growled and stomped out of the room, leading six men to what must be the front. The leader and two others carried the crossbows.

Somehow, she knew Henry was coming. She reached out to him, but only felt him getting closer. Maybe it was an effect from the ruby putting its mark on her, or more likely, her imagination.

"I gotta take a piss." One of the men got up from the table and tossed his cards down. "Cards are garbage anyway."

"Don't take all night." They watched him head for the door. An arrow of panic made her heart race. She screamed into the gag, then couldn't get enough air in through her nose. She wet herself, hot with shame.

"Oh, for..." Another man slapped his cards on the table. "She's choking." He stomped toward her as the other man lifted the bar from the inside of the door.

The door burst open, sending the man staggering back into the table. Henry came through the door the door like an avenging god. He sent an axe flying to crash into the back of the man coming to check on her. Breathing was impossible, and no matter how she fought it, the darkness claimed her.

***

Henry had killed one man before he'd fully entered the room. Allin followed him, axe in his right hand, knife in the other. He split one man's skull while another stumbled for the door. Allin chased him, flipped the knife to his right hand, and threw it. It chunked into the fleeing man's back and he fell. Allin pulled the knife out and stabbed him again for good measure.

In the room, Henry was holding Magpie with tears streaking down his face.

"She's gone, she's not breathing."

"Try breathing into her." Allin put the bar back on the door. "Talk to her. She'll hear you."

Henry sealed her mouth with his and breathed out. He did it again and yet again. "Magpie, your emperor commands you to live!" He breathed again, and she finally coughed, rolled to her side, and puked all over Henry.

"Let's get her back to the house and lay a trap for the others." Allin looked the bloody scene. "The others will be back soon."

"Crossbows, three." Magpie rasped.

"Magpie first, then we come back and finish this." Henry said.

"You're the boss." Allin shrugged and picked up a sword that leaned in the corner. "Not bad for a thief's weapon."

Henry picked up Magpie, and they slipped out the door, ducking into an alley when a drunk man staggered past. Henry got them out of the village and back to the farmhouse. No one was around. They slipped in quietly. Allin half expected thieves to jump out from every corner of the room, but the old man snored in his chair. A candle burned in the other room.

The old woman sat in a chair. "They'll be here soon. Take your friend and go, stay off the road. Head west. There's a bow and quiver of arrows in the corner." She went to shake Rebecca. "Time to wake, dear."

Rebecca stirred and opened her eyes. "Magpie!"

"She's safe." Allin offered his hand. "We have to get moving. There are more coming."

"We should kill all of them." Henry said. "What about the old people?"

"Don't worry about me, son." The old woman drank the tea that sat beside her and grimaced. "We knew tonight was our last on the land." She put her head back and closed her eyes.

"Right now, escape is more important than vengeance." Allin grabbed the packs and the oilskin cloaks. "If they come after us, we can hunt them in the forest." The old man had stopped snoring as Allin led the way out the door. Henry followed, still carrying Magpie, then Rebecca walking almost normally.

All night they walked west, away from the village, stopping only when the moon went down. They found a tiny clearing beside a creek. Allin and Rebecca sat with their backs to the creek as Magpie washed herself and her clothes, then put on spares from the pack, sewn together in between mending for other people.

***

Alekar pushed the door open and walked into the house. He tripped over a body, then smelled the blood. "Curse them, curse them to hell."

"Emperor," the man on the floor whispered, "we've attacked the emperor."

"How do you know?" Alekar grabbed.

"Th, they said. Been waiting to tell you." He choked and breathed out, but didn't take a breath in.

"What's up, boss?" Alekar's second stuck his head in the door.

"Grab your stuff. We're heading south to Dordnom. I need to have a chat with the emperor."

"What about that's more important than running down those four?"

"We'll stop at the farm on the way, find out what the old couple know."

"Jack and Sam were supposed to off them and burn the house."

Alekar pointed east. "Do you see the light of flames? They're dead, along with this useless crew. We'll need more resources to catch them."

"You sound like it will take an army."

"Fortunately, I know how to get an army." Alekar grinned. "We leave in five minutes. Anyone not ready, I'll leave them behind."

***

Allin stumbled over a branch and swore under his breath. His hand hurt like blazes, even after Magpie had stitched it up for him. They'd been walking along field lines and woodlots for two days.

"There's a farm." Henry pointed. "I'll check it out."

Allin wanted to go with him, but he could barely walk, never mind fight. Henry came back and waved them forward.

"We're good. We can sleep in the barn, and she'll feed us tonight." Henry shook his head. "She's got two daughters who look like they'd make decent warriors. They watched me like a hawk the whole time. Her husband will be home from the fields soon. We can relax in the barn until then."

They set up in a remote corner of the barn. Allin tried to relax, but his hand itched and burned the whole time. The others chatted about things he couldn't follow.

Henry had to pull him upright and Allin still almost fell again.

"You all right?" Henry asked. "You haven't been yourself all day."

"My hand is bothering me more than I expected." Allin straightened himself and took a deep breath. He couldn't afford to fall apart now.

"We'll have a look at it inside where the light will be better."

In the farmhouse, they pulled the bandage off to discover the cut had swollen over the stitches. The angry red of the wound made his hand look pale.

"It's festered," the woman said. "Girls, I need some boiling water and your dad's brandy. Bring my sharp knife"

"It's okay." Allin's heart sank as he spoke.

"You'll be dead within a week if we don't do something." She pointed to Henry. "You hold his hand in place. Don't let him move. If he passes out in the chair, worry about keeping the arm still."

Magpie and Rebecca moved around behind Allin, and one of them put a hand on his shoulder.

"Soldier I knew had a similar wound. Claimed a fae healed him by sniffing at his arm and cutting it open."

Henry tightened his grip on Allin's arm. "Maybe a rolled cloth, so he doesn't break his teeth?" He inserted a roll of leather which tasted ghastly and Allin bit down.

Cutting the stitches made him clamp hard on the leather and fight the need to scream. A nauseating smell almost made him vomit. He breathed past the leather in his teeth. A momentary relief came when the pressure lessened, but the knife kept cutting and he passed out.

***

Allin woke and immediately tried to lift his hand to look at it. All he could tell was it had been wrapped in clean white cloth. It still throbbed in agony.

Next time he woke, Rebecca was sitting at his side.

"You're awake." She put her hand on his forehead. "No fever, that's good. You had us worried for a bit."

"Hand?" He mouthed tasted horrible, but an herbal horrible.

"You still have it." Rebecca frowned and lowered her voice. "Whether or not it works, we won't know until it heals up some. Good thing Marta had plenty of mending to do. Magpie been busy teaching the girls to sew. Henry's out in the field with Jack. You'd think he'd grown up with physical labour."

"Strong."

"He is. I'd never thought about it before." Rebecca stood up. "I'll let the others know you're awake. There's herbal tea, tastes foul, but it helps. Try to drink some."

He stretched out his right hand and picked up a pottery cup. Rebecca was right. It tasted foul, but he'd never trusted medicine with a good taste.

The next day, he was able to walk to the front room and eat some bread and broth. He kept his eyes away from the bandage. Couldn't change things by worrying about it. Magpie and the girls giggled in a corner when Henry came in, freshly washed under the pump. He looked strong.

"Good, you're up." Henry put his shirt on and sat down across the table from him. "Should have taken a minute to have the witch look at your hand. Sorry."

"Not your fault." Allin finished his broth and chewed on the crust of bread. "Feeling better now. How long did I sleep?"

"Three days. Rebecca and Marta took turns watching you."

"So, if people are chasing us, they'll be well ahead."

"Haven't heard a peep. Jack says there are no strangers about. We told Jack and Marta what we thought safe about the situation. Looks like the people trying to collect on your father's debt have given up for now."

"That's good news. Wouldn't want to put our hosts at risk."

"Now that you're up and eating, shouldn't be long before you can return to your travels." Marta put more bread and broth in front of him. "We keep to ourselves here, but if any strangers show up, we'll know. Since the war, strangers have been bad news."

"Too many soldiers unable to go home." Allin sighed and dunked the bread into his bowl. "And too many homes with no soldiers coming home."

"You sound like you know about it."

"Read too many histories when I was young."

"You read?" Marta's eyebrows rose.

"I had strict parents. They had high expectations of me."

"Right."

He finished the broth while Marta puttered away in the kitchen. Rebecca helped, looking like she was born in a kitchen.

In two more days, Allin felt strong enough to continue their journey. Marta insisted on changing the bandage. He'd been trying not to think about what it would look like. The palm of his hand was a healthy pink, with a scar zigzagging across it. His first thought was about an old woman who used to read palms. What would she make of this? The second was to move his fingers. He could make his fingers wiggle a little.

"Move your fingers, clench your hand, you lost flesh, but I don't think the tendons were affected." Marta took his hand and closed his fingers. The hand ached, but there was no sharp pain.

"I will do so."

He flexed his hand as they walked across the land. With pursuit apparently stopped, they risked the road. Allin kept the thief's sword hidden under the cloak and in the evening ran through a few patterns in their camp where no one would be likely to see.

The left hand grew stronger, but not to the point Allin could hold anything in it.

A week or so after they left Jack and Marta's, Allin saw the city of Nordfin. High stone walls enclosed it. It had an ominous look, rising out of the farmland so abruptly. Past it lay the open plains.

Chapter 23

Hob watched Lady Robin's soldiers train the Free in a large yard near the west gate. The difference between learning in the midst of battle and having specific attacks and blocks for spear and sword could mean a major drop in their casualty rate. Currently, the Free's only choice was to overwhelm the enemy with numbers. But the previous battle showed how much discipline and tactics mattered.

As much as it tired him out, training on top of all the other work he did, he looked forward to it. The commanders were all learning as well, not just the fighting techniques, but some of the wisdom from Sarge. Lady Robin talked about him in a mixed way, sometimes as if he were already dead, and other times as if he were watching their discussion. The commanders then passed on the training to their hordes, group by group. With almost two hundred Fhayde soldiers, the training spread rapidly.

Those discussions solidified his intent to have the plains for the Free, but not expand past that. There were too many soldiers and generals who knew more about battles and killing than he did. He hoped that if they didn't cross the border, the others would eventually leave the Free alone.

Something he hadn't thought about was sending a delegation to Vilscape to update Lord Huddroc on what had happened and extend trade talks. Lady Robin wanted to send some of her people with them so they could ride to the capital and report to her king. He still found it strange to think of people like masters who cared about their people.

He found Lady Robin on the wall, staring north.

"Lady Robin," Hob said, "you look thoughtful."

"I told you to call me Robin. We are equals."

"I will try to remember." Hob leaned on the wall beside her. "What do you see to the north?"

"Someone, something is calling me, but it is dangerous to travel through Anca now, especially for the Fhayde."

"Because you aided me to survive."

"Partly, but also this Haffmon will weasel his way back into power. He corrupted two of the three commanders and enough soldiers to break the truce. He is a dangerous man, and I don't think you've seen the last of him. The major can't turn on him without revealing his part in the treachery. So he will be Haffmon's military mind. He was canny enough to get most of the Ancans out of what could easily have been a massacre."

"And because we were once peasants, they won't want to talk to us."

"Not Haffmon or his major, but others might. The general was truly ready to talk."

"So we need an enormous army to keep their army at bay."

"How quickly could you pull together your horde?"

"It would take two weeks of hard marching for the furthest villages to send their people. You're thinking we'd need to hold the city against experienced troops for the two weeks until the horde shows up."

"I think so. You could keep a reserve here. There is lots of work to be done in the forests and farms to keep the soldiers from getting bored and into trouble." The wind blew from the north, ruffling her short hair. She didn't appear to notice.

"We've already had some problems between people who still think of themselves as overseers or peasants."

"Talk to Marshal Hapten, she's the legal expert of the thousand. It would give her something to do until she recovers enough to take over command again."

"Are you still angry at her?"

"Don't think so, I may have made the same decision in her place. I think it is a matter of my attitude toward the thousand. I thought of them as mine, which is ridiculous, perhaps it would be better to think of me being theirs. I don't know." Lady Robin banged her fist on the wall.

"Confusion is painful." Hob turned to look at her. "But being not confused is difficult." He shrugged and looked north again. "I was never supposed to lead the Ancan army, it just happened."

By the time he'd finished telling the story of the army's campaign, the sun had all but set.

"I don't feel so bad." Lady Robin chuckled. "Let me tell you how I ended up commanding the thousand."

The quarter moon had risen by the time she finished.

"I think you should talk to our elders." Hob said when she'd finished. "I will see if I can set it up. The old stories talk about listening to the land."

"The land did say I wasn't the only one."

"All the more reason. I will talk to them and let you know."

"Thanks, Hob. I'd better go talk to Marshal Hapten before it gets too late." She saluted him as he was becoming used to and left.

Hob stayed on the wall, thinking. Perhaps there is something behind all this, the elders would know.

***

Robin found Marshal Hapten walking with crutches through the large room the Free had set up as a hospital, visiting the wounded Fhayden soldiers.

"Don't worry, I got the knacker's permission to walk."

Robin held up her hand. "That's not what I'm here about. I'm glad to see you recovering."

"Are you?" The marshal frowned at her.

"I took out my anger at myself on you." Robin said. "It just got overwhelming. I never really had any idea what I was doing. Less after Sarge got sick. What am here to do and why I have the thousand with me are two different questions. Hob told me confusion is painful. I'm sorry you paid the price."

"I keep forgetting how young you are." Marshal Hapten moved a bench. "Have a seat. Recent events pushed all this on you. I think we just took for granted that the land would fill in the blanks."

"Sending half the thousand home reminded me how little I know, about command, about the land. I'm supposed to figure out what the land is afraid of, but I can't separate its fears from mine."

"You're in a hard position, and speaking as the Marshal, you've been doing a good job of determining strategy. I still wonder if I really should be commanding, and I'm just about old enough to be your grandmother."

"Do you have a family?"

"A son and two daughters, all married with their own kids and their own worries. My husband died years ago. That's when I went full time with the Regulars. Most of what I did was paperwork. This whole situation is as new to me as it is to you."

"I'm not sure if that makes me feel better or worse." Robin laughed and got up to pace. "The thing to do now is determine our next strategic goal. I need to speak to the Free elders and learn what they have to say. I don't know if that will mean travelling out of the city. It is the first I've heard of them."

"If you have to travel, be sure to take someone with you for security." Marshal Hapten leaned back.

"Sargent Temajin won't be in shape to travel for a while and Ham is missing. If you have a suggestion of someone, I'd appreciate it."

"I will give it some thought." Marshal Hapten stared up at the rafters. "If you are planning on reinstating my command, I'd like a day or so to prepare myself. This break has allowed me to rediscover Emily Hapten. This is the first time in years I've not had to be considering the thousand every waking moment. I should thank you for the break. It has been so long, I began to act like Marshal is my name, not my rank."

"You shouldn't wait until your commander gets grumpy to take time for yourself."

"In the middle of a campaign is hardly the time for introspection." Emily snorted.

"We have paused while we wait for our people to heal, and things are quiet. Introspection is necessary to know what we are doing next. This campaign is as much about who we are as who we are helping, or fighting."

"And that is why you are my commander." Emily shook her head. "I would never have thought that."

"Okay, you have two days to prepare, Emily, before you become Marshal Hapten again." Robin waved and headed off to bed.

***

Robin visited the wounded and watched the training, even taking on a sparring match with Commander Betrice. A crowd gathered as Robin and the Commander circled and ran through the basic moves on to more complex moves, to finally fighting so quickly, Robin had a hard time keeping up even with her ability to read the rhythms.

It ended with them stepping back and saluting each other.

"It's been a while since someone fought me to a draw." Commander Betrice saluted. "It was a grand match."

"Thank you, it is good to be reminded there are people out there as fast or faster than I am. I need to spar with people who can beat me, so I don't get overconfident." Robin grinned at her.

"I can suggest a few, but there aren't many who could keep up with your sword work." Commander Betrice said.

"Maybe I should review some other weapons. I haven't shot a bow in ages, nor sparred with spear and shield."

"If you want to be truly challenged, try grappling."

"Grappling." Robin laughed and stretched her joints. "You want to see me hanging from one foot from some behemoth?"

"As amusing as that would be, practice with all kinds of partners, including the behemoths."

"If you will set me up with people to practice with, I'd appreciate it."

For the next few days, Robin practiced with the bow, rediscovering why she loved archery. She grappled with people who were only normally bigger than her up to Rick, the biggest man left in the thousand. He didn't hang her from one foot, but she couldn't budge him, and as soon as she tried, he had her pinned.

"Y're working too hard on being fast and strong." Rick told her. "Wrestling is as much a mind game as swordplay. Work through things in yer head, then try them. Someone as small as you needs to think about leverage more than strength." He showed her a few throws and Robin remembered how she'd grappled Hal what felt like years ago.

Rick worked her mercilessly for the next week until one evening on the wall, Hob announced that he'd received an invitation for her to meet the elders.

"It will take a week's travel there and back, but they are eager to talk to you." He stood with his back to the wall and stared south. "It is my home village. There are people I need to talk to there, so I will accompany you. We will take a half-squad."

"I would like a couple of my people to be included in that group." Robin had grown used to his presence as she stared north and tried to figure out what to do.

"That will be no problem."

They started out the next morning. Rick was one of her 'guards'. The other was a woman named Lace, who seemed to think her job was to remind Robin of her position and the need for dignity. She particularly didn't like the daily grappling matches with Rick and the Free.

"It doesn't become you as a commander to be forced to grovel in the dust." Lace frowned.

"I'm not being forced; I'm losing a wrestling match. It is no worse than losing a match with swords."

Lace pursed her lips, unconvinced. Robin gave up trying to change the woman's thinking.

The few days of travel reminded her of her time as a trainee when most of the group could defeat her in everything but archery. The matches were lasting longer. She didn't expect she'd ever beat Rick, but she won against the Free one out of three times.

The village wasn't what she expected. The wall around the village looked like it would make one feel trapped, but the gate was wide and open.

"They've made the gate bigger." Hob said as a woman walked over to him.

"So, you're back." She didn't sound happy about it.

"I am here to see the elders," Hob replied, "and to talk to you. I have a position I'd like you to consider."

"All about work, as usual."

"Willow, I can see you're angry with me, but you knew when we started out what I am like. We can talk about it more at length in more private circumstances."

"Fine then." Willow turned and walked away.

"Let us prepare to visit the elders." Hob led them up to the manor and its baths. "Wash the dust from your bodies and relax. There are rooms in the barracks for you to stay."

The bath reminded Robin of bathing as a trainee with Jalliet and Tamlyn, but Lace didn't relax or talk, as if she couldn't imagine Robin as anything but the commander of the thousand and shieldmaiden.

After they'd bathed, they met in a room in the manor to eat. The good, plain food was a sharp contrast with the luxury of the space.

"Come," Hob stood after they'd finished their meal. "I will introduce you to the elders." He walked with Robin through the gate into the village, then down a ladder into a pit where a stone had been removed from the wall. "The elders are most comfortable in the room they have lived in for many years. We kept their existence a secret from the masters."

She followed him down the stairs into a chamber lit by a lamp. The elders sat in chairs facing her. She had the feeling they lived in those chairs, but they didn't look unhappy.

"Welcome, shieldmaiden." The woman nodded gracefully at Robin. The man just lifted a hand in greeting. They were the oldest people she'd seen aside from Sarge.

"You look familiar." Robin sat on the floor in front of them. "I saw you when I was talking to the land."

"Which land?" The woman smiled slightly. "There are many lands as there are many peoples."

"It was on the border between Anca and the plains." Robin closed her eyes. "I was arguing with the land, then an old woman appeared and challenged me to imagine fighting on after losing my heart."

"The plains are wise. We Free were here when it was a verdant plain and seeds grew when scattered carelessly on the grown. There were herds then that roved the plain. The masters came and forced the plains to submit to them. The herds vanished over generations. Dust overran the green of the land."

"Is it possible to restore the plains?"

"A good question, and we do not yet know the answer. We will not until we have striven body and soul to restore them. We are not here to rule over the land, but to live on it as the grass and the herds once did."

"I can see how the land of the Ancans is confused and broken."

"Each land is itself." The old man frowned. "Our only interest in that land is to be sure we are never subjugated again."

"A people who live by subjugating each other will struggle to consider the land as an entity to itself."

"An entity of which we are part of. We are no more separate from the land than your hand is from your body."

"Or my heart." Robin mused out loud. "I still can't understand how a person, or a land, could continue after losing their heart."

"You're young yet." The old woman said. "You will learn."

"Will I learn in time?" Robin whispered.

"In time for what?" The old man's words rasped on her.

"In time to do whatever I'm here to do?"

The man laughed, but it felt kinder than his words. "You will do what you do, and it will be when it will be. The question of will it be enough is foolish."

"So it doesn't matter what I do?" Robin furrowed her brow. "Then why am I here?"

"What you do matters, what you choose matters." The old woman shook her head slowly. "Everything matters, when, where, especially why."

"Intention is everything." Robin put a hand on the amulet.

"See, you are already wise." The man teased her.

"Hardly." Robin smiled wryly. "I may know intention is important, but I rarely know what I'm doing."

"What you do and why you do are separate questions." The old woman looked over at Hob. "Isn't that right, Hob?"

"They are the same question." Hob frowned. "I do what I do because it needs to be done."

"Why does it need to be done?" Robin asked. "Is it because it is the only thing I can think of, or the least painful option, or what is going to keep me alive?"

"And thus you are on the path to knowing what it is you know." The old man gestured her forward. He put a hand on her head like Sarge used to do, and Robin had to fight back tears. "You have decided what you must do."

"I need to talk to Sarge."

***

Hob met Willow outside the gate of the village.

"I see you have found a new master to follow." Her mouth twisted.

"I have no master, nor do you. We are Free." Hob frowned. "The elders wanted to talk to Robin. From the sounds of it, she is important to the future, not just of the Free, but of the Ancans too. I don't envy her."

"I do; she has more of your time than I do." Willow crossed her arms and paced about. "I thought I would be happy just to be by your side, but here I am, angry and hollow."

"That's a hard place to be." Hob sighed. "But I can't fill you, only you can find the purpose which gives you life."

"What am I supposed to do?" Willow stomped her foot. "I don't want to hate you, but I can't be near you, and I can't stand to be away from you."

"You don't need me." Hob caught her hand and held it. "You need to find yourself, who you want to be. What do you need to do? Do that."

"I want to make a difference to the Free." Willow pulled her hand free. "But I don't know what I have to do."

"What needs to be done?" Hob asked her. "Something that is in front of you."

"I don't know." Willow put her hands over her face. "I'm not special like you. I just follow you around pining for your attention."

"You aren't special like me." He nodded and stared up at the stars coming out. "You are special like you."

"Give me a job to do. Something to help me find myself."

"I did have something I'd like you to do." Hob said. "It is up to you if you take it on."

"What is it?"

"Lady Robin has someone she calls a sergeant."

"What's that?"

"I'm not exactly sure. He seems to be someone she trusts to tell he when she's making a mistake. She talks out things with him."

"And you want me to be this sergeant for you?" Willow's brow furrowed.

"I trust you to speak your mind." Hob smiled wryly. "I'm sure we'll figure it out together."

"I will try to live up to your trust." Willow took his hand and squeezed. "Thank you for taking a chance on me."

Chapter 24

Commander Bodan Themson peered through the grass. The Ancan army moved at a snail's pace. He didn't like that Haffmon had gone on ahead with Major Sarigal and a hundred soldiers. Now they stopped and set up a semi-permanent camp.

He'd wanted to infiltrate the camp, but the Ancan's boredom made them put on extra security and kept the officers riding the troops to stay alert. For now, he'd watch and wait. He sent Maci at top speed to Ancanopolis on a horse they'd found wandering loose. Maybe she'd get there before Haffmon, but he didn't count on it.

The others camped a suitable distance from the army. The army didn't appear to have any scouts doing wide sweeps, so they were safe enough for now. In the centre of the army, the captured Fhayden soldiers had marched, unarmed and tied together with ropes, five columns with ten to a column. Behind them, Ham drove a wagon. Bodan wondered if it was holding wounded from the battle. They guarded it with the same boredom driven intensity. It wouldn't be long before some officer decided on wide sweeps to keep more soldiers at busy work.

Bodan calculated they could free the prisoners if they were lucky, but it would send the army after them like hounds on a rabbit. The five of them could play tag with the army, but not with fifty plus injured in a wagon. As much as he hated it, his people were better off as prisoners for the moment. Maybe if the Ancans moved closer to the city, the Fhaydens might make a dash for the camp and try to get behind the walls.

Those walls wouldn't stand against a genuine effort to push past them, so it might only make things worse. Maybe Maci would return soon and report on what was going on in Ancanopolis.

He waited until the dust settled from the last of the scouts before he moved away into the forest, staying alert for enemy soldiers. It wasn't the white banner that kept them from eliminating too-inquisitive soldiers, but the practical fact that missing scouts from a peaceful camp would quickly raise suspicions.

He reached his squad and reported.

"Might be better hopping it to the city ahead of them, find out what's going on there." Nascup said. "Wouldn't be the first time we infiltrated an Ancan city."

"True enough, but we'd need to get civilian clothes and work in pairs." Bodan rubbed his chin. "It's better than dawdling along with the army. If we get information that warrants it, we can always come back and break the prisoners out. Fandin and Sherr, you stay keep an eye on the Ancans. Don't get caught. Something happens. I'll leave it up to you to decide what to do."

They picked up their gear, made sure there was no sign of their presence, then loped past the army, swinging wide enough to stay unseen. The three of them soon outpaced the army enough that even the dust they created couldn't be seen. Late the next day, they arrived at the outskirts of Ancanopolis and headed for the walled camp. By now they'd acquired clothes which wouldn't give them away. There was sufficient diversity in the Ancan Empire that the Fhaydens didn't look out of place, dressed like everyone else.

Members of the city guard surrounded the camp. A dialogue took place by shouting at the gate and someone on a ladder sticking their head over to shout back.

"Look," a guard said. "We need to come in to secure the area, by the orders of the palace."

"You say you have orders from the palace, but we can't just take your word for it. Nobody from the palace has come to explain why you need to secure our camp. I assure you it is very secure."

"I have orders!" the guard shouted.

"But not in writing. Bring us back orders in writing, and we'll look at them and consider the situation carefully." Came the answer from the wall.

"We could simply come in by force. Your wall won't keep us out."

"True, true, but then you'd be in violation of that white banner flying there over the gate. A truce and contract signed by the bureaucrats at the palace. Get one of those people and we'll talk to them."

"We don't want to break into the compound, but you have one more day before we are forced to." Bodan stood in the crowd watching the show. He wasn't the only one snickering at the exchange.

"That's what you said yesterday." The voice floated back.

"Do you *want* us to break in?"

"No, but we should be clear. If you say one day, then we expect one day. Do you know how tiring it is to get all the soldiers geared up and ready to greet you, only for you to tell us we have to wait until tomorrow, again. That's tough on morale, it is."

"I need to speak to your senior officer." The guard shouted through clenched teeth.

"Not here," the man at the gate answered. "She went off with a bunch of your lot and we haven't had a word in days. We're soldiers following orders just like you, so come back with someone from the palace, or break in, or bugger off. Your racket is disturbing us."

"Disturbing you; what do you mean, what are you doing in there?"

"What do you think we're doing?"

For a moment Bodan thought the guards were going to charge the gate, but the shouter sputtered into silence, then yelled at the guard to be sure no one went in or out.

"They b'n at that for days now," a man behind Bodan said. "None of them haven't seen them Fhaydens skirmishing. They ain't eager to charge in and face that."

"Show's over for the day, I guess. How about we have a beer and prepare for tomorrow's negotiations?" Bodan turned to look at the man, who winked at him and led him away to an inn.

The place was so noisy with a bard singing badly in the front and people yelling to be heard over him that Bodan figured conversation was impossible, but then he wasn't here to talk.

His new friend ordered a pitcher of beer, and Bodan tossed a few coins on the table. The man picked through them and pushed one back.

"Don't need this." He swept the other coins up and put them in his pouch. The remaining coin was a Fhayden copper.

Bodan picked it up. "You're in with Betrice's aren't you?"

"Yup, sure am, boss." The man's voice was just audible over the racket. The pitcher of beer arrived, and they set to emptying it. Another one followed, and Bodan enjoyed the buzz.

"Happens, I need a place to stay." Bodan put his mug down.

"You can sleep on the floor where I'm at. A copper a night."

"Sounds good." The floor moved under Bodan when he stood, but it settled quickly, and he followed his drinking partner out of the bar and along the street.

They cut through an alley, and then another, through a tiny courtyard and up to a door which let them in as if someone was watching for them.

"Welcome, Commander Themson. I'm Tradkin." The man holding the door saluted. He stood tall and straight with an immaculate bearing.

"You'll want to let Sylve in, Tradkin." Bodan returned the salute. A quiet knock sounded at the door.

"Welcome, I guess." Tradkin scowled at her, and she smiled back.

"Spent many a year working special details, don't feel bad." Sylve stepped past them. "Nascup is holed up waiting for orders. Conversations on the street are split between people supporting Haffmon and people wanting to hang him."

"A lot of people don't like Haffmon," Bodan's drinking partner said. "But just as many people like money, and he's throwing around a lot of it. The farce outside the camp is because he has the guard under his thumb, but the palace won't give him the time of day. You may as well come in and sit down. It isn't fancy, but it's safe."

The room had a wobbly table and mismatched chairs that looked like they'd fall apart if sat on. A candle on the table lit the room. "I'll get some bread and cheese," Tradkin left the room.

"I'm Camron," the drinking partner said. "Commander Paychen has most of our people out in the city in tenements or safe houses. Seems he got a heads up about the guard trying to take over the camp from one of our agents. There's a skeleton crew running the show. The old man and the boys are still there too, hard to sneak out a bed."

"We may have to do something about that. Lady Robin will not be pleased if Sarge and the lads end up in enemy hands."

"I hear you." Camron plunked down on one of the rickety chairs. It creaked in protest, but didn't fall apart. Sylve sat on a chair held together with string. Bodan cautiously took a seat. "Maybe the palace can do something. They've been staying out of the politics and concentrating on running the city. If it weren't for the fire and all, you might never know the emperor is missing. Rumours are split between him being killed by one of the wives, generals or so on, or he's run away and is in hiding, building up an army to come and retake the city."

"He could walk in alone and the city would be his until someone else tries to kill him." Tradkin put a plate on the table. "Help yourself. I think Haffmon is trying to replace the emperor, or at least become his stand in. Nothing can happen with the succession without the imperial ruby, and it hasn't turned up."

"Likely the emperor took it with him." Bodan yawned. "Sorry, drink always makes me tired. Anyway, we know that Duke Allin, the emperor, and two women escaped and headed north. It isn't general knowledge, so keep it under your hats."

"General Ordamy is a hardliner. He took his legion and headed north to secure his north border. I don't know what he'd do if the emperor strolled into his province." Sylve helped herself to bread and cheese. "He's ambitious, so he might welcome the emperor and reinstall him as a puppet, or make him disappear completely and show up carrying the ruby. I was an agent here a few years back. I doubt he's changed much."

"So he wouldn't be pleased if Haffmon takes over the capital." Tradkin bit into a crust of bread.

"Not likely, but it might give him the excuse he needs to come down and take the city himself and become regent. Wouldn't be the first regent to become emperor." Sylve brushed crumbs off her clothes. "If there's a handy open spot on the floor, I could use some sleep."

Tradkin led her into another room.

"I forgot to ask, did Maci make it here?" Bodan yawned again.

"Just beat Haffmon here, had them shut up the camp tight. We'd been training at the arena until then," Camron replied.

"I'll need to get in to report to Commander Paychen. Tomorrow will be soon enough." Bodan looked around. Is there a room, or should I sleep under the table?"

Camron laughed and showed him to a room.

***

Sarge lay on his bed and listened to the boys talk. He couldn't move a muscle, but he could swallow and breath. Most of the time, he floated in a realm filled with ghosts of his past, but they held no fear for him. He and his ghosts had made peace a long time back.

"They still shouting outside the gate?" Rud asked.

"One more day when they give us one more day." Lencely snorted. "They should just give up and go back to doing their job. I walked the wall earlier, and the guard is still lined up all around us."

"You aren't supposed to be on the wall."

"How else am I supposed to know what is going on? No one will talk to us." A spoon clattered in a bowl. Must be feeding time.

"True." One boy lifted him while the other spooned soup carefully into Sarge's mouth. They had surprised him with the dedication of their care. They'd never voiced a complaint, even at the most undignified parts of caring for him.

For Sarge, this was just the next stage of the dissolution of his body. One day, his ghosts would take him away and that would be it. That would be a poor return for their efforts, but he'd given up on ever being able to move on his own again. Even if he miraculously 'woke', his muscles wouldn't have the strength to move.

He floated away to his ghosts.

They showed him Robin leading the thousand. He didn't care if it was real or his imagination; it allowed him to see Robin.

"I need to talk to Sarge." Robin knelt in front of an old man in what looked like a cave. The words set his heart racing in panic, though there was nothing he wanted more than to talk with Robin again and set things right between them.

"No." Sarge tried to shake his head, but his body wouldn't move. He didn't know why, but Robin coming to see him was a bad idea. "No, no, no."

"Did Sarge just say something?" Rud's voice grew louder as he leaned over Sarge.

"I wish." Lencely also approached.

Sarge tried his utmost, but couldn't make a sound.

Chapter 25

Robin stared up at the sky.

"Not paying attention when you're sparring is going to get you hurt." Rick reached down his huge hand and hoisted her to her feet.

"You're right." Robin rubbed her shoulder. "I have to think, and I'm avoiding it."

"You already know what you should do, but you can't find a reason to do something else."

"Pretty much."

"I have to talk to the land tonight. Don't freak out if I'm hard to wake in the morning." She sighed and scanned the plains. "Imagine this as all green with herds of animals wandering freely. How many generations will it take to return the plains to those days?"

"It will never happen." Hob came over to her. "We're ready to move as soon as you are."

"Let's get going." Robin stretched. "Why did you say the plain will never return?"

"Can't go backward. They will become something new, and if we are wise, we'll have some part in shaping it." Hob held her gaze.

"How can you know if you're wise?" Robin looked away.

"You don't." Rick nudged her shoulder. "Do what you can for the right reasons and let your grandkids decide if you're wise or not."

"Assuming I live that long." She snorted and picked up her pack and headed north toward Westburg.

That evening after supper, she sat in her tent and closed her eyes.

"You there?" Her face heated. That's right, just shout into the dark.

"What disturbs you, child?" The elder woman sat across from her.

"I still have no idea why I'm doing what I'm doing." Robin lost the fight to keep from whining.

"To know with certainty is a rare gift." The woman tilted her head.

"I thought I knew before I left Fhayde, now I'm wandering in a fog."

"Not completely aimless."

"Right, like 'go north and find the emperor' is clear. How will I know him when I meet him? What do I say to him? 'You're the emperor, fix the land.'?"

"If you are called to find him, then you'll figure out who he is, and you'll say what you say. As for fixing the land, no one human can fix what has been done."

"Then what's the point?" Robin jumped to her feet and flung her arms out. "Why does any of this matter?"

"Child." The elder frowned slightly. "In the south, there are mountains. A single pebble may begin a landslide, but a landslide may pass and leave the pebble undisturbed. What is important, the landslide or the pebble?"

"I guess it depends on whether you need a pebble or a landslide." Robin sat down. "My gut says to go north and find this emperor, alone if I have to, but my heart aches to be with Sarge and help him."

"And what is the worst that could happen?" The woman shrugged. "The pebble moves, or it doesn't. It isn't up to you to start the landslide. You can't achieve anything if you are pulled in two directions."

"I'm always pulled in two directions." Robin shouted.

"Then choose a direction and do what you are going to do."

"What if I choose wrong?"

"You can't choose wrong unless you intend to. Remember, the pebble will move, or it won't. Who's to say what is right or wrong?"

"Fat lot of help you are." Robin put her hands over her face.

"As you say." The woman's voice faded into silence.

Robin waited for someone else to come and torment her, but no one did. When she opened her eyes, her face was wet with tears and the smell of breakfast made her stomach rumble.

***

They arrived at Westburg with Robin no more decided about what she should do. The thought that Sarge might already be dead terrified her. She wanted to run to him, to sit at his feet like she once did and ask his advice.

Only he was never one for handing out advice. He made her think things through and decide for herself. She missed him.

She would go visit him and let the pebble fall where it may. The next question was what to do with the remnant of the thousand. Couldn't bring them with her, it would put them at too much risk. Robin rolled her eyes. She was worried about risk now, but it would be hard enough for her to sneak into the city without more than a hundred followers. Better go find Marshal Hapten and break the news.

She felt like she was floating with the weight of the decision off her shoulders. Sneak in talk to Sarge, make sure the boys were all right, then she could head north to find this blasted emperor. Simple.

"I'm going to slip into the capital, visit Sarge and make sure he's okay, then we'll head north."

"You what?" Marshal Hapten shouted. People on the wall turned to look, then carefully busied themselves with whatever was handy.

"Right, and what will we be doing here while you're gone?"

"What we are doing now, training with the Free."

"That's all very well, but I am charged with following you and do what we can to stop a full-fledged civil war from breaking out. Stopping and training a horde that may or may not become our enemies is not a part of that." Marshal Hapten stopped and took a deep breath. "Not that I think Hob will try to invade, but we have no truce with the Free, no trade agreements, no assurance they won't toss us out on our ears the moment you disappear."

"Then negotiate something with Hob. If I put my name on it, the king isn't likely to argue with the terms."

"And you will put your name on something you haven't read? Haven't been part of?" Marshal Hapten moved into Robin's face. "That doesn't sound like something to impress the king."

Robin stood with her mouth open, then shook her head. Nothing came into her head to make the situation anything but worse. "I'm not bound by your orders." She sputtered.

"No, you're not; you are supposed to be our commander and now you plan to hare off and abandon us to the mercy of the Free." Marshal Hapten moved even closer. "Why do you think that army is sitting there waiting only a two-day march from here? It isn't for their health. They are waiting on reinforcements. Something Haffmon is very sure he can get, or they wouldn't be there. He's a treacherous slime, but he's not stupid. What if they come back and attack with ten thousand trained troops? Bring siege equipment? The Free have only one advantage, numbers. If the Ancans can reduce the city before the horde gets here, what happens to us? To the Ancans, we're the enemy. You don't have to obey my orders, but by damn, you will listen to my advice and know what you're risking."

Robin fled, her face burning. She was failing as a commander. Again. Was she ever really commanding, or was she the thousand's mascot? Someone bumped into her and knocked her down.

"It is dangerous to run on the wall." Hob reached a hand to help her up. "I heard Marshal Hapten's voice. You are having a disagreement?"

"I want to go see Sarge, make sure he is okay. She doesn't understand."

"I think she understands all too well. I too dislike the idea of you Fhayden staying around without their commander. What happens if the rest of the thousand show up marching with the Ancans? Who will your people fight for? Without you to give the orders, they may switch sides again. I will not risk it. If you leave, you take your people with you, or I will send them home. I was thinking of a delegation to Lord Huddroc, in any case."

Robin stumbled away from him and walked until she found a corner to sit in, bury her face in her hands and cry.

***

Ham knew the Ancans were lying to him. The problem was he couldn't remember enough to know what was lie and what was truth. He was one of fifty healthy prisoners; a few more wounded lay on mats in the barracks. The Ancans made him their go between. He certainly wondered what he'd done to be abandoned to the mercy of the Ancans. The army had stopped partway to the capital and built a defensible camp. Maybe they were expecting the horde to attack and wanted someone to slow them down.

Lady Robin had turned on the Ancans, killing the general and one of the majors before the rest of the truce party had broken free and fled before the peasants could come and finish them. Or so said Captain Hervithon. Then the horde had arrived as the rest of the Fhaydens fought for the enemy.

The other Fhayde soldiers ignored the Ancans and resented Ham. He was a common soldier, but both sides were forcing him to be the go-between, and he didn't like it. Part of him wanted to put the blame on Lady Robin and the other commanders, but that was a waste of time.

"Ham." Captain Hervithon came over, looking as jolly as ever. "We'll be moving soon and expect cooperation from the prisoners. We would be within our rights to execute the lot of you, but we're civilized people. There will be a trial and a chance for you to plead for mercy. Of course, there may be something you can do to show you are not like the officers who left you for dead."

"I'm a common soldier." Ham kept his face stolid. "I wouldn't know about such things."

"You don't have to be a common soldier." The captain slapped him on the shoulder and laughed as he walked away.

"What did the clown want?" Befal stared at Ham doubtfully through the fence.

"The usual nonsense," Ham replied. "Hints and threats. They're up to something, but I have no idea what it is."

"Maybe it's time for you to learn."

"I'd agree with you, except my gut says it will get people killed. For now, I'm playing dumb as a post."

"They aren't feeding us for nothing." Befal frowned. "The bill is going to come due eventually, and I'm guessing we won't like it."

"I agree with you there." Ham sighed. "If I could just remember what happened, I might know what to do."

"What happened was Lady Robin changed sides. We don't know why. It might be one of those screw-the-soldier kind of politics, or she might have a good reason. She isn't here to explain, and I wouldn't understand if she were."

Shouting came from the compound where the Fhaydens milled endlessly through the day.

"Fighting again?" Ham scowled. "It ain't doing anyone any good."

"People are bored. What is there to do but fight?"

"Stupid, stupid, stupid." Ham stomped over to the gate, and the guards waved him in. He'd headed out to ask for more bandages, but the captain distracted him. Things just fell out of his mind now, as if the sword blow had actually split his head open.

Two women circled each other while others shouted jeers or encouragement.

"That's enough," Ham shouted. "You're just proving that we have no discipline."

"And you're going to discipline us?" One woman spat in his direction.

"If you're going to fight, you're going to do it properly." Ham growled. "Not this brawling."

"And what are you going to do about it?" the other said belligerently.

"You want to fight, you fight me, and we spar properly, like training."

"Just because you're big, you think you can order us around?"

"You want the job?" Ham loomed over her. "You want to be the one doing the balancing act trying to keep you alive?"

"No, Ham." The woman stepped back and glared at the other.

"Get everyone here." Ham ordered. "It's time we talked about how things are going to go."

The Fhaydens gathered in a half circle, their faces showing a mix of curiosity and disdain.

"The longer we lounge around without a plan, the more we play into whatever plan the Ancans have. Whatever you think of me, their use for us ranges from hostages to example. What if they march us up to the wall and ask Lady Robin to surrender or they kill us? You going to beg for mercy, or spit in their eyes?" Ham scanned the crowd. "We didn't beat the Empire back by being undisciplined slobs, and we won't get out of this without cooperation."

"What do you suggest?" someone asked.

"We train properly, become a unit, not a mish-mash of soldiers who don't know or trust each other."

"And you're going to do this?" another shouted.

"You want the job? Step up and take over." Ham stared them down. "First thing is we introduce ourselves properly. It doesn't matter what hundred we're from, we're stuck with each other now."

"Why should we listen to you?"

"Because I can and will beat you into the dust, one at a time or all at once." Ham challenged them. "Right here, right now."

No one stepped forward.

"Right then, introductions, what's your name, where you from, what's your specialty if you got one. I'll start. Ham, no fancy title. I'm from a tiny forest town in the northeast, not far from the sea. You can guess my specialty. I'm big and mean and the officers like to have me guarding their back."

One by one, the others put up a hand and introduced themselves. By the time they were done, they stood straighter. Most were spear or pike, but a few were archers and a couple were trackers and scouts.

"Good. First thing in the morning, we work with what we have. If we're gonna survive, we gotta do it ourselves."

***

"Been looking for you."

Robin looked up at Sargent Temajin, standing over her in the deepening twilight.

"Why? Are you going to yell at me too?"

"Do I need to?" He leaned against the wall. "Heard you've been told some tough things. You want me to pat you on the back and say you're right and they are all wrong?"

"I've had enough lectures."

"But did you listen?" Sargent Temajin asked. "You made me a Sargent because you thought I'd tell you the truth, like it or not. You saying you don't need a Sargent anymore?"

"I need Sarge."

"And what do you think Sarge would say about this?"

Robin stared at her feet until she wondered why Sargent Temajin hadn't left.

"I don't know what to do." She shook her head. "I know what I need to do, but I don't know why."

"So?" Sargent Temajin shrugged. "A lot of the time I know what to do, but not all the why. I know what I need to know, more than that just confuses things."

"Don't you want to know? What if the person giving you the order is wrong?"

"You mean, what if you are wrong?" He sighed and crouched down beside her. "You are going to be wrong sometimes. But you need to be wrong for the right reasons."

"That doesn't make any sense. Wrong is wrong."

"Is it?"

The chill air made her shiver, but there was something more there.

"Intention is everything." Robin put her head on her knees. "I'm so stupid. Are Hob and Marshal Hapten ever going to listen to me again?"

"Who do you think sent me to look for you? You are young, you're going to make mistakes. You're *supposed* to make mistakes. How else will you learn? Talk to them, listen, take it all in, then make your decision. They've been where you are now."

"I guess there is no time like the present." Robin stood and almost fell back down.

"Food first, then talk. You can't think properly hungry. They'll be there when you're ready."

Robin didn't taste the food, but it made her stomach calmer. "Sargent Temajin, please ask Marshal Hapten and Hob to meet with me tomorrow morning. Perhaps Hob will let us use a room in the manor."

She needed to prepare for the meeting. This needed to be more than a simple apology. In her room, she lay on the bed and concentrated on the land.

"What are you doing?" Sarge grumped, looking put out that in this darkness he had no cane to bang on a non-existent floor.

"I need to talk to you about what I'm doing."

"You going to yell and pout at me, too?"

"You'd never stand for that." Robin ignored the tears in her eyes. "I need to solve the question of what to do with what's left of the thousand. We can't depend on the Free's hospitality much longer."

"Then send them home." He waved dismissal.

"These are people who chose to stay with me. I won't insult them by sending them away for my convenience."

"You going to get together and invade Ancanopolis and rescue everyone like the hero everyone expects to you be?"

"Something like that. We will need to deal with Haffmon at some point. At the very least, he has prisoners with the army. At worst, he has everyone we left in the capital too. I thought about sending them to swing wide around the Ancan army. From the scouting reports, they are camped on the road, controlling the access between the cities. If we moved to the south bank of the river, we should avoid attention."

"Or end up in a battle you can't win." Sarge moved his hand to thump his non-existent cane. "Bah."

"It is possible, but I think Marshal Hapten can avoid that." Robin got up to pace.

"And what about the Free?"

"They aren't my responsibility, but I would like to have at least a draft agreement to build into a treaty. I will suggest that Marshal Hapten and Hob work something out to present to the king. Betrice can command the escort for the envoy to prevent any trouble."

"You've got rid of the marshal and Hob. What are you going to be doing?" Sarge leaned on an invisible cane.

"I'm going to do what I think I should have done from the start, head north on my own, or at least with only a half-squad of hunters experienced at staying out of sight. Having the thousand is fun, but it is a distraction from my being a shield maiden."

"Hurrah for you, you get to play at being the heroine again." Sarge sneered at her.

"It isn't my first choice of career." Robin said. "The land is broken and confused, doesn't know what it needs, so it is reaching out for the only bit of stability it had—the emperor."

"Marshal Hapten won't let you just disappear."

"It isn't up to her, but I want her advice."

"And what about Sarge?"

"He is either safe and doesn't need rescuing, or he's captured or dead and there is nothing I can do about it."

"If you going to make it to your meeting, you'd better wake up." Sarge turned and walked into the darkness.

Chapter 26

Allin showed his pass at the gate into Nordfin, expecting to answer questions about why they were there, but the guard barely glanced at it. They walked into the city half ready to meet a contingent of thieves waiting for their revenge. Nobody so much as glanced at them.

"Let's find a place to stay." Allin pointed to an inn. "But maybe something less ostentatious."

"Not a hostel with a nosy manager." Rebecca frowned. "We need to rest, and I want to check your hand."

"It itches." Allin refused the urge to scratch it.

"Good." Rebecca smiled at him. "It's a sign of healing."

They wandered until they found a market where they bought something to eat. Rebecca asked the vendor where they could stay for less than a fortune, but still be safe.

From the speed of his answer, he got asked that question a lot and probably got a cut from the inn he recommended. The place looked clean and the person running it was a matronly woman.

"A room is a silver a night, and that includes your evening meat. Ale is five penny a mug. Supper starts at the mid-afternoon bell." Allin made a show of reluctantly pulling coins out of his purse to pay for three nights.

"Come, Papa." Rebecca took his arm. "Let's walk around a bit more. It is better than you spending all our money on ale."

They walked to the western gate and scanned the dusty plain.

"Don't wanna go out there, the peasants will murder you," an old man said. "Rebelling, hmmph, wouldn't have been no rebellion in my day."

"A peasant uprising?" Allin smiled at the old man. "Thank you for the warning, good sir."

"Hmmph, peasants don't know their place these days."

"The inns must be full of displaced nobility." Rebecca said when they were out of earshot of the old man. "Everyone

212

will make money until the nobles run out of it. Can't see General Ordamy campaigning to re-install a few old families. If he takes the plain, he'll run it himself and let the nobles cry."

"That would involve settling matters here first. Don't want to send the legions away if there could be trouble at home." Allin looked around. "Don't see much of a guard here, so the general must think there isn't a risk of the peasants coming here."

"What risk could peasants present?" Henry asked. "The noble families have ruled the plains for generations. The plains will be in chaos, begging for the general to step in and create order."

"I'm not so sure." Allin turned to stare out the gate. "There is a change in the wind, and who knows where it will blow?"

They meandered through the streets and got so turned around they needed to ask directions again. A young boy took them there for a penny. The matron led them up to a room which was barely large enough for the four thin mats on the floor.

"I'm losing hope about the quality of the meal." Allin stretched out on a mat and sighed. "I think I'm going to catch forty winks until suppertime."

The others talked quietly enough for Allin not to be able to follow the conversation, but not enough to allow him to sleep. He didn't say anything. They were trying, and this was almost as good as a nap.

***

"Where are we supposed to go from here?" Rebecca's voice woke Allin. They'd spent three days wandering aimlessly through the city and knew it well enough they didn't have to hire an urchin to guide them. The good news was Allin's hand was close to normal, the bad was Rebecca got more restless by the day.

"Marta said to go east." Henry responded. "Maybe there is a road north from the plain?"

"Rebecca has a point." Allin sat up. "We need to decide our next move before we run out of coin, and there is still a chance the guild will catch up with us. I'd rather not flee another battle scene. Our luck will run out, eventually."

"I don't mind where we go." Henry took Magpie's hand.

"I do mind. I want to get home." Rebecca crossed her arms.

"I'm for moving on, but we need to get water skins and food, a map if there is one, any other gear we might need on the plains." Allin sighed and hefted his purse. "We don't have much coin left at all, never mind Ancan coin."

"Maybe split up the tasks." Rebecca stood up, ready to head out immediately. "I'll go find the gear we need."

"I'll go as well." Allin groaned and pushed to his feet. "Henry, you and Magpie hold down the fort here."

"Okay." Henry winked at Magpie and Rebecca huffed.

"Come, daughter." Allin led the way from the room while Magpie giggled.

"You know they will pay no attention to anything but each other." Rebecca said. "I'd be disgusted if I wasn't scheming for the same things only a few months ago."

Allin laughed as they headed out onto the street.

"The food and water skins will be easy enough to find. Let's look for a map first." Allin grinned. "I used to collect old maps and books. It will be interesting to see some old empire cartography."

Rebecca rolled her eyes but didn't object.

"I remember seeing an old bookstore this way." She pulled Allin down a street. They found a book merchant whose stock was piled in dusty mountains through the store. The proprietor sat in a corner and watched them, but didn't speak.

Allin soon lost himself in the store. He could have spent everything he had and more on books and still only scratched the surface. Maps lay in disordered rolls on a table. Most of them he immediately pushed aside. Poor copies of copies of old maps. Then he spotted a map on thicker parchment, almost leather. Unrolling it with shaking hands, he studied the faint lines.

"That doesn't look very helpful," Rebecca poked at the other rolls.

"If this is authentic, it is a veritable treasure." Allin leaned close to it. "I will have to get it back to our room and examine it properly, but I believe it is a map of the world before the Ancan Empire. Look here, it says 'here the people of the plains' I can't read the next word 'rule? wander?' Fierce warriors who keep to themselves.'"

"How is an ancient map going to help us?" Rebecca unrolled another one. "They all have the plains as a blank space as if there is nothing there."

"Here, it shows the road north from what must be Dordnom, then in the east another road from the plains heading north as well. In the south, it shows Caldera and Fhayde, but only warns of the fae and to stay away."

"The fae are just children's tales." Rebecca turned away. "My nurse used to scare me with stories of them being capricious and having a taste for poorly behaved children."

"I have history books from the time when the fae still walked the forest. They were genuine enough, but how much like the old tales I can't say. There are even a few paintings showing them, slight, pale with raven black hair, but the stories tell of them being fearsome in battle. Even then, the border between Fhayde and what is now the empire was troubled."

"Okay, you have me convinced, but do you have enough to buy this?" Rebecca touched it with the tip of a finger.

"Only way to find out is ask." Allin rolled the map up and carried it to the old man. "How much are you asking for this?"

"It is very old," the man said, "my grandfather had it for sale for a gold coin. My father for five silvers, I'll let you have it for two silvers."

Allin dropped the coins in the old man's hand. "Here you are, and worth every bit."

The old man frowned as he took the money.

"Two silvers for an old map? That's two nights at the inn."

"This is priceless." Allin held it with great care as if it would fall into dust at a heavy breath. They left the store and Allin headed back to the inn.

"What about food and water skins?" Rebecca caught up to him.

"We can go out again once this is safe." Allin caressed the roll of leather.

"Fine." Rebecca huffed and followed him.

They arrived at the inn. Allin stopped as soon as he set foot through the door, but someone was already behind him, blocking escape.

"I hear you like maps." A man sat at a table in the corner like he owned the place. He waved Allin over. "Your daughter is welcome to join the others upstairs. Don't be concerned, my orders are very specific. You are to be delivered alive and whole to the emperor."

"General Ordamy." Allin sat, still clutching the map.

"Precisely, he felt it necessary to fill a gap before the empire crumbled entirely."

"I see."

"He is very curious about four travellers who spend Fhayden coins and, according to a somewhat unreliable source, have been responsible for quite a few deaths in a certain guild. Unusual enough that the left hand of a certain guild came to the emperor looking for help capturing and punishing you. He said something about an emperor. You can imagine how the emperor felt about a spare emperor wandering the countryside."

"So why capture us rather than kill us?" Allin waved the serving girl over. "Do you mind if I have an ale?"

"Not at all." The man tossed a silver on the table. "Two ales. Now the emperor feels it is important to understand what is going on. There are a lot of stories going around. A Fhayden thousand marching under a white banner spreading peace and love wherever they go, at least until someone sets a foot wrong. His imperial majesty is concerned that this thousand apparently vanished after switching sides in a battle for a city. Can't have a thousand soldiers wandering around unaccounted for. Then there is the rumor that the emperor survived the fire that burned his city and headed north. My personal favourite story is that a fae is leading the thousand and personally killed a giant distressing a city to the south of Ancanopolis."

The girl put the ale on the table and retreated to the kitchen.

"You are an interesting man." The man picked up a mug and sipped from it. "Your companions have opinions about the emperor and the present situation. Opinions which run very close to what the emperor is thinking. Then you are discovered to be a collector of old maps and filled with stories about the fae from before the empire, even describing a painting of one. A description which matches the rumored fae general."

Allin took a long drink from his mug. "I haven't heard of any fae generals in recent times."

"No, I don't expect you have. Two soldiers returned from the forests of Fhayde with a tale about a fae who killed imperial soldiers like they were raw recruits and sent a message to the emperor to 'consider carefully'."

"I would wager a month's salary that you are the Fhayde envoy who supposedly died tragically in the fire. What was his name again..." the man took another long drink.

"Lord Allin, Duke of Fhayde." Allin poured the ale down his throat. Rich and bitter, it didn't replace the wine vintages of his home.

"That's right." The man smiled slightly. "I am General Mihone, Lord Allin, and the emperor sent me to issue an invitation to you and the emperor, along with the women, to return to Dordnom and meet his imperial majesty."

"An invitation which we have no choice about accepting."

"Exactly. The emperor is most eager to meet you." General Mihone stood. "We leave in the morning. Please bring whatever possessions you have. I'm glad you understand the situation."

"Til the morning then." Allin saluted the general with his mug and drained it. "I will talk to the others and make sure they understand the situation."

***

Allin rubbed his temples. "That's why we will need to go with them and cooperate. Any trouble and we go from guests to prisoners. The advantage is we will be safe from the guild at least until the emperor releases us."

"I don't like it. I need to travel north." Rebecca frowned as she paced in their small room in the inn.

"True, but if we cooperate, we might convince the emperor to open the border for you." Henry leaned his head against the wall. "I remember General Ordamy. He is very strict and by the book. He wasn't in favour of the invasion of Fhayde, but I don't know his reasoning."

"He's calling himself 'Emperor' now. We'd better keep that in mind." Allin sighed. "We want to be polite, but not fawning. I'm an envoy from Fhayde, officially recognized by the palace. That should count for something."

"Maybe not, considering it was the previous emperor who welcomed you." Rebecca's frown deepened.

"Was he at the palace when I was there?" Allin's head ached. He didn't like the situation any more than Rebecca.

"No, he likes to stay in Dordnom, away from the politics of the palace." Rebecca said. "At least in the time I was there. He is mostly interested in the north."

"He thinks the palace is decadent and weak." Henry sighed. "He is not wrong about the decadence, but it is more powerful than most people give credit to. Whoever sits on the throne, it is the same bureaucrats who run the empire. I expect even now, as the empire crumbles, the bureaucrats are still doing their job."

"I still don't like it." Rebecca sat down and crossed her arms. "But I guess we have no choice. I will behave."

They packed up and prepared for the morning.

***

General Mihone welcomed them in the morning. Allin kept a smile on his face, even as doubts assaulted his stomach.

"I will ask you to ride in the coach with me." The general opened the door and waved them into its luxurious interior. The polished wood was carved, and the seats covered with fine leather. It took Allin back to when he rode in the coach with Jecquillane and her Nana. He didn't think any knives would change hands this time. Their packs were secured in a compartment at the back of the coach.

"Nice." Henry nodded in approval. "More comfortable than walking in ditches and sleeping in barns."

"I am glad you approve, your majesty."

Henry winced. "Please, I am no longer the emperor. Call me Henry. It will be easier than having two imperial majesties in the same room."

"Very well, Henry." The general frowned, as if he expected a rebuke. "I know, Lord Allin, but who are the ladies?"

"I'm Rebecca, once the emperor's third wife." Rebecca nodded regally.

"I am Magpie." She said quietly, but Henry took her hand and smiled.

"She owns my heart," he said.

"I've never met people so intent on not taking advantage of their social position." The general smiled and tapped the window. As the coach started off, the padding on the benches was needed, as they could feel every cobble through the seats. The Marques' coach had better springs. Clearly, the innovation hadn't made it to the north.

They stopped at a waystation while the horses were changed over, and the squad rested their mounts.

"Come in and have a meal." The general climbed out and offered a hand to Rebecca, who accepted it as her due, then Magpie, who looked over to Henry before taking the hand and stepping down.

The dining room was spartan, but well built. Stew and bread was set in front of them. Magpie sat close to Henry, looking around nervously.

"I need to use the privy." Magpie whispered to Henry.

"I will go with you." Rebecca stood up. "You will be quite safe."

The women left the room after getting directions from the server.

"What brought you to the Empire as envoy?" The general dipped bread in his stew.

"We are aware of the poor harvests in the empire for the last few years. I thought maybe we could work a trade agreement out instead of a war. Sadly, we didn't get the chance to discuss anything before the generals started the war."

"I've heard reports that the real fighting only lasted a day, and by attacking Fhayde, the empire doomed itself to collapse."

"I wouldn't know. I was in Ancanopolis during the fighting."

"Of course," the general said. "I hoped you knew something of the fae who fought and killed the foolish general who attacked the Fhayde."

"As I said yesterday—" Allin was cut off by a scream. The general jumped to his feet, but Henry had already vanished down the hall. The screaming cut off suddenly, then there was a shout, also cut short.

When Allin and the general reached the hallway outside the privy, two men lay on the floor. Henry bled from a cut on his arm, but he held Magpie tightly as she trembled in his arms. Rebecca lay on the floor. Allin checked and found she was still alive, though already a bruise was forming on her cheek. He picked her up and carried her out to the dining room. Her breathing was strong and steady. Henry followed with Magpie.

"We will hang them both." General Mihone's face darkened as he strode back into the room. "I should have sent a guard. The emperor may hang me as well when he finds out."

"I hope not." Allin looked down at the unconscious Rebecca. "But I am glad they will face the consequences of their actions. I have played Rebecca's father for so long, I begin to feel like her father in fact."

"Stay here until I return." General Mihone frowned. "I will check that we are ready to start off again."

Rebecca stirred in Allin's arms. "Magpie, they took her."

"It's all right. Henry stopped them, and they won't be bothering either of you again."

She put her head on his chest. "My father died the year after I went to the palace as third wife. I miss him still. You are like him in many ways."

"We are ready to go." General Mihone stepped into the room. "I have asked our surgeon to look at Rebecca and Henry as we travel."

As he carried Rebecca to the coach, Allin saw two men hanging from a nearby tree.

"To be honest," General Mihone climbed up and took Rebecca from Allin and placed her on the seat. "The men were already dead, but a message needed to be given. Guests of the emperor are sacrosanct. The way stations are extensions of the emperor's palace."

The surgeon fussed over Rebecca, then pronounced that she would be fine in a day or two. He stitched up Henry's wound before sitting in the corner of the coach and apparently falling asleep.

Rebecca lay with her head on Allin's leg, and Magpie clung to Henry.

General Mihone stared out the window, face like a thundercloud as they rolled ever closer to the self-declared emperor.

Chapter 27

Ham worked the Fhaydens until they were ready to drop. The yard was packed dirt with an eight-foot fence around it. A walkway ran around the outside of the yard and the one barracks tent they used for eating and sleeping. Empire soldiers lined it, pointing and laughing.

The Ancans watched some jeering at the sight of people practicing unarmed combat. The wounded Fhayden who could followed the training intently.

"You aren't going to punch your way out of here."

"Try to grab me and watch me cut your throat."

Ham gritted his teeth and ignored them. The Fhaydens knew better than to allow anything to distract them. How did he come to be the leader of the motley bunch? There were people who outranked him, but all insisted that since he was Lady Robin's personal guard, he was the top of the heap.

He hated command. Years he had been a squad leader, and every night worried he would lead them wrong and cause someone's death. That had been before the war when all they did was patrol for bandits and watch the north for Ancans crossing into Fhayde. Now they were in the middle of a war, and they didn't know what side they were on. Not the Ancans according to their captors, but that didn't mean they were going to make nice—.

Ham's sparring partner punched through his distraction and clipped his shoulder.

"Sorry, I didn't mean..." she sputtered to a stop as Ham unleashed his full fury on her. To her credit, she didn't run away, but hunkered down and defended. She'd have bruises on her arms.

"Never apologise for landing a strike, not until after you've won. Follow through, continue the attack. The referee will tell you if there's a problem."

"Y,yes, sir."

"Don't call me sir, I'm just a grunt soldier." Ham stepped back. "Now it's your turn. See if you can land another blow on me. Don't hold back." He let her chase him around the yard and the others stopped to watch. She relied too much on punches and arm blocks, quick though. The woman darted in and struck at his face as he lifted his arms to take the punch. Next thing, she landed a kick to the back of his leg. A little higher and he might have gone down.

"Hold." Ham stepped back and shouted to the crowd. "That's how it's done, people. Think and act, you can't win on instinct, nor brains, alone. What's your name?"

"Merideth." She snapped her mouth shut before the 'sir' came out. She was quick in more ways than one.

"Okay Merideth, as of now, you are my assistant instructor. Watch the others and make them work. Get in there and make them sweat."

"Her?" one of the men in the crowd said. "She's too weak."

"Come here." Ham waved him over. "Land a strike on me and you get her job." The man jumped to the attack. Ham used what he'd learned from working Lady Robin into a quivering wreck. Move just enough to get out of the way, block only enough to make the punch or kick go wide. The man had stamina; he'd give him that. He tried punches, kicks, combos, even tried a grappling move.

"Hold." Ham stepped back. "You're not bad, but you're throwing attacks at me like a handful of pebbles. Watch your opponent, learn from them, then use it against them."

"You must have let her land that blow."

"Not likely." Merideth stomped over to him. "You and me. We'll see what happens."

"Fight." Ham said.

The man attacked almost before the word was out of Ham's mouth, but Merideth slipped away to the side and stung him in the ribs. She danced away, grinning malevolently.

"Damn." The man attacked her again, but she dropped under his swing and this time her kick landed exactly on target. The leg flew out from under him, and he landed on his back.

"What's your name?" Merideth stood ready for another attack.

"Job." He pushed to his feet and bowed. His leg flashed out in a vicious roundhouse kick. Merideth ducked under it and kicked his leg out from under him again.

"That's the match." Merideth stepped back. "You aren't bad, but you're predictable."

"You—" Job surged off the dirt and Ham caught him by the shoulder and spun him around, swept Job's legs from under him, then landed on him and pinned him to the ground.

"The match was over. If you're fighting for your life, then a sneak attack is commendable, but stupid. Don't force your opponent to kill you." Ham stood up and glared down at Job. "But she wasn't about to kill you, so what you did was just stupid. Don't do it again." He looked around. "What are you doing? Back to work; Merideth is going to run you ragged."

The Fhaydens went back to sparring while Meridith wandered through them, making comments and suggestions.

Ham hoisted Job to his feet. "Do something like that again and I will pitch over the fence and hope you don't land on anyone important. Your enemies aren't in this yard."

"Hey, big man." An Ancan clambered over the fence. He stood almost as tall as Ham, but was broader in the shoulders. "How about you fight a real man?"

"No." Ham scowled at the man. "I might lose my temper and hurt you, and that would be bad for my people. Now get out of my yard."

The Ancan charged at Ham.

"Hold!" Captain Hervithon pushed through the gate. "No fighting with the prisoners." A glower replaced his usual kindly face.

"Ahh, Captain. I'm bored and no one will wrestle me."

"You have only yourself to thank for that. You aren't here to be entertained. Do extra duty in the kitchen if you're so bored."

"Captain—"

"You want latrine duty?" Captain Hervithon swatted the man on the side of the head. "Now get out of here. The rest of you find something to do, or I'll find it for you."

The crowd vanished like smoke.

"If it is going to distract soldiers from their duty, I will have to order you to stop the training. I know you are trying to hold things together, but the camp discipline comes first."

"Your troop's lack of discipline is not my problem." Ham clenched his fists.

"You're not here for fun." Captain Hervithon poked Ham. "You're prisoners, alive only because the major wants it so. Any more problems and I will have to make an example Major Sarigal won't miss one of you." He turned and walked away through the gate. The archers on the walkway relaxed. Guards shut the gate and dropped the bar in with a thump.

"You heard the man. Fun's over, back to the barracks."

The Fhaydens slumped and walked into the barracks. Ham wondered if the whole thing had been a setup, an excuse to stop the training. It wouldn't surprise him. He wouldn't underestimate Hervithon. The man was a snake wearing a smile.

Inside the barracks, Ham scanned the disconsolate faces.

"Clear the mats out of the way. We'll train in here. Fight in silence. We don't want to give him an excuse to shut us down again. This time you will spar in fours. Learn to work with your partner on attack and defense. We're not going to be prisoners forever." That they would likely die as prisoners, Ham left unsaid.

***

"You're telling me there is no way to communicate with the people inside the fence?" Bodan growled. "Whose idea was that?"

"Commander Paychen didn't want to risk people coming and going. It could give away the hoax." Tradkin didn't sound convinced.

"What about talking with the other members of the hundred?"

"We keep it to a minimum. They all know you're here, but anything more and they'd start thinking there was something they could do. We're a hundred people in a city of thousands. The gang they have outside the gate isn't even all the guards on shift."

"Are all the guards with Haffmon?" Bodan slouched against the wall. The tiny rooms made it stuffy, and the place reeked of something unnameable, which made his throat sore.

"The guards have taken an oath to obey commands. It doesn't matter what they think about it." Tradkin shrugged.

"Would they obey a command to kill unarmed people?"

"Probably, the guards tend to recruit men who like to throw their weight around. Haffmon has surrounded himself with those whose morals aren't any better than his."

"Perhaps we can use that to our advantage." Bodan stared up at the grimy ceiling. "If we can sow dissension in the ranks, it will give us more time to come up with a plan."

"What kind of plan?"

"Don't know yet." Bodan shrugged. "But we have to come up with something. The farce at the gate isn't going to last forever."

"All it would take is one higher up at the palace to kick the doors in and arrest everyone. Any threat to the bureaucratic power will bring the palace guard into the picture, and no one is eager to have blood run in the streets, especially not their own." Tradkin sighed and leaned back in the rickety chair. "We cause any trouble and they'll be on us like hounds on a hare."

"What if we went home?" Bodan put his head in his hands. "I hate to suggest it, but half the thousand is on their way home."

"I would like nothing more than to head home, Commander Themson, but it would mean abandoning those in the camp. I won't leave until we all can leave."

"I suspect it won't be long before some start thinking about it." Bodan said. "Even the most loyal soldier is going to lose morale. We're down to a remnant, but even the full thousand couldn't do much here. Yet a few may do what a thousand cannot." He sat on the floor and tapped the floor with his finger. "First thing is to get Commander Paychen and the others out so they can't be used as hostages against us."

"Easier said than done." Tradkin coughed. "Blasted gas."

"Where does the gas come from?" Bodan suppressed the urge to cough.

"Think it's from the sewer, but can't find where it's getting in."

"Let me have a go, a sewer could be useful as a back door."

"If you don't die from breathing the gas, it's flammable. Strike a spark and the whole thing goes up."

"Interesting, so why aren't we exploding?" Bodan pointed to the candle in a sconce on the wall.

"Beats me, was a sewer explosion in Fhayde in my dad's time. That's all I know about it."

Bodan walked over to the candle and plucked it out of the sconce. "Air's better here. Sewer entrance would be downstairs." He muttered to himself. "Is there any way down?" Opening and closing doors finally brought him to a steep staircase cut into the rock.

"The air is really bad down there. We lost a guy who decided to explore."

"Interesting. Did he take a candle or a torch with him?

"Yeah, got halfway down the stair and poof, there's this flash of heat, then the candle goes out and the guy fell down the stairs like a rag doll." Tradkin closed the door. "Let's not play with it."

"Right." Bodan closed the door. "An escape route that kills you is no good."

They walked out to the courtyard and heard a roar in the distance.

"That came from the direction of the camp." Tradkin began running and Bodan chased after him through the maze of streets until they stopped in an alley across from the camp. The guards had a ram and had already smashed most of the gate. As they watched, guards flooded into the camp, shouting and waving swords.

***

Sarge talked with his ghosts; he'd learned early on that none of them had much original to say. Other than listening to Lencely and Rud, it was the only entertainment he had. He'd never seen Robin among the ghosts more than once, which led him to believe that something else had been going on.

Suddenly bored with the repetitious dialogue, Sarge walked away into the dark. He didn't need a cane in whatever this place was, but he missed it anyway. The thing had been good for emphasizing a point or getting attention.

He didn't walk in the darkness much, partly because he feared getting lost and not being able to return, but mostly because the unrelieved black made him feel like he was the ghost.

Today he walked until he saw a light ahead. It might have been minutes or days before he arrived. Images of Robin surrounded him, some with her neck broken, others with a sword through her back. One had a lance piercing her chest. The Robins were different ages. The sword killed a matronly Robin in an elegant dress. The one with a snapped neck showed Robin covered with scars and wearing what looked like gladiatorial amour.

The longer he looked, the more the pictures spread. Some of them moved as she gasped her last breath. One of them, he was sure, whispered 'Sarge' as she died.

Sarge turned and fled back into the darkness. He didn't know what direction the ghosts were. All he wanted was to get away from the terrible images of Robin dead and dying.

He didn't know how long he ran, his heart raced, and he struggled to catch his breath, but he couldn't stop. Then, far in the distance, he spotted a light and ran toward it, praying it wasn't the images of Robin's death.

The ghosts surrounded him, babbling all at once. Gord's ghost stood to the side, silent, his eyes dark.

"Back off!" Sarge shouted. They muttered as they faded, leaving only Gord behind.

"You saw the scenes of death." Gord didn't move. "Not your own, or you wouldn't be here."

"What is that? Why are so many ways Robin dies in my mind?" Sarge gasped for air.

"This isn't just your mind; it connects with other things. Some of them delight in reflecting our fears, or the fears of the person you see. Sometimes it shows what is real, sometimes not." Gord gazed at him with dead eyes. "And sometimes they show the future, just as the ghosts are your past."

"You mean Robin is going to die?"

"Everybody dies, Sarge, everybody except you. You drag on watching everyone you care about dying." He began bleeding from a wound in his chest, then to fade. Sarge reached for him, but Gord laughed and vanished.

"No!" Sarge's hand dripped with blood. "Robin!"

The darkness shattered like glass and Sarge found himself sitting up in bed with Rud staring at him wide eyed.

"Lencely, he's awake, Sarge is awake."

"If you woke me up because of some dream..." Lencely trailed off. "Sarge," he whispered. "I'm not dreaming?"

"I hope not." Sarge said, and the fear of returning to the darkness made him throw off the covers and try to stand.

Lencely and Rud caught him and helped him to a chair.

"How long have I been lying here?"

"It was fall when you collapsed. They were harvesting the fields. Now the fields have been planted for the summer."

"I shouldn't be able to move, never mind sit up in a chair."

"Maybe it wasn't an ordinary sleep." Rud turned away. "What's that sound?"

"They've finally broken the gate." Lencely shouted. "Get our swords."

"No," Sarge lifted his hand. "Sit on the bed, your hands in sight. Quickly."

The boys did as he ordered, and a few minutes later, the door burst open.

A guard holding a sword shouted. "More in here."

Other guards flooded the room. They tied Lencely and Rud hand and foot and carried them out as the boys shouted for Sarge.

"What about this one?" The first guard through the door asked.

"He's just an old man. Bring him along. We'll let the captain decide."

"Up you get, and walk ahead of us, and no tricks." The guards laughed.

"If you want me to walk, I will need my cane." Sarge pointed to where it leaned in the corner.

A guard handed it to him, then pulled him out of the chair. Sarge expected to collapse, but his legs held firm and he walked out of the room followed by the city guards. He was afraid he'd see bodies all over, but the camp looked empty.

Outside, the sun made him squint, so he couldn't count how many were held at sword point.

"Where is everyone else?" A guard with a gold badge on his tunic held a sword at Commander Paychen's throat.

"When I learned you were coming, I sent everyone but a few volunteers home. They should be well south of Lord

Edward's city by now." The commander didn't sound at all nervous.

"Well, we don't need to tell the others we didn't net them all. If they think we have all the hostages, the plan will work. Haffmon won't be pleased, but he'll get over it. Take them to the city jail. No rough stuff until I say so."

"Yes, Major Saligar." Guards pulled the captives to their feet and marched them off.

"Now, who are you?"

"Master Sargent Christopher Severson."

"And what is a Master Sargent?"

"I am."

"Take him to Haffmon. Let him figure it out."

Guards formed a square around Sarge, and they started out, Sarge walking as slowly as he dared.

***

Bodan saw Tradkin move forward out of their hiding place.

"We need to help them."

Bodan grabbed his arm and pulled him back into the alley.

"If we don't stop to think, we'll end up prisoners as well. We talk to the others and make a plan." They walked through the maze of streets. "I think the first thing we'll need is a few of those guard uniforms. I'm going to follow them, see where they take the old man. You let the others know what's happened."

Bodan jogged back to the street, then sauntered out and headed in the direction they'd taken Sarge. At the speed the old man was moving, it should be easy to catch up.

It took longer than he'd expected, and he discovered them rushing Sarge with hands on his arms, half carrying him. They weren't heading for a guard post, and it was the wrong direction for the palace. Since they were taking him to Haffmon, it would be the house or the company offices. Maybe Haffmon had another residence hidden away. He'd check with

Fabell. She, Merle, and Eric had been among the first to escape, according to Tradkin.

They stopped at an inn, walking straight in as if they owned the place. Most of the guard stayed outside. Only the major, Sarge, and his carriers went through the door. Bodan didn't slow as he passed on the far side of the street, studiously not watching the guard.

***

A heavy-set man sat at a table in the inn. Sarge couldn't see much, as he was shaking with exhaustion. He dropped into a chair without permission and concentrated on breathing.

"What is this?" the man waved a hand in Sarge's direction.

"He says he is a Master Sargent, Master Haffmon." Major Saligar pointed at the door and the two guards left them alone. "We found him in the Fhayden camp. He isn't Fhayden, but he had two attendants. It suggests he is important."

"Where are the attendants?" Haffmon huffed a sigh.

"With the other prisoners in the cells."

"What do you have to say for yourself?" Haffmon slapped the table in front of Sarge.

"I am the reason the Fhaydens routed the Empire at the border and in Vilscape." Sarge's voice was surprisingly steady, given the banging of his heart in his chest.

"You?" Haffmon scoffed. "I doubt you could even lift a sword."

"You'd be right, but there is more to a war than people swinging swords." Sarge glanced over at the major, who was nodding his head. "I taught them strategy and tactics."

"You taught them?" Haffmon laughed and drank from a tankard beside him. "What can you teach me?"

"The empire is collapsing; it is a time of opportunity and danger. You already have the guard behind you, but not the palace. Otherwise, I'd be sitting in much grander surroundings." Sarge met Haffmon's eyes. "I think you are trying to carve out a piece of the empire for yourself. There are three things you need. The first you have - the army is behind you. The second is out of reach, - the bureaucracy won't support you, so you need the third, which is to have the public acclaim of the people, especially the ones with money and influence." Sarge coughed until his whole body shook. "Perhaps some water. Sadly, I no longer drink ale."

"You religious or something?" Haffmon stared at Sarge.

"Or something." Sarge straightened up, gasping.

"Get the man some water." Haffmon ordered the major. "You brought him here. Don't let him die on you." Haffmon looked like a cat eyeing a canary. "We might find him very useful."

When Major Saligar returned with a tankard of water, he set it in front of Sarge. "Master Haffmon, I have work to do."

"More important than this prisoner you brought me?"

"I need to question the other prisoners. There was only a handful left in the camp. They claim the rest were sent home."

"But we still have hostages," Haffmon didn't look away from Sarge, "and we have their Master Sargent. "I will tell the innkeeper's daughter to care for the old man for now. Maybe suggest that the quality of his care depends on their cooperation. Master Sargent, there is a city I want, unfortunately it is held by a rabble of peasants."

"Fortified cities are a challenge. Most fall to treachery rather than to a direct attack."

"I have a plan for that." Haffmon leaned forward. "I think we're going to get along just fine."

Sarge swallowed the foul taste in his mouth and put on a smile. There was more to wars than armies and emperors.

Chapter 28

Robin took extra care with her uniform but didn't put on her armour, though she was sorely tempted. She met Sargent Temajin, who led her to the meeting. Marshal Hapten sat with a cup of tea. Hob arrived behind Robin. Like the other rooms in the manor house, it was richly decorated in stark contrast to the utilitarian purpose of the meeting, matching Robin's mood.

"Good morning. Lady Robin." Hob nodded to her and sat by the table.

"I will start by apologizing for my behaviour yesterday." Robin poured herself a cup of tea and relished the warmth in her hands. "But we have more important things to discuss today."

"Robin, we need to talk about yesterday." Marshal Hapten put her tea down.

"Marshal Hapten, there are more important things than rehashing my outbursts. I am well aware of the root cause, and while I cannot promise something similar won't recur, it will not be for the same reasons."

"Robin—" Marshal Hapten frowned.

"Lady Robin." Robin said. "I am being judged on my behaviour based on that title. Let's use it as a reminder."

"What do you have to say?" Hob's face showed no emotion.

"We have several problems." Robin held up a finger. "First, the thousand has lost direction and the people who remain are here because of me, right or wrong. When I am overwhelmed by circumstance, it has a negative effect on the morale."

She lifted another finger. "Morale is also affected by the knowledge that members of the thousand are prisoners of the Ancans, at least some from the battle, but possibly the hundred left behind in Ancanopolis are restrained or captured, including the Master Sargent, Lencely and Rud.

There is nothing we can do about the prisoners at this time. Any action to rescue them would start a battle we cannot win. I don't want to start any fights. My opinion is the contract we have with the palace is in effect until they cancel it."

Another finger. "The truce under which we have entered and worked in Anca has been broken. They broke it by their treachery, and they will argue we broke it by our actions in response to that treachery. We can no longer march about the country under the white banner and expect it to protect us."

Robin paused for a breath to calm the whirlwind in her gut, then raised another finger. "The truce between the thousand and the Free is a result of circumstance and is unsustainable as it stands. It needs to be negotiated and entered into freely by both sides or dissolved."

Hob nodded his head, and Marshal Hapten's frown deepened.

Robin deliberately relaxed her hand. "Lastly, the command structure is untenable. It needs to be clarified and held to. Have I missed anything?" She waited for an agonizing two breaths for a response.

"Very well. Let's take the items in order. The thousand was assigned to support my quest, and to do what it could to prevent civil war. What remains of the thousand cannot achieve either of those goals. The sensible action is to recover our people who are imprisoned or threatened with imprisonment, then retreat. Next, the breaking of the truce has made that aim difficult, with a genuine possibility that any overt action will worsen the situation. Thus, any retreat needs to be through neutral territory, which brings up the next issue, the truce between the Free and the thousand. It needs to be clarified and signed, with open negotiation by both sides. There is much we can offer each other, but continuing the ad hoc truce we have now is unworkable."

Robin closed her eyes and quieted her stomach. "That brings us to the command structure. This is not specifically an issue for the Free, except as it affects the negotiation of a mutually beneficial truce. For the thousand, the problem is we have two people in the top position. When our goals aligned, that worked reasonably well, but our goals no longer lie in the same direction. The thousand's goal must be a retreat with a minimum number of people left behind. My task is to follow the direction of the land. The thousand has become a distraction from the purpose of my quest. My superior officer at this moment is the land, and any action away from that could trigger the very thing we are trying to prevent, the outbreak of civil war and its attendant risk to Fhayde and Caldera.

"As such, I am ordering Marshal Hapten to take command of the thousand with two tasks to undertake. The first is to strike a proper truce between the thousand and the Free and open the possibility of a treaty between the Free and Caldera. I suggest you send a delegation to the king through Vilscape after the truce is completed. The second task is to retreat with the thousand, leaving no one behind to face the Ancan's ire for the action of their commanders."

"And what will you be doing?" Marshal Hapten spoke sharply.

"What I should have been doing from the beginning, tracking the nudging of the land north to the emperor to discover what his part to play in Ancan's future may be." Robin swallowed but refused to back down.

"Robin." Marshal Hapten stood up.

"Emily, you continue to be familiar with me while we are discussing matters of import. If you are not willing to speak to me as an equal, I will relieve you of command and give my instructions to Commander Betrice." Robin's heart beat painfully in her chest as the marshal's face reddened, then paled.

"Very well, Lady Robin. I respectfully refuse to take command under these circumstances. You are overtired—" Her voice was icy and hard.

"That's enough." Robin stepped up close to the marshal. "The king gave me command. I am living my responsibilities to the best of my ability. If you refuse my orders, I have no more to discuss with you. You are dismissed."

They stood for a long moment, eye to eye, then the marshal deflated and sat down. "My apologies, Lady Robin. I was out of line."

"Then you will obey my orders?"

"Yes, my Lady."

"Thank you." Robin suppressed a sigh. "Hob, I asked you here to find out if you were willing as the leader of the Free to enter a formal truce with the thousand?"

"If I am not?" Hob asked.

"Then we will leave immediately and leave any relations between our people to a future time."

"I will talk to my council and give you their answer by sundown."

"Thank you, Hob."

"Robin." He nodded and left the room.

"If I may." Marshal Hapten saluted. "I have work to do to fulfill your orders." She followed Hob from the room.

Robin collapsed in a chair and put her hands over her face. *What have I done?* She allowed herself a moment of weakness before she stood up and shook herself. *I have work to do.*

***

Robin put on her travelling uniform and carefully checked off the things she needed to pack. Food, water, a bow and arrows, her sword. She'd take her chain mail but leave the plate armour. Speed was more important than safety now. Since she'd decided to follow the call north, it had sharpened and grown more urgent.

"You don't think you're going to leave me behind?" Sargent Temajin stood in front of her.

"You won't be able to keep up with me." Robin said. "Your job is to find Ham and the both of you protect Sarge and the boys."

"Very well, Lady Robin." He stepped back and saluted. "Travel well."

She met Hob on the wall. The sun settled in the west.

"We will negotiate with you." Hob leaned on the parapet. "If we are to survive, we will need friends."

"Don't hold back. You are the leader of the Free. Think of that as you talk."

"I will remember, Robin."

She left him there at the wall and walked down the stair and out the gate, just as the guards were closing it.

"Are you sure you want to go out now?" One asked. "We have to close it sundown."

"I am travelling north. Close the gate behind me and don't worry about me."

"It's up to you." The guard waved her through, then shut the gate. The thud of the bar dropping made her shiver.

She loped north across the plain, following a call as urgent as the one taking her to the northern border. She had a message to give to someone. Time was precious.

The ground blurred as she passed. The moon rose and set before she allowed herself a rest and a chance to drink and eat. She followed the call like an arrow from her bow as it moved towards the west.

***

Robin stopped to rest in a small clearing in the forest. She had a long way to go yet and arriving exhausted wouldn't be smart. A small fire and a bit of the food from her pack made for a cheerful camp. Robin couldn't sleep for worrying about Sarge. Though she told herself there was nothing she could do, her heart wanted to dash straight to his side. She pulled out her smaller knife and whittled a stick to toast a chunk of bread. A snap of a twig behind her made her jump up and spin, knife at the ready.

A boy, probably younger even than her, stood staring at her wide eyed.

"You might as well sit." Robin waved with the knife. "You hungry?"

He nodded slowly. "Are you a fae?"

"And if I was, would I tell you?" Robin finished whittling her stick. "I said sit." She put the knife in its sheath and tossed it to the boy. "Carve yourself a stick to toast bread with."

He stared at the knife and slowly stretched out his hand.

"Don't worry, I'm not going to eat you, boy." She stabbed the crust onto her stick and held it to the fire. "You do know how to use a knife?"

He nodded and snatched the knife up, picking up a stick and whittling a point in it. "My name is Adam."

"You should be careful about giving your name to strangers in the forest, especially if you think they are fae."

"Gran said I had to be polite to the fae." Adam blushed, and the knife slipped, slicing his finger open.

"Oh, for the land's sake." Robin reached into her satchel and grabbed some moss and herbs, then bandaged the hand. "You want to be careful with that knife. It's sharper than you're used to."

"Sorry, I'm not used to knives much. Da wouldn't give me one when I left. Said if I was daft enough to wander the world alone, I couldn't be trusted with a knife." He put the blade back in the sheath and held it out to Robin.

"I don't need it. You keep it now that you've blooded the blade. Don't be losing it now. It's a good knife and will be helpful to you." Robin handed him a crust of bread and broke off a chunk of cheese to go with it. She broke off one for herself and put it on the now toasted crust and bit into it, sighing with pleasure.

"Thanks." Adam toasted his bread and put the cheese on it, biting into immediately. He made a face as the heat burned his mouth, but he didn't spit it out. "All my brothers laugh at me, but I'm going to make something of myself and show them all."

"What do you plan to be?" Robin took another bite of the bread and cheese.

"Don't know." Adam said. "Gran said I'd have to find my way."

"And she told you how to talk to the fae?"

"Yes'm" He blew on the bread and cheese and took another bite.

"Did she give you anything aside from advice?" Robin wondered how Adam had survived this long alone. Maybe he was only a day out from his home and could be convinced to return to it.

"I've been wandering lost in the forest for days and ate all the food she packed for me, drank all my water too." Adam finished his bread and cheese in one last bite. "Didn't know what I was going to do until I saw your fire."

"You're lucky I'm in a good mood." Robin handed him a waterskin. "I have a spare. Fill it every chance you get." She pointed to a plant. "Dig up the root with a stick and shake the dirt from it."

Adam shrugged and did as she told him and handed it to her. She tossed it into the fire.

"You need to let these cook for several hours, even overnight, but they will keep you from starving. Don't eat too many or you'll start seeing things, never eat them raw. Here's a bit of cheese to go with it in the morning. Break it open and eat the white part." Robin tossed her stick into the fire. "May as well sleep. Keep that knife and waterskin safe. Don't be afraid to offer to work for people you meet. Build some muscle on that body."

"Thank you, mistress." Adam jumped up. "I can fetch you more wood."

"I have enough for my need, but I appreciate the offer. Sleep for now." He lay down and started snoring almost immediately. She worried about leaving him alone in the forest, but where she was going would be more dangerous. She banked the fire so it would burn through the night without spreading. He curled up on the ground, hugging the knife and the waterskin. Robin drew a sigil on his hand. The cut would heal without infection. Maybe he'd find a nice farming couple who needed an extra hand. She drew another one in the dirt beside him. If he was lucky, the land would watch out for him.

Something tugged at her, and she made an arrow of sticks pointing west. Some direction was the least she could do. She stood up and checked her gear, settled her pack and bow into place along with the quiver of arrows. Robin loped north and was soon miles away from the boy. She put him out of her mind. Nothing more she could do for him.

Robin was alone, but for the occasional connection with the land. So far, the land hadn't given her any useful direction. Through the night she ran, each step bringing her closer to where she needed to be. Too bad she had no idea what to do when she arrived.

Other books by Alex

Series:

Calliope Books
Calliope and the Sea Serpent
Calliope and the Royal Engineers
The Third Prince and the Enemy's Daughter
Calliope and the Kershan Empire

Spruce Bay Books
Wendigo Whispers
Cry of the White Moose
Disputed Rock

The Belandria Tarot
The Devil Reversed
The Regent's Reign
The Empire Unbalanced
The World Widens
The Fury Unleashed

Blue in Kamloops
Tranquille Dark
Columbia Smoke
Victoria Run

The Fae
Call of a Hero
Shieldmaiden's Quest

Stand-alone books:

Leedles and the Golden Tree
Generation Gap
The Gods Above
Tales of Light and Dark
Like Mushrooms (poetry and photography)
The Heronmaster
Blood and Sparkles, and other stories
Princess of Boring
By the Book
Sarcasm is My Superpower
Playing on Yggdrasil
The Unenchanted Princess

Read short stories and excerpts from his novels at alexmcgilvery.com